PANDEMONIUM!

When I got down to my place of business the next morning, I found a surprise waiting for me—several of them, in fact. It was as if it had been ransacked by burglars, set fire to, then gutted by a flood.

Jedson watched me with a sardonic grin. "Don't you see?" he said. "It's magic, all right.

"Archie, you've been kicked in the teeth by at least three of the four elements—earth, fire, and water. Maybe there was sylph of the air in on it, too, but I can't prove it. First the gnomes came and cleaned out everything you had that came out of the ground, except cold iron. A salamander followed them and set fire to the place. Then an undine turned the place into a swamp, ruining anything that wouldn't burn, like cement and lime.

"You insured?"

By Robert A. Heinlein
Published by Ballantine Books:

Robert A. Heinlein
WALDO & MAGIC, INC.

A Del Rey Book

BALLANTINE BOOKS • NEW YORK

A Del Rey Book
Published by Ballantine Books

ISBN 0-345-33015-3

This edition published by arrangement with Doubleday and Co.,
Inc.

Printed in Canada

First Ballantine Books Edition: November 1986
Second Printing: February 1990

Cover Art by Barclay Shaw

To
John and Doña

Contents

Waldo

T HE ACT WAS BILLED AS BALLET TAP—WHICH DOES not describe it.

His feet created an intricate tympany of crisp, clean taps. There was a breath-catching silence as he leaped high into the air, higher than a human being should—and performed, while floating there, a fantastically improbable *entrechats douze*.

He landed on his toes, apparently poised, yet producing a fortissimo of thunderous taps.

The spotlights cut, the stage lights came up. The audience stayed silent a long moment, then realized it was time to applaud, and *gave*.

He stood facing them, letting the wave of their emotion sweep through him. He felt as if he could lean against it; it warmed him through to his bones.

It was wonderful to dance, glorious to be applauded, to be *liked*, to be *wanted*.

When the curtain rang down for the last time he let his dresser lead him away. He was always a little bit drunk at the end of a performance; dancing was a joyous intoxication even in rehearsal, but to have an audience lifting him, carrying him along, applauding him—he never grew jaded to it. It was always new and heartbreakingly wonderful.

"This way, chief. Give us a little smile." The flash bulb flared. "Thanks."

"Thank *you*. Have a drink." He motioned toward one end of his dressing room. They were all such nice fellows, such grand guys—the reporters, the photographers—all of them.

"How about one standing up?" He started to comply, but his dresser, busy with one slipper, warned him:

"You operate in half an hour."

"Operate?" the news photographer said. "What's it this time?"

"A left cerebrectomy," he answered.

"Yeah? How about covering it?"

"Glad to have you—if the hospital doesn't mind."

"We'll fix that."

Such grand guys.

"—trying to get a little different angle on a feature article." It was a feminine voice, near his ear. He looked around hastily, slightly confused.

"For example, what made you decide to take up dancing as a career?"

"I'm sorry," he apologized. "I didn't hear you. I'm afraid it's pretty noisy in here."

"I said, why did you decide to take up dancing?"

"Well, now, I don't quite know how to answer that. I'm afraid we would have to go back quite a way——"

James Stevens scowled at his assistant engineer. "What have you got to look happy about?" he demanded.

"It's just the shape of my face," his assistant apologized. "Try laughing at this one: there's been another crash."

"Oh, cripes! Don't tell me—let me guess. Passenger or freight?"

"A Climax duo-freighter on the Chicago-Salt Lake shuttle, just west of North Platte. And, chief——"

"Yes?"

"The Big Boy wants to see you."

"That's interesting. That's very, very interesting. Mac——"

"Yeah, chief."

"How would you like to be Chief Traffic Engineer of North American Power-Air? I hear there's going to be a vacancy."

Mac scratched his nose. "Funny that you should mention that, chief. I was just going to ask you what kind of a recommendation you could give me in case I went back into civil engineering. Ought to be worth something to you to get rid of me."

"I'll get rid of you—right now. You bust out to Nebraska, find that heap before the souvenir hunters tear it apart, and bring back its deKalbs and its control board."

"Trouble with cops, maybe?"

"You figure it out. Just be sure you come back."

Stevens's office was located immediately adjacant to the zone power plant; the business offices of North American were located in a hill, a good three quarters of a mile away. There was the usual interconnecting tunnel; Stevens entered it and deliberately chose the low-speed slide in order to have more time to think before facing the boss.

By the time he arrived he had made up his mind, but he did not like the answer.

The Big Boy—Stanley F. Gleason, Chairman of the Board—greeted him quietly. "Come in, Jim. Sit down. Have a cigar."

Stevens slid into a chair, declined the cigar and pulled out a cigarette, which he lit while looking around. Besides the chief and himself, there were present Harkness, head of the legal staff, Dr. Rambeau, Stevens's opposite number for research, and Striebel, the chief engineer for city power. Us five and no more, he thought grimly—all the heavyweights and none of the middleweights. Heads will roll!—starting with mine.

"Well," he said, almost belligerently, "we're all here. Who's got the cards? Do we cut for deal?"

Harkness looked faintly distressed by the

impropriety; Rambeau seemed too sunk in some personal gloom to pay any attention to wisecracks in bad taste. Gleason ignored it. "We've been trying to figure a way out of our troubles, James. I left word for you on the chance that you might not have left."

"I stopped by simply to see if I had any personal mail," Stevens said bitterly. "Otherwise I'd be on the beach at Miami, turning sunshine into vitamin D."

"I know," said Gleason, "and I'm sorry. You deserve that vacation, Jimmie. But the situation has gotten worse instead of better. Any ideas?"

"What does Dr. Rambeau say?"

Rambeau looked up momentarily. "The deKalb receptors can't fail," he stated.

"But they do."

"They can't. You've operated them improperly." He sunk back into his personal prison.

Stevens turned back to Gleason and spread his hands. "So far as I know, Dr. Rambeau is right—but if the fault lies in the engineering department, I haven't been able to locate it. You can have my resignation."

"I don't want your resignation," Gleason said gently. "What I want is results. We have a responsibility to the public."

"And to the stockholders," Harkness put in.

"That will take care of itself if we solve the other," Gleason observed. "How about it, Jimmie? Any suggestions?"

Stevens bit his lip. "Just one," he announced,

5

"and one I don't like to make. Then I look for a job peddling magazine subscriptions."

"So? Well, what is it?"

"We've got to consult Waldo."

Rambeau suddenly snapped out of his apathy. "What! That charlatan? This is a matter of *science*."

Harkness said, "Really, Dr. Stevens——"

Gleason held up a hand. "Dr. Stevens' suggestion is logical. But I'm afraid it's a little late, Jimmie. I talked with him last week."

Harkness looked surprised; Stevens looked annoyed as well. "Without letting me know?"

"Sorry, Jimmie. I was just feeling him out. But it's no good. His terms, to us, amount to confiscation."

"Still sore over the Hathaway patents?"

"Still nursing his grudge."

"You should have let me handle the matter," Harkness put in. "He can't do this to us—there is public interest involved. Retain him, if need be, and let the fee be adjudicated in equity. I'll arrange the details."

"I'm afraid you would," Gleason said dryly. "Do you think a court order will make a hen lay an egg?"

Harkness looked indignant, but shut up.

Stevens continued, "I would not have suggested going to Waldo if I had not had an idea as how to approach him. I know a friend of his——"

"A friend of *Waldo*? I didn't know he had any."

"This man is sort of an uncle to him—his first

physician. With his help I might get on Waldo's good side."

Dr. Rambeau stood up. "This is intolerable," he announced. "I must ask you to excuse me." He did not wait for an answer, but strode out, hardly giving the door time to open in front of him.

Gleason followed his departure with worried eyes. "Why does he take it so hard, Jimmie? You would think he hated Waldo personally."

"Probably he does, in a way. But it's more than that; his whole universe is toppling. For the last twenty years, ever since Pryor's reformulation of the General Field Theory did away with Heisenberg's Uncertainty Principle, physics has been considered an exact science. The power failures and transmission failures we have been suffering are a terrific nuisance to you and to me, but to Dr. Rambeau they amount to an attack on his faith. Better keep an eye on him."

"Why?"

"Because he might come unstuck entirely. It's a pretty serious matter for a man's religion to fail him."

"Hm-m-m. How about yourself? Doesn't it hit you just as hard?"

"Not quite. I'm an engineer—from Rambeau's point of view just a high-priced tinker. Difference in orientation. Not but what I'm pretty upset."

The audio circuit of the communicator on Gleason's desk came to life. "Calling Chief Engineer Stevens—calling Chief Engineer Stevens." Gleason flipped the tab.

"He's here. Go ahead."

"Company code, translated. Message follows: 'Cracked up four miles north of Cincinnati. Shall I go on to Nebraska, or bring in the you-know-what from my own crate?' Message ends. Signed 'Mac.'"

"Tell him to *walk* back!" Stevens said savagely.

"Very well, sir." The instrument cut off.

"Your assistant?" asked Gleason.

"Yes. That's about the last straw, chief. Shall I wait and try to analyze this failure, or shall I try to see Waldo?"

"Try to see Waldo."

"O.K. If you don't hear from me, just send my severance pay care of Palmdale Inn, Miami. I'll be the fourth beachcomber from the right."

Gleason permitted himself an unhappy smile. "If you *don't* get results, I'll be the fifth. Good luck."

"So long."

When Stevens had gone, Chief Stationary Engineer Striebel spoke up for the first time. "If the power to the cities fails," he said softly, "you know where I'll be, don't you?"

"Where? Beachcomber number six?"

"Not likely. I'll be number one in my spot—first man to be lynched."

"But the power to the cities *can't* fail. You've got too many cross-connects and safety devices."

"Neither can the deKalbs fail, supposedly. Just the same—think about Sublevel 7 in Pittsburgh, with the lights out. Or, rather, don't think about it!"

Doc Grimes let himself into the aboveground access which led into his home, glanced at the announcer, and noted with mild, warm interest that someone close enough to him to possess his house combination was inside. He moved ponderously downstairs, favoring his game leg, and entered the lounging room.

"Hi, Doc!" James Stevens got up when the door snapped open and came forward to greet him.

"H'lo, James. Pour yourself a drink. I see you have. Pour me one."

"Right."

While his friend complied, Grimes shucked himself out of the outlandish anachronistic greatcoat he was wearing and threw it more or less in the direction of the robing alcove. It hit the floor heavily, much more heavily than its appearance justified, despite its unwieldy bulk. It clunked.

Stooping, he peeled off thick overtrousers as massive as the coat. He was dressed underneath in conventional business tights in blue and sable. It was not a style that suited him. To an eye unsophisticated in matters of civilized dress—let us say the mythical man-from-Antares—he might have seemed uncouth, even unsightly. He looked a good bit like an elderly fat beetle.

James Stevens's eye made no note of the tights, but he looked with disapproval on the garments

9

which had just been discarded. "Still wearing that fool armor," he commented.

"Certainly."

"Damn it, Doc—you'll make yourself sick, carrying that junk around. It's unhealthy."

"Danged sight sicker if I don't."

"Rats! *I* don't get sick, and *I* don't wear armor—outside the lab."

"You should." Grimes walked over to where Stevens had reseated himself. "Cross your knees." Stevens complied; Grimes struck him smartly below the kneecap with the edge of his palm. The reflex jerk was barely perceptible. "Lousy," he remarked, then peeled back his friend's right eyelid.

"You're in poor shape," he added after a moment.

Stevens drew away impatiently. "*I'm* all right. It's you we're talking about."

"What about me?"

"Well— Damnation, Doc, you're throwing away your reputation. They talk about you."

Grimes nodded. "I know. 'Poor old Gus Grimes—a slight touch of cerebral termites.' Don't worry about my reputation; I've always been out of step. What's your fatigue index?"

"I don't know. It's all right."

"It is, eh? I'll wrestle you, two falls out of three."

Stevens rubbed his eyes. "Don't needle me, Doc. I'm run-down. I know that, but it isn't anything but overwork."

"Humph! James, you are a fair-to-middlin' radiation physicist——"

"Engineer."

"—engineer. But you're no medical man. You can't expect to pour every sort of radiant energy through the human system year after year and not pay for it. It wasn't designed to stand it."

"But I wear armor in the lab. You know that."

"Surely. But how about outside the lab?"

"But——Look, Doc—I hate to say it, but your whole thesis is ridiculous. Sure there is radiant energy in the air these days, but nothing harmful. All the colloidal chemists agree——"

"Colloidal, fiddlesticks!"

"But you've got to admit that biological economy is a matter of colloidal chemistry."

"I've got to admit nothing. I'm not contending that colloids are not the fabric of living tissue— they are. But I've maintained for forty years that it was dangerous to expose living tissue to assorted radiation without being sure of the effect. From an evolutionary standpoint the human animal is habituated to and adapted to only the natural radiation of the sun—and he can't stand that any too well, even under a thick blanket of ionization. Without that blanket——Did you ever see a solar-X type cancer?"

"Of course not."

"No, you're too young. *I* have. Assisted at the autopsy of one, when I was an intern. Chap was on the Second Venus Expedition. Four hundred and thirty-eight cancers we counted in him, then gave up."

"Solar-X is whipped."

"Sure it is. But it ought to be a warning. You bright young squirts can cook up things in your labs that we medicos can't begin to cope with. We're behind—bound to be. We usually don't know what's happened until the damage is done. This time you've torn it." He sat down heavily and suddenly looked as tired and whipped as did his younger friend.

Stevens felt the sort of tongue-tied embarrassment a man may feel when a dearly beloved friend falls in love with an utterly worthless person. He wondered what he could say that would not seem rude.

He changed the subject. "Doc, I came over because I had a couple of things on my mind—"

"Such as?"

"Well, a vacation for one. I know I'm run-down. I've been overworked, and a vacation seems in order. The other is your pal, Waldo."

"Huh?"

"Yeah. Waldo Farthingwaite-Jones, bless his stiff-necked, bad-tempered heart."

"Why Waldo? You haven't suddenly acquired an interest in *myasthenia gravis*, have you?"

"Well, no. I don't care what's wrong with him physically. He can have hives, dandruff, or the galloping never-get-overs, for all I care. I hope he has. What I want is to pick his brains."

"So?"

"I can't do it alone. Waldo doesn't help people; he *uses* them. You're his only normal contact with people."

"That is not entirely true—"

"Who else?"

"You misunderstand me. He has *no* normal contacts. I am simply the only person who dares to be rude to him."

"But I thought— Never mind. D'you know, this is an inconvenient setup? Waldo is the man we've got to have. Why should it come about that a genius of his caliber should be so unapproachable, so immune to ordinary social demands? Oh, I know his disease has a lot to do with it, but why should *this* man have *this* disease? It's an improbable coincidence."

"It's not a matter of his infirmity," Grimes told him. "Or, rather, not in the way you put it. His weakness *is* his genius, in a way——"

"Huh?"

"Well——" Grimes turned his sight inward, let his mind roam back over his long association— lifelong, for Waldo—with this particular patient. He remembered his subliminal misgivings when he delivered the child. The infant had been sound enough, superficially, except for a slight blueness. But then lots of babies were somewhat cyanotic in the delivery room. Nevertheless, he had felt a slight reluctance to give it the tunk on the bottom, the slap which would shock it into taking its first lungful of air.

But he had squelched his own feelings, performed the necessary "laying on of hands," and the freshly born human had declared its independence with a satisfactory squall. There was nothing else he could have done; he was a young G.P. then, who took his Hippocratic oath seriously. He still took it seriously, he supposed, even though he sometimes referred to it as the "hypocritical" oath. Still, he had been right in his feelings; there *had* been something rotten about that child— something that was not entirely *myasthenia gravis*.

He had felt sorry for the child at first, as well as having an irrational feeling of responsibility for its condition. Pathological muscular weakness is an almost totally crippling condition, since the patient has no unaffected limbs to retrain into substitutes. There the victim must lie, all organs, limbs, and functions present, yet so pitifully, completely weak as to be unable to perform any normal function. He must spend his life in a condition of exhausted collapse, such as you or I might reach at the finish line of a grueling cross-country run. No help for him, and no relief.

During Waldo's childhood he had hoped constantly that the child would die, since he was so obviously destined for tragic uselessness, while simultaneously, as a physician, doing everything within his own skill and the skill of numberless consulting specialists to keep the child alive and cure it.

Naturally, Waldo could not attend school; Grimes ferreted out sympathetic tutors. He could indulge in no normal play; Grimes invented sickbed games which would not only stimulate Waldo's imagination but encourage him to use his flabby muscles to the full, weak extent of which he was capable.

Grimes had been afraid that the handicapped child, since it was not subjected to the usual maturing stresses of growing up, would remain infantile. He knew now—had known for a long time—that he need not have worried. Young Waldo grasped at what little life was offered him, learned thirstily, tried with a sweating tenseness of will to force his undisciplined muscles to serve him.

He was clever in thinking of dodges whereby to circumvent his muscular weakness. At seven he devised a method of controlling a spoon with two hands, which permitted him—painfully—to feed himself. His first mechanical invention was made at ten.

It was a gadget which held a book for him, at any angle, controlled lighting for the book, and turned its pages. The gadget responded to finger tip pressure on a simple control panel. Naturally, Waldo could not build it himself, but he could conceive it, and explain it; the Farthingwaite-Joneses could well afford the services of a designing engineer to build the child's conception.

Grimes was inclined to consider this incident, in which the child Waldo acted in a role of intellectual domination over a trained mature adult neither blood relation nor servant, as a landmark in the psychological process whereby Waldo eventually came to regard the entire human race as his servants, his *hands*, present or potential.

* * *

"What's eating you, Doc?"

"Eh? Sorry, I was daydreaming. See here, son—you mustn't be too harsh on Waldo. I don't *like* him myself. But you must take him as a whole."

"*You* take him."

"*Shush*. You spoke of needing his genius. He wouldn't have a genius if he had not been crippled. You didn't know his parents. They were good stock—fine, intelligent people—but nothing spectacular. Waldo's potentialities weren't any greater than theirs, but he had to do more with them to accomplish anything. He had to do everything the hard way. He *had* to be clever."

"Sure. Sure, but why should he be so utterly poisonous? Most big men aren't."

"Use your head. To get anywhere in his condition he had to develop a will, a driving one-track mind, with a total disregard for any other considerations. What would you expect him to be but stinking selfish?"

"I'd— Well, never mind. We need him and that's that."

"Why?"

Stevens explained.

It may plausibly be urged that the shape of a culture—its mores, evaluations, family organizations, eating habits, living patterns, pedagogical methods, institutions, forms of government, and so forth—arise from the economic necessities of its technology. Even though the thesis be too broad and much oversimplified, it is nonetheless true that much which characterized the long peace which followed the constitutional establishment of the United Nations grew out of the technologies which were hothouse-forced by the needs of the belligerents in the war of the forties. Up to that time broadcast and beamcast were used only for commercial radio, with rare exceptions. Even telephony was done almost entirely by actual metallic connection from one instrument to another. If a man in Monterey wished to speak to his wife or partner in Boston, a physical, copper neuron stretched bodily across the continent from one to the other.

Radiant power was then a hop dream, found in Sunday supplements and comic books.

A concatenation—no, a meshwork—of new developments was necessary before the web of copper covering the continent could be dispensed with. Power could not be broadcast economically; it was necessary to wait for the co-axial beam—a direct result of the imperative military shortages of the Great War. Radio telephony could not replace wired telephony until ultra micro-wave techniques made room in the ether, so to speak, for the traffic load. Even then it was necessary to invent a tuning device which could be used by a nontechnical person—a ten-year-old child, let us say—as easily as the dial selector which was characteristic of the commercial wired telephone of the era then terminating.

Bell Laboratories cracked that problem; the solution led directly to the radiant power receptor,

17

domestic type, keyed, sealed, and metered. The way was open for commercial radio power transmission—except in one respect: efficiency. Aviation waited on the development of the Otto-cycle engine; the Industrial Revolution waited on the steam engine; radiant power waited on a really cheap, plentiful power source. Since radiation of power is inherently wasteful, it was necessary to have power cheap and plentiful enough to waste.

The same year brought atomic energy. The physicists working for the United States Army—the United States of North America had its own army then—produced a superexplosive; the notebooks recording their tests contained, when properly correlated, everything necessary to produce almost any other sort of nuclear reaction, even the so-called Solar Phoenix, the hydrogen-helium cycle, which is the source of the sun's power.

Radiant power became economically feasible—and inevitable.

The reaction whereby copper is broken down into phosphorus, silicon29 and helium3, plus degenerating chain reactions, was one of the several cheap and convenient means developed for producing unlimited and practically free power.

Of course Stevens included none of this in his explanation to Grimes. Grimes was absentmindedly aware of the whole dynamic process; he had seen radiant power grow up, just as his grandfather had seen the development of aviation. He had seen the great transmission lines removed from the sky—"mined" for their copper; he had

seen the heavy cables being torn from the dug-up
streets of Manhattan. He might even recall his
first independent-unit radiotelephone with its
somewhat disconcerting double dial—he had gotten a lawyer in Buenos Aires on it when attempting to reach his neighborhood delicatessen. For
two weeks he made all his local calls by having
them relayed back from South America before he
discovered that it made a difference which dial he
used first.

At that time Grimes had not yet succumbed to
the new style in architecture. The London Plan
did not appeal to him; he liked a house aboveground, where he could see it. When it became
necessary to increase the floor space in his offices,
he finally gave in and went subsurface, not so
much for the cheapness, convenience, and general
all-around practicability of living in a tri-
conditioned cave, but because he had already
become a little worried about the possible conse-
quences of radiation pouring through the human
body. The fused-earth walls of his new residence
were covered with lead; the roof of the cave had
a double thickness. His hole in the ground was as
near radiationproof as he could make it.

"—the meat of the matter," Stevens was saying,
"is that the delivery of power to transportation
units has become erratic as the devil. Not enough
yet to tie up traffic, but enough to be very disconcerting. There have been some nasty accidents;

we can't keep hushing them up forever. I've got to do something about it."

"Why?"

"'Why?' Don't be silly. In the first place as traffic engineer for NAPA my bread and butter depends on it. In the second place the problem is upsetting in itself. A properly designed piece of mechanism ought to work—all the time, every time. These don't, and we can't find out why not. Our staff mathematical physicists have about reached the babbling stage."

Grimes shrugged. Stevens felt annoyed by the gesture. "I don't think you appreciate the importance of this problem, Doc. Have you any idea of the amount of horsepower involved in transportation? Counting both private and commercial vehicles and common carriers, North American Power-Air supplies more than half the energy used in this continent. We *have* to be right. You can add to that our city-power affiliate. No trouble there—yet. But we don't *dare* think what a city-power breakdown would mean."

"I'll give you a solution."

"Yeah? Well, give."

"Junk it. Go back to oil-powered and steam-powered vehicles. Get rid of these damned radiant-powered deathtraps."

"Utterly impossible. You don't know what you're saying. It took more than fifteen years to make the changeover. Now we're geared to it. Gus, if NAPA closed up shop, half the population of the northwest seaboard would starve, to say nothing of the lake states and the Philly-Boston axis."

"Hrrmph—— Well, all I've got to say is that that might be better than the slow poisoning that is going on now."

Stevens brushed it away impatiently. "Look, Doc, nurse a bee in your bonnet if you like, but don't ask me to figure it into my calculations. Nobody else sees any danger in radiant power."

Grimes answered mildly. "Point is, son, they aren't looking in the right place. Do you know what the high jump record was last year?"

"I never listen to the sport news."

"Might try it sometime. The record leveled off at seven foot two, 'bout twenty years back. Been dropping ever since. You might try graphing athletic records against radiation in the air— artificial radiation. Might find some results that would surprise you."

"Shucks, everybody knows there has been a swing away from heavy sports. The sweat-and-muscles fad died out, that's all. We've simply advanced into a more intellectual culture."

"Intellectual, hogwash! People quit playing tennis and such because they are tired all the time. Look at you. You're a mess."

"Don't needle me, Doc."

"Sorry. But there has been a clear deterioration in the performance of the human animal. If we had decent records on such things I could prove it, but any physician who's worth his salt can *see* it, if he's got eyes in him and isn't wedded to a lot of fancy instruments. I can't prove what causes it, not yet, but I've a damned good hunch that it's caused by the stuff you peddle."

"Impossible. There isn't a radiation put on the air that hasn't been tested very carefully in the bio labs. We're neither fools nor knaves."

"Maybe you don't test 'em long enough. I'm not talking about a few hours, or a few weeks; I'm talking about the cumulative effects of years of radiant frequencies pouring through the tissues. What does that do?"

"Why, nothing—I believe."

"You believe, but you don't know. Nobody has ever tried to find out. F'rinstance—what effect does sunlight have on silicate glass? Ordinarily you would say 'none,' but you've seen desert glass?"

"That bluish-lavender stuff? Of course."

"Yes. A bottle turns colored in a few months in the Mojave Desert. But have you ever seen the windowpanes in the old houses on Beacon Hill?"

"I've never been on Beacon Hill."

"O.K., then I'll tell you. Same phenomena—only it takes a century or more, in Boston. Now tell me—you savvy physics—could you measure the change taking place in those Beacon Hill windows?"

"Mm-m-m—probably not."

"But it's going on just the same. Has anyone ever tried to measure the changes produced in human tissue by thirty years of exposure to ultra short-wave radiation?"

"No, but——"

"No 'buts.' I see an effect. I've made a wild guess at a cause. Maybe I'm wrong. But I've felt a lot more spry since I've taken to invariably wearing my lead overcoat whenever I go out."

Stevens surrendered the argument. "Maybe you're right, Doc. I won't fuss with you. How about Waldo? Will you take me to him and help me handle him?"

"When do you want to go?"

"The sooner the better."

"Now?"

"Suits."

"Call your office."

"Are you ready to leave right now? It would suit me. As far as the front office is concerned, I'm on vacation; nevertheless, I've got this on my mind. I want to get at it."

"Quit talking and git."

They went topside to where their cars were parked. Grimes headed toward his, a big-bodied, old-fashioned Boeing family landau. Stevens checked him. "You aren't planning to go in that? It 'u'd take us the rest of the day."

"Why not? She's got an auxiliary space drive, and she's tight. You could fly from here to the Moon and back."

"Yes, but she's so infernal slow. We'll use my 'broomstick.'"

Grimes let his eyes run over his friend's fusiformed little speedster. It's body was as nearly invisible as the plastic industry could achieve. A surface layer, two molecules thick, gave it a refrac-

23

tive index sensibly identical with that of air. When perfectly clean it was very difficult to see. At the moment it had picked up enough casual dust and water vapor to be faintly seen—a ghost of a soap bubble of a ship.

Running down the middle, clearly visible through the walls, was the only metal part of the ship—the shaft, or, more properly, the axis core, and the spreading sheaf of deKalb receptors at its terminus. The appearance was enough like a giant witch's broom to justify the nickname. Since the saddles, of transparent plastic, were mounted tandem over the shaft so that the metal rod passed between the legs of the pilot and passengers, the nickname was doubly apt.

"Son," Grimes remarked, "I know I ain't pretty, nor am I graceful. Nevertheless, I retain a certain residuum of self-respect and some shreds of dignity. I am *not* going to tuck that thing between my shanks and go scooting through the air on it."

"Oh, rats! You're old-fashioned."

"I may be. Nevertheless, any peculiarities I have managed to retain to my present age I plan to hang onto. No."

"Look—I'll polarize the hull before we raise. How about it?"

"Opaque?"

"Opaque."

Grimes slid a regretful glance at his own frumpish boat, but assented by fumbling for the barely visible port of the speedster. Stevens assisted him; they climbed in and straddled the stick.

24

"Atta boy, Doc," Stevens commended, "I'll have you there in three shakes. That tub of yours probably won't do over five hundred, and Wheelchair must be all of twenty-five thousand miles up."

"I'm never in a hurry," Grimes commented, "and don't call Waldo's house 'Wheelchair'—not to his face."

"I'll remember," Stevens promised. He fumbled, apparently in empty air; the hull suddenly became dead black, concealing them. It changed as suddenly to mirror bright; the car quivered, then shot up out of sight.

Waldo F. Jones seemed to be floating in thin air at the center of a spherical room. The appearance was caused by the fact that he was indeed floating in air. His house lay in a free orbit, with a period of just over twenty-four hours. No spin had been impressed on his home; the pseudo gravity of centrifugal force was the thing he wanted least. He had left earth to get away from its gravitational field; he had not been down to the surface once in the seventeen years since his house was built and towed into her orbit; he never intended to do so for any purpose whatsoever.

Here, floating free in space in his own air-conditioned shell, he was almost free of the unbearable lifelong slavery to his impotent muscles. What little strength he had he could spend economically, in movement, rather than in fighting against the tearing, tiring weight of the Earth's thick field.

Waldo had been acutely interested in space flight since early boyhood, not from any desire to explore the depths, but because his boyish, overtrained mind had seen the enormous advantage—to him—in weightlessness. While still in his teens he had helped the early experimenters in space flight over a hump by supplying them with a control system which a pilot could handle delicately while under the strain of two or three gravities.

Such an invention was no trouble at all to him; he had simply adapted manipulating devices which he himself used in combating the overpowering weight of one gravity. The first successful and safe rocket ship contained relays which had once aided Waldo in moving himself from bed to wheelchair.

The deceleration tanks, which are now standard equipment for the lunar mail ships, traced their parentage to a flotation tank in which Waldo habitually had eaten and slept up to the time when he left the home of his parents for his present, somewhat unique, home. Most of his basic inventions had originally been conceived for his personal convenience, and only later adapted for commercial exploitation. Even the ubiquitous and grotesquely humanoid gadgets known universally as "waldoes"—Waldo F. Jones's Synchronous Reduplicating Pantograph, Pat. #296,001,437, new series, *et al*—passed through several generations of development and private use in Waldo's machine shop before he redesigned them for mass production. The first of them, a primitive gadget compared with the waldoes now to be found in every shop, factory, plant, and warehouse in the country, had been designed to enable Waldo to operate a metal lathe.

Waldo had resented the nickname the public had fastened on them—it struck him as overly familiar—but he had coldly recognized the business advantage to himself in having the public identify him verbally with a gadget so useful and important.

When the newscasters tagged his spacehouse "Wheelchair," one might have expected him to regard it as more useful publicity. That he did not so regard it, that he resented it and tried to put a stop to it, arose from another and peculiarly Waldo-ish fact: Waldo did not think of himself as a cripple.

He saw himself not as a crippled human being, but as something higher than human, the next step up, a being so superior as not to need the coarse, brutal strength of the smooth apes. Hairy apes, smooth apes, then Waldo—so the progression ran in his mind. A chimpanzee, with muscles that hardly bulge at all, can tug as high as fifteen hundred pounds with one hand. This Waldo had proved by obtaining one and patiently enraging it into full effort. A well-developed man can grip one hundred and fifty pounds with one hand. Waldo's own grip, straining until the sweat sprang out, had never reached fifteen pounds.

Whether the obvious inference were fallacious or true, Waldo believed in it, evaluated by it. Men were overmuscled canaille, smooth chimps. He felt himself at least ten times superior to them.

He had much to go on.

Though floating in air, he was busy, quite busy. Although he never went to the surface of the Earth his business was there. Aside from managing his many properties he was in regular practice as a consulting engineer, specializing in motion analysis. Hanging close to him in the room were the paraphernalia necessary to the practice of his profession. Facing him was a four-by-five color-stereo television receptor. Two sets of co-ordinates, rectilinear and polar, crosshatched it. Another smaller receptor hung above it and to the right. Both receptors were fully recording, by means of parallel circuits conveniently out of the way in another compartment.

The smaller receptor showed the faces of two men watching him. The larger showed a scene inside a large shop, hangarlike in its proportions. In the immediate foreground, almost full size, was a grinder in which was being machined a large casting of some sort. A workman stood beside it, a look of controlled exasperation on his face.

"He's the best you've got," Waldo stated to the two men in the smaller screen. "To be sure, he is clumsy and does not have the touch for fine work, but he is superior to the other morons you call machinists."

The workman looked around, as if trying to locate the voice. It was evident that he could hear Waldo, but that no vision receptor had been provided for him. "Did you mean that crack for me?" he said harshly.

"You misunderstand me, my good man," Waldo said sweetly. "I was complimenting you. I actually have hopes of being able to teach you the rudiments of precision work. Then we shall expect you to teach those butterbrained oafs around you. The gloves, please."

Near the man, mounted on the usual stand, were a pair of primary waldoes, elbow length and human digited. They were floating on the line, in parallel with a similar pair physically in front of Waldo. The secondary waldoes, whose actions could be controlled by Waldo himself by means of his primaries, were mounted in front of the power tool in the position of the operator.

Waldo's remark had referred to the primaries near the workman. The machinist glanced at them, but made no move to insert his arms in them. "I don't take no orders from nobody I can't see," he said flatly. He looked sidewise out of the scene as he spoke.

"Now, Jenkins," commenced one of the two men in the smaller screen.

Waldo sighed. "I really haven't the time or the inclination to solve your problems of shop discipline. Gentlemen, please turn your pickup, so that our petulant friend may see me."

The change was accomplished; the workman's face appeared in the background of the smaller of Waldo's screens, as well as in the larger. "There—

is that better?" Waldo said gently. The workman grunted.

"Now ... your name, please?"

"Alexander Jenkins."

"Very well, friend Alec—the gloves."

Jenkins thrust his arms into the waldoes and waited. Waldo put his arms into the primary pair before him; all three pairs, including the secondary pair mounted before the machine, came to life. Jenkins bit his lip, as if he found unpleasant the sensation of having his fingers manipulated by the gauntlets he wore.

Waldo flexed and extended his fingers gently; the two pairs of waldoes in the screen followed in exact, simultaneous parallelism. "Feel it, my dear Alec," Waldo advised. "Gently, gently—the sensitive touch. Make your muscles work for you." He then started hand movements of definite pattern; the waldoes at the power tool reached up, switched on the power, and began gently, gracefully, to continue the machining of the casting. A mechanical hand reached down, adjusted a vernier, while the other increased the flow of oil cooling the cutting edge. "Rhythm, Alec, rhythm. No jerkiness, no unnecessary movement. Try to get in time with me."

The casting took shape with deceptive rapidity, disclosed what it was—the bonnet piece for an ordinary three-way nurse. The chucks drew back from it; it dropped to the belt beneath, and another rough casting took its place. Waldo continued with unhurried skill, his finger motions within his waldoes exerting pressure which would need to be measured in fractions of ounces, but the two sets of waldoes, paralleled to him thousands of miles below, followed his motions accurately and with force appropriate to heavy work at hand.

Another casting landed on the belt—several more. Jenkins, although not called upon to do any work in his proper person, tired under the strain of attempting to anticipate and match Waldo's motions. Sweat dripped down his forehead, ran off his nose, accumulated on his chin. Between castings he suddenly withdrew his arms from the paralleled primaries. "That's enough," he announced.

"One more, Alec. You are improving."

"No!" He turned as if to walk off. Waldo made a sudden movement—so sudden as to strain him, even in his weight-free environment. One steel hand of the secondary waldoes lashed out, grasped Jenkins by the wrist.

"Not so fast, Alec."

"Let go of me!"

"Softly, Alec, softly. You'll do as you are told, *won't you*?" The steel hand clamped down hard, twisted. Waldo had exerted all of two ounces of pressure.

Jenkins grunted. The one remaining spectator—one had left soon after the lesson started—said, "Oh, I say, Mr. Jones!"

"Let him obey, or fire him. You know the terms of my contract."

There was a sudden cessation of stereo and sound, cut from the Earth end. It came back on a few seconds later. Jenkins was surly, but no longer recalcitrant. Waldo continued as if nothing had happened. "Once more, my dear Alec."

When the repetition had been completed, Waldo directed, "Twenty times, wearing the wrist and elbow lights with the chronanalyzer in the picture. I shall expect the superposed strips to match, Alec." He cut off the larger screen without further words and turned to the watcher in the smaller screen. "Same time tomorrow, McNye. Progress is satisfactory. In time we'll turn this madhouse of yours into a modern plant." He cleared that screen without saying good-by.

Waldo terminated the business interview somewhat hastily, because he had been following with one eye certain announcements on his own local information board. A craft was approaching his house. Nothing strange about that; tourists were forever approaching and being pushed away by his autoguardian circuit. But this craft had the approach signal, was now clamping to his threshold flat. It was a broomstick, but he could not place the license number. Florida license. Whom did he know with a Florida license?

He immediately realized that he knew no one who possessed his approach signal—that list was *very* short—and who could also reasonably be expected to sport a Florida license. The suspicious defensiveness with which he regarded the entire world asserted itself; he cut in the circuit whereby he could control by means of his primary waldoes the strictly illegal but highly lethal inner defenses of his home. The craft was opaqued; he did not like that.

A youngish man wormed his way out. Waldo looked him over. A stranger—face vaguely familiar perhaps. An ounce of pressure in the primaries and the face would cease to be a face, but Waldo's actions were under cold cortical control; he held his fire. The man turned, as if to assist another passenger. Yes, there was another. Uncle Gus!—but the doddering old fool had brought a stranger with him. He knew better than that. He knew how Waldo felt about strangers!

Nevertheless, he released the outer lock of the reception room and let them in.

Gus Grimes snaked his way through the lock, pulling himself from one handrail to the next, and panting a little as he always did when forced to move weight free. Matter of diaphragm control, he told himself as he always did; can't be the exertion. Stevens streaked in after him, displaying a groundhog's harmless pride in handling himself well in space conditions. Grimes arrested himself just inside the reception room, grunted, and spoke to a man-sized dummy waiting there. "Hello, Waldo."

The dummy turned his eyes and head slightly. "Greetings, Uncle Gus. I do wish you would remember to phone before dropping in. I would have had your special dinner ready."

"Never mind. We may not be here that long. Waldo, this is my friend, Jimmie Stevens."

The dummy faced Stevens. "How do you do, Mr.

Stevens," the voice said formally. "Welcome to Freehold."

"How do you do, Mr. Jones," Stevens replied, and eyed the dummy curiously. It was surprisingly lifelike; he had been taken in by it at first, A "reasonable facsimile." Come to think of it, he had heard of this dummy. Except in vision screen few had seen Waldo in his own person. Those who had business at Wheelchair—no, "Freehold," he must remember that—those who had business at Freehold heard a voice and saw this simulacrum.

"But you *must* stay for dinner, Uncle Gus," Waldo continued. "You can't run out on me like that; you don't come often enough for that. I can stir something up."

"Maybe we will," Grimes admitted. "Don't worry about the menu. You know me. I can eat a turtle *with* the shell."

It had really been a bright idea, Stevens congratulated himself, to get Doc Grimes to bring him. Not here five minutes and Waldo was insisting on them staying for dinner. Good omen!

He had not noticed that Waldo had addressed the invitation to Grimes alone, and that it had been Grimes who had assumed the invitation to be for both of them.

"Where are you, Waldo?" Grimes continued. "In the lab?" He made a tentative movement, as if to leave the reception room.

"Oh, don't bother," Waldo said hastily. "I'm sure you will be more comfortable where you are. Just a moment and I will put some spin on the room so that you may sit down."

"What's eating you, Waldo?" Grimes said testily. "You know I don't insist on weight. And I don't care for the company of your talking doll. I want to see you." Stevens was a little surprised by the older man's insistence; he had thought it considerate of Waldo to offer to supply acceleration. Weightlessness put him a little on edge.

Waldo was silent for an uncomfortable period. At last he said frigidly, "Really, Uncle Gus, what you ask is out of the question. You must be aware of that."

Grimes did not answer him. Instead, he took Stevens's arm. "Come on, Jimmie. We're leaving."

"Why, Doc! What's the matter?"

"Waldo wants to play games. I don't play games."

"But—"

"Ne' mind! Come along. Waldo, open the lock."

"Uncle Gus!"

"Yes, Waldo?"

"Your guest—you vouch for him?"

"Naturally, you dumb fool, else I wouldn't have brought him."

"You will find me in my workshop. The way is open."

Grimes turned to Stevens. "Come along, son."

Stevens trailed after Grimes as one fish might follow another, while taking in with his eyes as much of Waldo's fabulous house as he could see. The place was certainly unique, he conceded to himself—unlike anything he had ever seen. It

35

completely lacked up-and-down orientation. Space craft, even space stations, although always in free fall with respect to any but internally impressed accelerations, invariably are designed with up-and-down; the up-and-down axis of a ship is determined by the direction of its accelerating drive; the up-and-down of a space station is determined by its centrifugal spin.

Some few police and military craft use more than one axis of acceleration; their up-and-down shifts, therefore, and their personnel, must be harnessed when the ship maneuvers. Some space stations apply spin only to living quarters. Nevertheless, the rule is general; human beings are used to weight; all their artifacts have that assumption implicit in their construction—except Waldo's house.

It is hard for a groundhog to dismiss the notion of weight. We seem to be born with an instinct which demands it. If one thinks of a vessel in a free orbit around the Earth, one is inclined to think of the direction toward the Earth as "down," to think of oneself as standing or sitting on that wall of the ship, using it as a floor. Such a concept is completely mistaken. To a person inside a freely falling body there is no sensation of weight whatsoever and no direction of up-and-down, except that which derives from the gravitational field of the vessel itself. As for the latter, neither Waldo's house nor any space craft as yet built is massive enough to produce a field dense enough for the human body to notice it. Believe it or not, that is true. It takes a mass as gross as a good-sized planetoid to give the human body a feeling of weight.

It may be objected that a body in a free orbit around the Earth is not a freely falling body. The concept involved is human, Earth surface in type, and completely erroneous. Free flight, free fall, and free orbit are equivalent terms. The Moon falls constantly toward the Earth; the Earth falls constantly toward the Sun, but the sidewise vector of their several motions prevents them from approaching their primaries. It is free fall nonetheless. Consult any ballistician or any astrophysicist.

When there is free fall there is no sensation of weight. A gravitational field must be opposed to be detected by the human body.

Some of these considerations passed through Stevens's mind as he handwalked his way to Waldo's workshop. Waldo's home had been constructed without any consideration being given to up-and-down. Furniture and apparatus were affixed to any wall; there was no "floor." Decks and platforms were arranged at any convenient angle and of any size or shape, since they had nothing to do with standing or walking. Properly speaking, they were bulkheads and working surfaces rather than decks. Furthermore, equipment was not necessarily placed close to such surfaces; frequently it was more convenient to locate it with space all around it, held in place by light guys or slender stanchions.

The furniture and equipment was all odd in design and frequently odd in purpose. Most furniture on Earth is extremely rugged, and at least 90 per cent of it has a single purpose—to oppose, in one way or another, the acceleration of gravity. Most of the furniture in an Earth-surface—or subsurface—house is stator machines intended to oppose gravity. All tables, chairs, beds, couches, clothing racks, shelves, drawers, et cetera, have that as their one purpose. All other furniture and equipment have it as a secondary purpose which strongly conditions design and strength.

The lack of need for the rugged strength necessary to all terrestrial equipment resulted in a fairylike grace in much of the equipment in Waldo's house. Stored supplies, massive in themselves, could be retained in convenient order by compartmentation of eggshell-thin transparent plastic. Ponderous machinery, which on Earth would necessarily be heavily cased and supported, was here either open to the air or covered by gossamerlike envelopes and held stationary by light elastic lines.

Everywhere were pairs of waldoes, large, small and life-size, with vision pickups to match. It was evident that Waldo could make use of the compartments through which they were passing without stirring out of his easy chair—if he used an easy chair. The ubiquitous waldoes, the insubstantial quality of the furniture, and the casual use of all walls as work or storage surfaces, gave the place a madly fantastic air. Stevens felt as if he were caught in a Disney.

So far the rooms were not living quarters. Stevens wondered what Waldo's private apartments could be like and tried to visualize what equipment would be appropriate. No chairs, no rugs, no bed. Pictures, perhaps. Something pretty clever in the way of indirect lighting, since the eyes might be turned in any direction. Communication instruments might be much the same. But what could a washstand be like? Or a water tumbler? A trap bottle for the last—or would any container be necessary at all? He could not decide and realized that even a competent engineer may be confused in the face of mechanical conditions strange to him.

What constitutes a good ash tray when there is no gravity to hold the debris in place? Did Waldo smoke? Suppose he played solitaire; how did he handle the cards? Magnetized cards, perhaps, and a magnetized playing surface.

"In through here, Jim." Grimes steadied himself with one hand, gesturing with the other. Stevens slid through the manhole indicated. Before he had had time to look around he was startled by a menacing bass growl. He looked up; charging through the air straight at him was an enormous mastiff, lips drawn back, jaws slavering. Its front legs were spread out stiffly as if to balance in flight; its hind legs were drawn up under its lean belly. By voice and manner it announced clearly its intention of tearing the intruder into pieces, then swallowing the pieces.

"Baldur!" A voice cut through the air from some point beyond. The dog's ferocity wilted, but it could not check its lunge. A waldo snaked out a good thirty feet and grasped it by the collar. "I am sorry, sir," the voice added. "My friend was not expecting you."

Grimes said, "Howdy, Baldur. How's your conduct?" The dog looked at him, whined, and wagged his tail. Stevens looked for the source of the commanding voice, found it.

The room was huge and spherical; floating in its center was a fat man—Waldo.

He was dressed conventionally enough in shorts and singlet, except that his feet were bare. His hands and forearms were covered by metallic gauntlets—primary waldoes. He was softly fat, with double chin, dimples, smooth skin; he looked like a great, pink cherub, floating attendance on a saint. But the eyes were not cherubic, and the forehead and skull were those of a man. He looked at Stevens. "Permit me to introduce you to my pet," he said in a high, tired voice. "Give the paw, Baldur."

The dog offered a foreleg, Stevens shook it gravely. "Let him smell you, please."

The dog did so, as the waldo at his collar permitted him to come closer. Satisfied, the animal bestowed a wet kiss on Stevens's wrist. Stevens noted that the dog's eyes were surrounded by large circular patches of brown in contrast to his pre-

40

vailing white, and mentally tagged it the Dog with Eyes as Large as Saucers, thinking of the tale of the soldier and the flint box. He made noises to it of "Good boy!" and "That's a nice old fellow!" while Waldo looked on with faint distaste.

"Heel, sir!" Waldo commanded when the ceremony was complete. The dog turned in midair, braced a foot against Stevens's thigh, and shoved, projecting himself in the direction of his master. Stevens was forced to steady himself by clutching at the handgrip. Grimes shoved himself away from the manhole and arrested his flight on a stanchion near their host. Stevens followed him.

Waldo looked him over slowly. His manner was not overtly rude, but was somehow, to Stevens, faintly annoying. He felt a slow flush spreading out from his neck; to inhibit it he gave his attention to the room around him. The space was commodious, yet gave the impression of being cluttered because of the assemblage of, well, *junk* which surrounded Waldo. There were half a dozen vision receptors of various sizes around him at different angles, all normal to his line of sight. Three of them had pickups to match. There were control panels of several sorts, some of which seemed obvious enough in their purpose—one for lighting, which was quite complicated, with little ruby telltales for each circuit, one which was the keyboard of a voder, a multiplex television control panel, a board which seemed to be power relays, although its design was unusual. But there were

41

at least half a dozen which stumped Stevens completely.

There were several pairs of waldoes growing out of a steel ring which surrounded the working space. Two pairs, mere monkey fists in size, were equipped with extensors. It had been one of these which had shot out to grab Baldur by his collar. There were waldoes rigged near the spherical wall, too, including one pair so huge that Stevens could not conceive of a use for it. Extended, each hand spread quite six feet from little finger tip to thumb tip.

There were books in plenty on the wall, but no bookshelves. They seemed to grow from the wall like so many cabbages. It puzzled Stevens momentarily, but he inferred—correctly it turned out later—that a small magnet fastened to the binding did the trick.

The arrangement of lighting was novel, complex, automatic, and convenient for Waldo. But it was not so convenient for anyone else in the room. The lighting was of course, indirect; but, furthermore, it was subtly controlled, so that none of the lighting came from the direction in which Waldo's head was turned. There was no glare— for Waldo. Since the lights behind his head burned brightly in order to provide more illumination for whatever he happened to be looking at, there was glare aplenty for anyone else. An electric eye circuit, obviously. Stevens found himself wondering just how simple such a circuit could be made.

Grimes complained about it. "Damn it, Waldo;

get those lights under control. You'll give us head-aches."

"Sorry, Uncle Gus." He withdrew his right hand from its gauntlet and placed his fingers over one of the control panels. The glare stopped. Light now came from whatever direction none of them happened to be looking, and much more brightly, since the area source of illumination was much reduced. Lights rippled across the walls in pleasant patterns. Stevens tried to follow the ripples, a difficult matter, since the setup was made *not* to be seen. He found that he could do so by rolling his eyes without moving his head. It was movement of the head which controlled the lights; movement of an eyeball was a little too much for it.

"Well, Mr. Stevens, do you find my house interesting?" Waldo was smiling at him with faint superciliousness.

"Oh—quite! Quite! I believe that it is the most remarkable place I have ever been in."

"And what do you find remarkable about it?"

"Well—the lack of definite orientation, I believe. That and the remarkable mechanical novelties. I suppose I am a bit of a groundlubber, but I keep expecting a floor underfoot and a ceiling overhead."

"Mere matters of functional design, Mr. Stevens; the conditions under which I live are unique; therefore, my house is unique. The novelty you speak of consists mainly in the elimination of unnecessary parts and the addition of new conveniences.

"To tell the truth, the most interesting thing I have seen yet is not a part of the house at all."

"Really? What is it, pray?"

"Your dog, Baldur." The dog looked around at the mention of his name. "I've never before met a dog who could handle himself in free flight."

Waldo smiled; for the first time his smile seemed gentle and warm. "Yes, Baldur is quite an acrobat. He's been at it since he was a puppy." He reached out and roughed the dog's ears, showing momentarily his extreme weakness, for the gesture had none of the strength appropriate to the size of the brute. The finger motions were flaccid, barely sufficient to disturb the coarse fur and to displace the great ears. But he seemed unaware, or unconcerned, by the disclosure. Turning back to Stevens, he added, "But if Baldur amuses you, you must see Ariel."

"Ariel?"

Instead of replying, Waldo touched the keyboard of the voder, producing a musical whistling pattern of three notes. There was a rustling near the wall of the room "above" them; a tiny yellow shape shot toward them—a canary. It sailed through the air with wings folded, bullet fashion. A foot or so away from Waldo it spread its wings, cupping the air, beat them a few times with tail down and spread, and came to a dead stop, hovering in the air with folded wings. Not quite a dead stop, perhaps, for it drifted slowly, came within an inch of Waldo's shoulder, let down its landing gear, and dug its claws into his singlet.

44

Waldo reached up and stroked it with a fingertip. It preened. "No earth-hatched bird can learn to fly in that fashion," he stated. "I know. I lost half a dozen before I was sure that they were incapable of making the readjustment. Too much thalamus."

"What happened to them?"

"In a man you would call it acute anxiety psychosis. They try to fly; their own prime skill leads them to disaster. Naturally, everything they do is wrong and they don't understand it. Presently they quit trying; a little later they die. Of a broken heart, one might say, poetically." He smiled thinly. "But Ariel is a genius among birds. He came here as an egg; he invented, unassisted, a whole new school of flying." He reached up a finger, offering the bird a new perch, which it accepted.

"That's enough, Ariel. Fly away home."

The bird started the "Bell Song" from *Lakmé*.

He shook it gently. "No, Ariel. Go to bed."

The canary lifted its feet clear of the finger, floated for an instant, then beat its wings savagely for a second or two to set course and pick up speed, and bulleted away whence he had come, wings folded, feet streamlined under.

"Jimmie's got something he wants to talk with you about," Grimes commenced.

"Delighted," Waldo answered lazily, "but shan't we dine first? Have you an appetite, sir?"

Waldo full, Stevens decided, might be easier to cope with than Waldo empty. Besides, his own mid-section informed him that wrestling with a calorie or two might be pleasant. "Yes, I have."

"Excellent." They were served.

Stevens was never able to decide whether Waldo had prepared the meal by means of his many namesakes, or whether servants somewhere out of sight had done the actual work. Modern food-preparation methods being what they were, Waldo could have done it alone; he, Stevens, batched it with no difficulty, and so did Gus. But he made a mental note to ask Doc Grimes at the first opportunity what resident staff, if any, Waldo employed. He never remembered to do so.

The dinner arrived in a small food chest, propelled to their midst at the end of a long, telescoping, pneumatic tube. It stopped with a soft sigh and held its position. Stevens paid little attention to the food itself—it was adequate and tasty, he knew—for his attention was held by the dishes and serving methods. Waldo let his own steak float in front of him, cut bites from it with curved surgical shears, and conveyed them to his mouth by means of dainty tongs. He made hard work of chewing.

"You can't get good steaks any more," he remarked. "This one is tough. God knows I pay enough—and complain enough."

Stevens did not answer. He thought his own steak had been tenderized too much; it almost fell apart. He was managing it with knife and fork, but the knife was superfluous. It appeared that Waldo did not expect his guests to make use of his own admittedly superior methods and utensils. Stevens ate from a platter clamped to his thighs, making a lap for it after Grimes's example by squatting in mid air. The platter itself had been thoughtfully provided with sharp little prongs on its service side.

Liquids were served in small flexible skins, equipped with nipples. Think of a baby's plastic nursing bottle.

The food chest took the utensils away with a dolorous insufflation. "Will you smoke, sir?"

"Thank you." He saw what a weight-free ash tray necessarily should be: a long tube with a bell-shaped receptacle on its end. A slight suction in the tube, and ashes knocked into the bell were swept away, out of sight and mind.

"About the matter—" Grimes commenced again. "Jimmie here is Chief Engineer for North American Power-Air."

"What?" Waldo straightened himself, became rigid; his chest rose and fell. He ignored Stevens entirely. "Uncle Gus, do you mean to say that you have introduced an officer of *that* company into my—home?"

"Don't get your dander up. Relax. Damn it, I've warned you not to do anything to raise your blood pressure." Grimes propelled himself closer to his host and took him by the wrist in the age-old fashion of a physician counting pulse. "Breathe slower. Whatcha trying to do? Go on an oxygen jag?"

Waldo tried to shake himself loose. It was a

rather pitiful gesture; the old man had ten times his strength. "Uncle Gus, you—"

"Shut up!"

The three maintained a silence for several minutes, uncomfortable for at least two of them. Grimes did not seem to mind it.

"There," he said at last. "That's better. Now keep your shirt on and listen to me. Jimmie is a nice kid, and he has never done anything to you. And he has behaved himself while he's been here. You've got no right to be rude to him, no matter who he works for. Matter of fact, you owe him an apology."

"Oh, really now, Doc," Stevens protested. "I'm afraid I *have* been here somewhat under false colors. I'm sorry, Mr. Jones. I didn't intend it to be that way. I tried to explain when we arrived."

Waldo's face was hard to read. He was evidently trying hard to control himself. "Not at all, Mr. Stevens. I am sorry that I showed temper. It is perfectly true that I should not transfer to you any animus I feel for your employers...though God knows I bear no love for them."

"I know it. Nevertheless, I am sorry to hear you say it."

"I was cheated, do you understand? *Cheated*— by as rotten a piece of quasi-legal chicanery as has ever——"

"Easy, Waldo!"

"Sorry, Uncle Gus." He continued, his voice less shrill. "You know of the so-called Hathaway patents?"

"Yes, of course."

"'So-called' is putting it mildly. The man was a mere machinist. Those patents are mine."

Waldo's version, as he proceeded to give it, was reasonably factual, Stevens felt, but quite biased and unreasonable. Perhaps Hathaway had been working, as Waldo alleged, simply as a servant— a hired artisan, but there was nothing to prove it, no contract, no papers of any sort. The man had filed certain patents, the only ones he had ever filed and admittedly Waldo-ish in their cleverness. Hathaway had then promptly died, and his heirs, through their attorneys, had sold the patents to a firm which had been dickering with Hathaway.

Waldo alleged that this firm had put Hathaway up to stealing from him, had caused him to hire himself out to Waldo for that purpose. But the firm was defunct; its assets had been sold to North American Power-Air. NAPA had offered a settlement; Waldo had chosen to sue. The suit went against him.

Even if Waldo were right, Stevens could not see any means by which the directors of NAPA could, legally, grant him any relief. The officers of a corporation are trustees for other people's money; if the directors of NAPA should attempt to give away property which had been adjudicated as belonging to the corporation, any stockholder could enjoin them before the act or recover from them personally after the act.

At least so Stevens thought. But he was no lawyer, he admitted to himself. The important point was that he needed Waldo's services, whereas

Waldo held a bitter grudge against the firm he worked for.

He was forced to admit that it did not look as if Doc Grimes's presence was enough to turn the trick. "All that happened before my time," he began, "and naturally I know very little about it. I'm awfully sorry it happened. It's pretty uncomfortable for me, for right now I find myself in a position where I need your services very badly indeed."

Waldo did not seem displeased with the idea. "So? How does this come about?"

Stevens explained to him in some detail the trouble they had been having with the deKalb receptors. Waldo listened attentively. When Stevens had concluded he said, "Yes, that is much the same story your Mr. Gleason had to tell. Of course, as a technical man you have given a much more coherent picture than that money manipulator was capable of giving. But why do you come to me? I do not specialize in radiation engineering, nor do I have any degrees from fancy institutions."

"I come to you," Stevens said seriously, "for the same reason everybody else comes to you when they are really stuck with an engineering problem. So far as I know, you have an unbroken record of solving any problem you cared to tackle. Your record reminds me of another man——"

"Who?" Waldo's tone was suddenly sharp.

"Edison. He did not bother with degrees either, but solved all the hard problems of his day."

"Oh, Edison——I thought you were speaking of

a contemporary. No doubt he was all right in his day," he added with overt generosity.

"I was not comparing him to you. I was simply recalling that Edison was reputed to prefer hard problems to easy ones. I've heard the same about you; I had hopes that this problem might be hard enough to interest you."

"It is mildly interesting," Waldo conceded. "A little out of my line, but interesting. I must say, however, that I am surprised to hear you, an executive of North American Power-Air, express such a high opinion of my talents. One would think that, if the opinion were sincere, it would not have been difficult to convince your firm of my indisputable handiwork in the matter of the so-called Hathaway patents."

Really, thought Stevens, the man is impossible. A mind like a weasel. Aloud, he said, "I suppose the matter was handled by the business management and the law staff. They would hardly be equipped to distinguish between routine engineering and inspired design."

The answer seemed to mollify Waldo. He asked, "What does your own research staff say about the problem?"

Stevens looked wry. "Nothing helpful. Dr. Rambeau does not really seem to believe the data I bring him. He says it's impossible, but it makes him unhappy. I really believe that he has been living on aspirin and Nembutal for a good many weeks."

"Rambeau," Waldo said slowly. "I recall the man.

A mediocre mind. All memory and no intuition. I don't think I would feel discouraged simply because Rambeau is puzzled."

"You really feel that there is some hope?"

"It should not be too difficult. I had already given the matter some thought, after Mr. Gleason's phone call. You have given me additional data, and I think I see at least two new lines of approach which may prove fruitful. In any case, there is always some approach—the correct one."

"Does that mean you will accept?" Stevens demanded, nervous with relief.

"Accept?" Waldo's eyebrows climbed up. "My dear sir, what in the world are you talking about? We were simply indulging in social conversation. I would not help your company under any circumstances whatsoever. I hope to see your firm destroyed utterly, bankrupt and ruined. This may well be the occasion."

Stevens fought to keep control of himself. Tricked! The fat slob had simply been playing with him, leading him on. There was no decency in him. In careful tones he continued, "I do not ask that you have any mercy on North American, Mr. Jones, but I appeal to your sense of duty. There is public interest involved. Millions of people are vitally dependent on the service we provide. Don't you see that the service *must* continue, regardless of you or me?"

Waldo pursed his lips. "No," he said, "I'm afraid that does not affect me. The welfare of those nameless swarms of Earth crawlers is, I fear, not my concern. I have done more for them already than there was any need to do. They hardly deserve help. Left to their own devices, most of them would sink back to caves and stone axes. Did you ever see a performing ape, Mr. Stevens, dressed in a man's clothes and cutting capers on roller skates? Let me leave you with this thought: I am not a roller-skate mechanic for apes."

If I stick around here much longer, Stevens advised himself, there will be hell to pay. Aloud, he said, "I take it that is your last word?"

"You may so take it. Good day, sir. I enjoyed your visit. Thank you."

"Good-by. Thanks for the dinner."

"Not at all."

As Stevens turned away and prepared to shove himself toward the exit, Grimes called after him, "Jimmie, wait for me in the reception room."

As soon as Stevens was out of earshot, Grimes turned to Waldo and looked him up and down. "Waldo," he said slowly, "I always did know that you were one of the meanest, orneriest men alive, but—"

"Your compliments don't faze me, Uncle Gus."

"Shut up and listen to me. As I was saying, I knew you were too rotten selfish to live with, but this is the first time I ever knew you to be a four-flusher to boot."

"What do you mean by that? Explain yourself."

"Shucks! You haven't any more idea of how to crack the problem that boy is up against than I have. You traded on your reputation as a miracle man just to make him unhappy. Why, you cheap tinhorn bluffer, if you——"

"Stop it!"

"Go ahead," Grimes said quietly. "Run up your blood pressure. I won't interfere with you. The sooner you blow a gasket the better."

Waldo calmed down. "Uncle Gus—what makes you think I was bluffing?"

"Because I know you. If you had felt able to deliver the goods, you would have looked the situation over and worked out a plan to get NAPA by the short hair, through having something they had to have. That way you would have *proved* your revenge."

Waldo shook his head. "You underestimate the intensity of my feeling in the matter."

"I do like hell! I hadn't finished. About that sweet little talk you gave him concerning your responsibility to the race. You've got a head on you. You know damned well, and so do I, that of all people you can least afford to have anything serious happen to the setup down on Earth. That means you don't see any way to prevent it."

"Why, what do you mean? I have no interest in such troubles; I'm independent of such things. You know me better than that."

"Independent, eh? Who mined the steel in these walls? Who raised that steer you dined on tonight? You're as independent as a queen bee, and about as helpless."

Waldo looked startled. He recovered himself and

answered, "Oh no, Uncle Gus. I really am independent. Why, I have supplies here for years."

"How many years?"

"Why ... uh, five, about."

"And then what? You may live another *fifty*— *if* you have regular supply service. How do you prefer to die—starvation or thirst?"

"Water is no problem," Waldo said thoughtfully; "as for supplies, I suppose I could use hydroponics a little more and stock up with some meat animals—"

Grimes cut him short with a nasty laugh. "Proved my point. You don't *know* how to avert it, so you are figuring some way to save your own skin. I know you. You wouldn't talk about starting a truck garden if you knew the answers."

Waldo looked at him thoughtfully. "That's not entirely true. I don't know the solution, but I do have some ideas about it. I'll bet you a half interest in hell that I can crack it. Now that you have called my attention to it, I must admit I am rather tied in with the economic system down below, and"— he smiled faintly—"I was never one to neglect my own interests. Just a moment—I'll call your friend."

"Not so fast. I came along for another reason, besides introducing Jimmie to you. It can't be just any solution; it's got to be a particular solution."

"What do you mean?"

"It's got to be a solution that will do away with the need for filling up the air with radiant energy."

"Oh, *that*. See here, Uncle Gus, I know how

interested you are in theory, and I've never disputed the possibility that you may be right, but you can't expect me to mix that into another and very difficult problem."

"Take another look. You're in this for self-interest. Suppose everybody was in the shape you are in."

"You mean my *physical condition*?"

"I mean just that. I know you don't like to talk about it, but we blamed well need to. If everybody was as weak as you are—presto! No coffee and cakes for Waldo. And that's just what I see coming. You're the only man I know of who can appreciate what it means."

"It seems fantastic."

"It is. But the signs are there for anybody to read who wants to. Epidemic *myasthenia*, not necessarily acute, but enough to raise hell with our mechanical civilization. Enough to play hob with your supply lines. I've been collating my data since I saw you last and drawing some curves. You should see 'em."

"Did you bring them?"

"No, but I'll send 'em up. In the meantime, you can take my word for it." He waited. "Well, how about it?"

"I'll accept it as a tentative working hypothesis," Waldo said slowly, "until I see your figures. I shall probably want you to conduct some further research for me, on the ground—if your data is what you say it is."

"Fair enough. G'by." Grimes kicked the air a couple of times as he absent-mindedly tried to walk.

Stevens's frame of mind as he waited for Grimes is better left undescribed. The mildest thought that passed through his mind was a plaintive one about the things a man had to put up with to hold down what seemed like a simple job of engineering. Well, he wouldn't have the job very long. But he decided not to resign—he'd wait until they fired him; he wouldn't run out.

But he would damn well get that vacation before he looked for another job.

He spent several minutes wishing that Waldo were strong enough for him to be able to take a poke at him. Or kick him in the belly—that would be more fun!

He was startled when the dummy suddenly came to life and called him by name. "Oh, Mr. Stevens."

"Huh? Yes?"

"I have decided to accept the commission. My attorneys will arrange the details with your business office."

He was too surprised to answer for a couple of seconds; when he did so the dummy had already gone dead. He waited impatiently for Grimes to show up.

"Doc!" he said, when the old man swam into view. "What got into him. How did you do it?"

"He thought it over and reconsidered," Grimes said succinctly. "Let's get going."

Stevens dropped Dr. Augustus Grimes at the

doctor's home, then proceeded to his office. He had no more than parked his car and entered the tunnel leading toward the zone plant when he ran into his assistant. McLeod seemed a little out of breath. "Gee, chief," he said, "I hoped that was you. I've had 'em watching for you. I need to see you."

"What's busted now?" Stevens demanded apprehensively. "One of the cities?"

"No. What made you think so?"

"Go ahead with your story."

"So far as I know ground power is humming sweet as can be. No trouble with the cities. What I had on my mind is this: *I fixed my heap.*"

"Huh? You mean you fixed the ship you crashed in?"

"It wasn't exactly a crash. I had plenty of power in the reserve banks; when reception cut off, I switched to emergency and landed her."

"But you fixed it? Was it the deKalbs? Or something else?"

"It was the deKalbs all right. And they're fixed. But I didn't exactly do it myself. I got it done. You see——"

"What was the matter with them?"

"I don't know exactly. You see I decided that there was no point in hiring another skycar and maybe having another forced landing on the way home. Besides, it was my own crate I was flying, and I didn't want to dismantle her just to get the deKalbs out and have her spread out all over the countryside. So I hired a crawler, with the idea of taking her back all in one piece. I struck a deal with a guy who had a twelve-ton semitractor combination, and we——"

"For criminy's sake, make it march! What happened?"

"I'm trying to tell you. We pushed on into Pennsylvania and we were making pretty fair time when the crawler broke down. The right lead wheel, ahead of the treads. Honest to goodness, Jim, those roads are something fierce."

"Never mind that. Why waste taxes on roads when 90 per cent of the traffic is in the air? You messed up a wheel. So then what?"

"Just the same, those roads are a disgrace," McLeod maintained stubbornly. "I was brought up in that part of the country. When I was a kid the road we were on was six lanes wide and smooth as a baby's fanny. They ought to be kept up; we might need 'em someday." Seeing the look in his senior's eye, he went on hastily: "The driver mugged in with his home office, and they promised to send a repair car out from the next town. All told, it would take three, four hours—maybe more. Well, we were laid up in the county I grew up in. I says to myself, 'McLeod, this is a wonderful chance to return to the scenes of your childhood and the room where the sun came peeping in the morn.' Figuratively speaking, of course. Matter of fact, our house didn't have any windows."

"I don't care if you were raised in a barrel!"

"Temper...temper——" McLeod said imperturbably. "I'm telling you this so you will understand what happened. But you aren't going to like it."

"I don't like it now."

"You'll like it less. I climbed down out of the cab and took a look around. We were about five miles from my home town—too far for me to want to walk it. But I thought I recognized a clump of trees on the brow of a little rise maybe a quarter of a mile off the road, so I walked over to see. I was right; just over the rise was the cabin where Gramps Schneider used to live."

"Gramps Snyder?"

"Not Snyder—*Sch*neider. Old boy we kids used to be friendly with. Ninety years older than anybody. I figured he was dead, but it wouldn't hurt any to walk down and see. He wasn't. 'Hello, Gramps,' I said. 'Come in, Hugh Donald,' he said. 'Wipe the feet on the mat.'

"I came in and sat down. He was fussing with something simmering in a stewpan on his baseburner. I asked him what it was. 'For morning aches,' he said. Gramps isn't exactly a hex doctor."

"Huh?"

"I mean he doesn't make a living by it. He raises a few chickens and garden truck, and some of the Plain People—House Amish, mostly—give him pies and things. But he knows a lot about herbs and such.

"Presently he stopped and cut me a slice of shoofly pie. I told him *danke*. He said, 'You've been upgrowing, Hugh Donald,' and asked me how I was doing in school. I told him I was doing pretty well.

He looked at me again and said, 'But you have trouble fretting you.' It wasn't a question; it was a statement. While I finished the pie I found myself trying to tell him what kind of troubles I had.

"It wasn't easy. I don't suppose Gramps has ever been off the ground in his life. And modern radiation theory isn't something you can explain in words of one syllable. I was getting more and more tangled up when he stood up, put on his hat and said, 'We will see this car you speak about.'

"We walked over to the highway. The repair gang had arrived, but the crawler wasn't ready yet. I helped Gramps up onto the platform and we got into my bus. I showed him the deKalbs and tried to explain what they did—or rather what they were supposed to do. Mind you, I was just killing time.

"He pointed to the sheaf of antennae and asked, 'These fingers—they reach out for the power?' It was as good an explanation as any, so I let it ride. He said, 'I understand,' and pulled a piece of chalk out of his trousers, and began drawing lines on each antenna, from front to back. I walked up front to see how the repair crew were doing. After a bit Gramps joined me. 'Hugh Donald,' he says, 'the fingers—now they will make.'

"I didn't want to hurt his feelings, so I thanked him plenty. The crawler was ready to go; we said good-by, and he walked back toward his shack. I went back to my car, and took a look in, just in case. I didn't think he could hurt anything, but I wanted to be sure. Just for the ducks of it. I tried out the receptors. They worked!"

"What!" put in Stevens. "You don't mean to stand there and tell me an old witch doctor fixed your deKalbs?"

"Not witch doctor—*hex* doctor. But you get the idea."

Stevens shook his head. "It's simply a coincidence. Sometimes they come back into order as spontaneously as they go out."

"That's what you think. Not this one. I've just been preparing you for the shock you're going to get. *Come take a look.*"

"What do you mean? Where?"

"In the inner hangar." While they walked to where McLeod had left his broomstick, he continued, "I wrote out a credit for the crawler pilot and flew back. I haven't spoken to anyone else about it. I've been biting my nails down to my elbows waiting for you to show up."

The skycar seemed quite ordinary. Stevens examined the deKalbs and saw some faint chalk marks on their metal sides—nothing else unusual. "Watch while I cut in reception," McLeod told him.

Stevens waited, heard the faint hum as the circuits became activized, and looked.

The antennae of the deKalbs, each a rigid pencil of metal, were bending, flexing, writhing like a cluster of worms. They were *reaching out*, like fingers.

Stevens remained squatting down by the deKalbs, watching their outrageous motion.

McLeod left the control saddle, came back, and joined him. "Well, chief," he demanded, "tell me about it. Whaduh yuh make of it?"

"Got a cigarette?"

"What are those things sticking out of your pocket?"

"Oh! Yeah—sure." Stevens took one out, lighted it, and burned it halfway down, unevenly, with two long drags

"Go on," McLeod urged. "Give us a tell. What makes it do that?"

"Well," Stevens said slowly, "I can think of three things to do next——"

"Yeah?"

"The first is to fire Dr. Rambeau and give his job to Gramps Schneider."

"That's a good idea in any case."

"The second is to just wait here quietly until the boys with the straitjackets show up to take us home."

"And what's the third?"

"The third," Stevens said savagely, "is to take this damned heap out and sink it in the deepest part of the Atlantic Ocean and pretend like it never happened!"

A mechanic stuck his head in the door of the car. "Oh, Dr. Stevens——"

"Get out of here!"

The head hastily withdrew; the voice picked up in aggrieved tones. "Message from the head office."

Stevens got up, went to the operator's saddle, cleared the board, then assured himself that the antennae had ceased their disturbing movements. They had; in fact, they appeared so beautifully straight and rigid that he was again tempted to doubt the correctness of his own senses. He climbed out to the floor of the hangar, McLeod behind him. "Sorry to have blasted at you, Whitey," he said to the workman in placating tones. "What is the message?"

"Mr. Gleason would like for you to come into his office as soon as you can."

"I will at once. And, Whitey, I've a job for you."

"Yeah?"

"This heap here—seal up its doors and don't let anybody monkey with it. Then have it dragged, dragged, mind you; don't try to start it—have it dragged over into the main lab."

"O.K."

Stevens started away; McLeod stopped him. "What do I go home in?"

"Oh yes, it's your personal property, isn't it? Tell you what, Mac—the company needs it. Make out a purchase order and I'll sign it."

"Weeeell, now—I don't rightly know as I want to sell it. It might be the only job in the country working properly before long."

"Don't be silly. If the others play out, it won't do you any good to have the only one in working order. Power will be shut down."

"I suppose there's that," McLeod conceded. "Still," he said, brightening visibly, "a crate like that, with its special talents, ought to be worth a good deal more than list. You couldn't just go out and buy one."

"Mac," said Stevens, "you've got avarice in your heart and thievery in your finger tips. How much do you want for it?"

"Suppose we say twice the list price, new. That's letting you off easy."

"I happen to know you bought that job at a discount. But go ahead. Either the company can stand it, or it won't make much difference in the bankruptcy."

Gleason looked up as Stevens came in. "Oh, there you are, Jim. You seemed to have pulled a miracle with our friend Waldo the Great. Nice work."

"How much did he stick us for?"

"Just his usual contract. Of course his usual contract is a bit like robbery with violence. But it will be worth it if he is successful. And it's on a straight contingent basis. He must feel pretty sure of himself. They say he's never lost a contingent fee in his life. Tell me—what is he like? Did you really get into his house?"

"I did. And I'll tell you about it—sometime. Right now another matter has come up which has me talking to myself. You ought to hear about it at once."

"So? Go ahead."

Stevens opened his mouth, closed it again, and realized that it had to be seen to be believed. "Say, could you come with me to the main lab? I've got something to show you."

"Certainly."

Gleason was not as perturbed by the squirming metal rods as Stevens had been. He was surprised, but not upset. The truth of the matter is that he lacked the necessary technical background to receive the full emotional impact of the inescapable implications of the phenomenon. "That's pretty unusual, isn't it?" he said quietly.

"Unusual! Look, chief, if the sun rose in the west, what would you think?"

"I think I would call the observatory and ask them why."

"Well, all I can say is that I would a whole lot rather that the sun rose in the west than to have this happen."

"I admit it is pretty disconcerting," Gleason agreed. "I can't say that I've ever seen anything like it. What is Dr. Rambeau's opinion?"

"He hasn't seen it."

"Then perhaps we had better send for him. He may not have gone home for the night as yet."

"Why not show it to Waldo instead?"

"We will. But Dr. Rambeau is entitled to see it first. After all, it's his bailiwick, and I'm afraid the poor fellow's nose is pretty well out of joint as it is. I don't want to go over his head."

Stevens felt a sudden flood of intuition. "Just a second, chief. You're right, but if it's all the same to you I would rather that you showed it to him than for me to do it."

"Why so, Jimmie? You can explain it to him."

"I can't explain a damn thing to him I haven't

66

already told you. And for the next few hours I'm going to be very, very busy indeed."

Gleason looked him over, shrugged his shoulders, and said mildly, "Very well, Jim, if you prefer it that way."

Waldo was quite busy, and therefore happy. He would never have admitted—he did not admit even to himself, that there were certain drawbacks to his self-imposed, withdrawal from the world and that chief among these was boredom. He had never had much opportunity to enjoy the time-consuming delights of social intercourse; he honestly believed that the smooth apes had nothing to offer him in the way of companionship. Nevertheless, the pleasure of the solitary intellectual life can pall.

He repeatedly urged Uncle Gus to make his permanent home in Freehold, but he told himself that it was a desire to take care of the old man which motivated him. True—he enjoyed arguing with Grimes, but he was not aware how much those arguments meant to him. The truth of the matter was that Grimes was the only one of the human race who treated him entirely as another human and an equal—and Waldo wallowed in it, completely unconscious that the pleasure he felt in the old man's company was the commonest and most precious of all human pleasures.

But at present he was happy in the only way he knew how to be happy—working.

There were two problems: that of Stevens and

that of Grimes. Required: a single solution which would satisfy each of them. There were three stages to each problem; first, to satisfy himself that the problems really did exist, that the situations were in fact as they had been reported to him verbally; second, to undertake such research as the preliminary data suggested; and third, when he felt that his data was complete, to invent a solution.

"Invent," not "find." Dr. Rambeau might have said "find," or "search for." To Rambeau the universe was an inexorably ordered cosmos, ruled by unvarying law. To Waldo the universe was the enemy, which he strove to force to submit to his will. They might have been speaking of the same thing, but their approaches were different.

There was much to be done. Stevens had supplied him with a mass of data, both on the theoretical nature of the radiated power system and the deKalb receptors which were the keystone of the system, and also on the various cases of erratic performance of which they had lately been guilty. Waldo had not given serious attention to power radiation up to this time, simply because he had not needed to. He found it interesting but comparatively simple. Several improvements suggested themselves to his mind. That standing wave, for example, which was the main factor in the co-axial beam—the efficiency of reception could be increased considerably by sending a message back over it which would automatically correct the aiming of the beam. Power delivery to moving vehicles could be made nearly as efficient as the power reception to stationary receivers.

Not that such an idea was important at present. Later, when he had solved the problem at hand, he intended to make NAPA pay through the nose for the idea; or perhaps it would be more amusing to compete with them. He wondered when their basic patents ran out—must look it up.

Despite inefficiencies the deKalb receptors should work every time, all the time, without failure. He went happily about finding out why they did not.

He had suspected some obvious—obvious to *him*—defect in manufacture. But the inoperative deKalbs which Stevens had delivered to him refused to give up their secret. He X-rayed them, measured them with micrometer and interferometer, subjected them to all the usual tests and some that were quite unusual and peculiarly Waldoish. They would not perform.

He built a deKalb in his shop, using one of the inoperative ones as a model and using the reworked metal of another of the same design, also inoperative, as the raw material. He used his finest scanners to see with and his smallest waldoes—tiny pixy hands, an inch across—for manipulation in the final stages. He created a deKalb which was as nearly identical with its model as technology and incredible skill could produce.

It worked beautifully.

Its elder twin still refused to work. He was not discouraged by this. On the contrary, he was elated.

He had proved, proved with certainty, that the failure of the deKalbs was not a failure of workmanship, but a basic failure in theory. The problem was real.

Stevens had reported to him the scandalous performance of the deKalbs in McLeod's skycar, but he had not yet given his attention to the matter. Presently, in proper order, when he got around to it, he would look into the matter. In the meantime he tabled the matter. The smooth apes were an hysterical lot; there was probably nothing to the story. Writhing like Medusa's locks, indeed!

He gave fully half his time to Grimes's problem.

He was forced to admit that the biological sciences—if you could call them science!—were more fascinating than he had thought. He had shunned them, more or less; the failure of expensive "experts" to do anything for his condition when he was a child had made him contemptuous of such studies. Old wives' nostrums dressed up in fancy terminology! Grimes he liked and even respected, but Grimes was a special case.

Grimes's data had convinced Waldo that the old man had a case. Why, this was serious! The figures were incomplete, but nevertheless convincing. The curve of the third decrement, extrapolated not too unreasonably, indicated that in twenty years there would not be a man left with strength enough to work in heavy industries. Button pushing would be all they would be good for.

It did not occur to him that all he was good for was button pushing; he regarded weakness in the smooth apes as an old-style farmer might regard weakness in a draft animal. The farmer did not expect to pull the plow—that was the horse's job.

Grimes's medical colleagues must be utter fools.

Nevertheless, he sent for the best physiologists, neurologists, brain surgeons, and anatomists he could locate, ordering them as one might order goods from a catalogue. He must understand this matter.

He was considerably annoyed when he found that he could not make arrangements, by any means, to perform vivisection on human beings. He was convinced by this time that the damage done by ultra short-wave radiation was damage to the neurological system, and that the whole matter should be treated from the standpoint of electromagnetic theory. He wanted to perform certain delicate manipulations in which human beings would be hooked up directly to apparatus of his own design to find out in what manner nerve impulses differed from electrical current. He felt that if he could disconnect portions of a man's nervous circuit, replace it in part with electrical hookups, and examine the whole matter *in situ*, he might make illuminating discoveries. True, the man might not be much use to himself afterward.

But the authorities were stuffy about it; he was forced to content himself with cadavers and with animals.

Nevertheless, he made progress. Extreme short-wave radiation had a definite effect on the nervous system—a double effect: it produced "ghost" pulsations in the neurons, insufficient to accomplish muscular motor response, but, he suspected, strong enough to keep the body in a continual state of inhibited nervous excitation; and, secondly, a living specimen which had been subjected to this process for any length of time showed a definite, small but measurable, lowering in the efficiency of its neural impulses. If it had been an electrical circuit, he would have described the second effect as a decrease in insulating efficiency.

The sum of these two effects on the subject individual was a condition of mild tiredness, somewhat similar to the malaise of the early stages of pulmonary tuberculosis. The victim did not feel sick; he simply lacked pep. Strenuous bodily activity was not impossible; it was simply distasteful; it required too much effort, too much will power.

But an orthodox pathologist would have been forced to report that the victim was in perfect health—a little run-down, perhaps, but nothing wrong with him. Too sedentary a life, probably. What he needed was fresh air, sunshine, and healthy exercise.

Doc Grimes alone had guessed that the present, general, marked preference for a sedentary life was the effect and not the cause of the prevailing lack of vigor. The change had been slow, at least as slow as the increase in radiation in the air. The individuals concerned had noticed it, if at all, simply as an indication that they were growing a little bit older, "slowing down, not so young as I used to be." And they were content to slow down; it was more comfortable than exertion.

Grimes had first begun to be concerned about it when he began to notice that *all* of his younger patients were "the bookish type." It was all very well for a kid to like to read books, he felt, but a normal boy ought to be out doing a little hell raising too. What had become of the sand-lot football games, the games of scrub, the clothes-tearing activity that had characterized his own boyhood?

Damn it, a kid ought not to spend *all* his time poring over a stamp collection.

Waldo was beginning to find the answer.

The nerve network of the body was not dissimilar to antennae. Like antennae, it could and did pick up electromagnetic waves. But the pickup was evidenced not as induced electrical current, but as nerve pulsation—impulses which were maddeningly similar to, but distinctly different from, electrical current. Electromotive force could be used in place of nerve impulses, to activate muscle tissue, but e.m.f. was *not* nerve impulse. For one thing they traveled at vastly different rates of speed. Electrical current travels at a speed approaching that of light; neural impulse is measured in feet per second.

Waldo felt that somewhere in this matter of speed lay the key to the problem.

He was not permitted to ignore the matter of McLeod's fantastic skycar as long as he had intended to. Dr. Rambeau called him up. Waldo accepted the call, since it was routed from the laboratories of NAPA. "Who are you and what do you want?" he demanded of the image.

Rambeau looked around cautiously. *"Sssh!* Not so loud," he whispered. "They might be listening."

"Who might be? And who are you?"

"'They' are the ones who are doing it. Lock your doors at night. I'm Dr. Rambeau."

"Dr. Rambeau? Oh yes. Well, Doctor, what is the meaning of this intrusion?"

The doctor leaned forward until he appeared about to fall out of the stereo picture. "I've learned how to do it," he said tensely.

"How to do what?"

"Make the deKalbs work. The dear, dear deKalbs." He suddenly thrust his hands at Waldo, while clutching frantically with his fingers. "They go like this: *Wiggle, wiggle, wiggle!*"

Waldo felt a normal impulse to cut the man off, but it was overruled by a fascination as to what he would say next. Rambeau continued. "Do you know why? Do you? Riddle me that."

"Why?"

Rambeau placed a finger beside his nose and smiled roguishly. "Wouldn't you like to know? Wouldn't you give a pretty to know? *But I'll tell you!*"

"Tell me, then."

Rambeau suddenly looked terrified. "Perhaps I shouldn't. Perhaps they are listening. But I will, I will! Listen carefully: Nothing is certain."

"Is that all?" inquired Waldo, now definitely amused by the man's antics.

"'Is that all?' Isn't that enough? Hens will crow and cocks will lay. You are here and I am there. Or maybe not. Nothing is certain. Nothing, *nothing*, NOTHING is certain! Around and around the little ball goes, and where it stops nobody knows. Only I've learned how to do it."

"How to do what?"

"How to make the little ball stop where I want it to. Look." He whipped out a penknife. "When you cut yourself, you bleed, don't you? Or do you?" He sliced at the forefinger of his left hand. "See?" He held the finger close to the pickup; the cut, though deep, was barely discernible and it was bleeding not at all.

Capital! thought Waldo. Hysteric vascular control—a perfect clinical case. "Anybody can do that," he said aloud. "Show me a hard one."

"Anybody? Certainly anybody can—if they know how. Try this one." He jabbed the point of the penknife straight into the palm of his left hand, so that it stuck out the back of his hand. He wiggled the blade in the wound, withdrew it, and displayed the palm. No blood, and the incision was closing rapidly. "Do you know why? The knife is only probably there, *and I've found the improbability!*"

Amusing as it had been, Waldo was beginning to be bored by it. "Is that all?"

"There is no end to it," pronounced Rambeau, "for nothing is certain any more. Watch this." He held the knife flat on his palm, then turned his hand over.

The knife did not fall, but remained in contact with the underside of his hand.

Waldo was suddenly attentive. It might be a trick; it probably was a trick—but it impressed him more, much more, than Rambeau's failure to bleed when cut. One was common to certain types of psychosis; the other should not have happened. He cut in another viewphone circuit. "Get me Chief Engineer Stevens at North American Power-Air," he said sharply. "At once!"

Rambeau paid no attention, but continued to speak of the penknife. "It does not know which way is down," he crooned, "for nothing is certain any more. Maybe it will fall—maybe not. I think it will. There—it has. Would you like to see me walk on the ceiling?"

"You called me, Mr. Jones?" It was Stevens.

Waldo cut his audio circuit to Rambeau. "Yes. That jumping jack, Rambeau. Catch him and bring him to me at once. I want to see him."

"But Mr. Jo——"

"Move!" He cut Stevens off, and renewed the audio to Rambeau.

"—uncertainty. Chaos is King, and Magic is loose in the world!" Rambeau looked vaguely at Waldo, brightened, and added, "Good day, Mr. Jones. Thank you for calling."

The screen went dead.

Waldo waited impatiently. The whole thing had been a hoax, he told himself. Rambeau had played a gigantic practical joke. Waldo disliked practical jokes. He put in another call for Stevens and left it in.

When Stevens did call back his hair was mussed and his face was red. "We had a bad time of it," he said.

"Did you get him?"

"Rambeau? Yes, finally."

"Then bring him up."

"To Freehold? But that's impossible. You don't understand. He's blown his top; he's crazy. They've taken him away to a hospital."

"You assume too much," Waldo said icily. "I know he's crazy, but I meant what I said. Arrange it. Provide nurses. Sign affidavits. Use bribery. Bring him to me at once. It is necessary."

"You really mean that?"

"I'm not in the habit of jesting."

"Something to do with your investigations? He's in no shape to be useful to you, I can tell you that."

"That," pronounced Waldo, "is for me to decide."

"Well," said Stevens doubtfully, "I'll try."

"See that you succeed."

Stevens called back thirty minutes later. "I can't bring Rambeau."

"You clumsy incompetent."

Stevens turned red, but held his temper. "Never mind the personalities. He's gone. He never got to the hospital."

"What?"

"That's the crazy part about it. They took him away in a confining stretcher, laced up like a corset. I saw them fasten him in myself. But when

77

they got there he was gone. And the attendants claim *the straps weren't even unbuckled*."

Waldo started to say, "Preposterous," thought better of it. Stevens went on.

"But that's not the half of it. I'd sure like to talk to him myself. I've been looking around his lab. You know that set of deKalbs that went nuts—the ones that were hexed?"

"I know to what you refer."

"Rambeau's got a second set to doing the same thing!"

Waldo remained silent for several seconds, then said quietly, "Dr. Stevens—"

"Yes."

"I want to thank you for your efforts. And will you please have both sets of receptors, the two sets that are misbehaving, sent to Freehold at once?"

There was no doubt about it. Once he had seen them with his own eyes, watched the inexplicable squirming of the antennae, applied such tests as suggested themselves to his mind, Waldo was forced to conclude that he was faced with new phenomena, phenomena for which he did not know the rules.

If there were rules....

For he was honest with himself. If he saw what he thought he saw, then rules were being broken by the new phenomena, rules which he had considered valid, rules to which he had never previously encountered exceptions. He admitted to himself that the original failures of the deKalbs should have been considered just as overwhelmingly upsetting to physical law as the unique behavior of these two; the difference lay in that one alien phenomenon was spectacular, the other was not.

Quite evidently Dr. Rambeau had found it so; he had been informed that the doctor had been increasingly neurotic from the first instance of erratic performance of the deKalb receptors.

He regretted the loss of Dr. Rambeau. Waldo was more impressed by Rambeau crazy than he had ever been by Rambeau sane. Apparently the man had had some modicum of ability after all; he had found out *something*—more, Waldo admitted, than he himself had been able to find out so far, even though it had driven Rambeau insane.

Waldo had no fear that Rambeau's experience, whatever it had been, could unhinge his own reason. His own self-confidence was, perhaps, fully justified. His own mild paranoid tendency was just sufficient to give him defenses against an unfriendly world. For him it was healthy, a necessary adjustment to an otherwise intolerable situation, no more pathological than a callus, or an acquired immunity.

Otherwise he was probably more able to face disturbing facts with equanimity than 99 per cent of his contemporaries. He had *been* born to disaster; he had met it and had overcome it, time and again. The very house which surrounded him was testimony to the calm and fearless fashion in which he had defeated a world to which he was not adapted.

He exhausted, temporarily, the obvious lines of direct research concerning the strangely twisting metal rods. Rambeau was not available for questioning. Very well, there remained one other man who knew more about it than Waldo did. He would seek him out. He called Stevens again.

"Has there been any word of Dr. Rambeau?"

"No word, and no sign. I'm beginning to think the poor old fellow is dead."

"Perhaps. That witch doctor friend of your assistant—was Schneider his name?"

"Gramps Schneider."

"Yes indeed. Will you please arrange for him to speak with me?"

"By phone, or do you want to see him in person?"

"I would prefer for him to come here, but I understand that he is old and feeble; it may not be feasible for him to leave the ground. If he is knotted up with spacesickness, he will be no use to me."

"I'll see what can be done."

"Very good. Please expedite the matter. And, Dr. Stevens—"

"Well?"

"If it should prove necessary to use the phone, arrange to have a portable full stereo taken to his home. I want the circumstances to be as favorable as possible."

"O.K."

"Imagine that," Stevens added to McLeod when the circuit had been broken. "The Great-I-Am's showing consideration for somebody else's convenience."

"The fat boy must be sick," McLeod decided.

"Seems likely. This chore is more yours than mine, Mac. Come along with me; we'll take a run over into Pennsylvania."

"How about the plant?"

"Tell Carruthers he's 'It.' If anything blows, we couldn't help it anyway."

Stevens mugged back later in the day. "Mr. Jones—"

"Yes, Doctor?"

"What you suggest can't be arranged."

"You mean that Schneider can't come to Freehold?"

"I mean that and I mean that you can't talk with him on the viewphone."

"I presume that you mean he is dead."

"No, I do not. I mean that he will not talk over the viewphone under any circumstances whatsoever, to you or to anyone. He says that he is sorry not to accommodate you, but that he is opposed to everything of that nature—cameras, cinécams, television, and so forth. He considers them dangerous. I am afraid he is set in his superstition."

"As an ambassador, Dr. Stevens, you leave much to be desired."

Stevens counted up to ten, then said, "I assure you that I have done everything in my power to comply with your wishes. If you are dissatisfied with the quality of my co-operation, I suggest that you speak to Mr. Gleason." He cleared the circuit.

"How would you like to kick him in the teeth?" McLeod said dreamily.

"Mac, you're a mind reader."

Waldo tried again through his own agents, received the same answer. The situation was, to him, almost intolerable; it had been years since he had encountered a man whom he could not buy, bully, nor—in extremity—persuade. Buying had failed; he had realized instinctively that Schneider would be unlikely to be motivated by greed. And how can one bully, or wheedle, a man who cannot be seen to be talked with?

It was a dead end—no way out. Forget it.

Except, of course, for a means best classed as a Fate-Worse-Than-Death.

No. No, not that. Don't think about it. Better to drop the whole matter, admit that it had him licked, and tell Gleason so. It had been seventeen years since he had been at Earth surface; nothing could induce him to subject his body to the intolerable demands of that terrible field. Nothing!

It might even kill him. He might choke to death, suffocate. No.

He sailed gracefully across his shop, an over-padded Cupid. Give up this freedom, even for a time, for that torturous bondage? Ridiculous! It was not worth it.

Better to ask an acrophobe to climb Half Dome, or demand that a claustrophobe interview a man in the world's deepest mine.

* * *

"Uncle Gus?"

"Oh, hello, Waldo. Glad you called."

"Would it be safe for me to come down to Earth?"

"Eh? How's that? Speak up, man. I didn't understand you."

"I said would it hurt me to make a trip down to Earth."

"This hookup," said Grimes, "is terrible. It sounded just like you were saying you wanted to come down to Earth."

"That's what I did say."

"What's the matter, Waldo? Do you feel all right?"

"I feel fine, but I have to see a man at Earth surface. There isn't any other way for me to talk to him, and I've got to talk to him. Would the trip do me any harm?"

"Ought not to, if you're careful. After all, you were born there. Be careful of yourself, though. You've laid a lot of fat around your heart."

"Oh dear. Do you think it's *dangerous*?"

"No. You're sound enough. Just don't overstrain yourself. And be careful to keep your temper."

"I will. I most certainly will. Uncle Gus?"

"Yes?"

"Will you come along with me and help me see it through?"

"Oh, I don't think that's necessary."

"Please, Uncle Gus. I don't trust anybody else."

"Time you grew up, Waldo. However, I will, this once."

"Now remember," Waldo told the pilot, "the absolute acceleration must never exceed one and one tenth gs, *even in landing*. I'll be watching the accelograph the whole time."

"I've been driving ambulances," said the pilot, "for twelve years, and I've never given a patient a rough ride yet."

"That's no answer. Understand me? One and one tenth; and it should not even approach that figure until we are under the stratosphere. Quiet, Baldur! Quit snuffling."

"I get you."

"Be sure that you do. Your bonuses depend on it."

"Maybe you'd like to herd it yourself."

"I don't like your attitude, my man. If I should die in the tank, you would never get another job."

The pilot muttered something.

"What was that?" Waldo demanded sharply.

"Well, I said it might be worth it."

Waldo started to turn red, opened his mouth.

Grimes cut in, "Easy, Waldo! Remember your heart."

"Yes, Uncle Gus."

Grimes snaked his way forward, indicated to the pilot that he wanted him to join him there.

"Don't pay any attention to anything he says," he advised the man quietly, "except what he said about acceleration. He really can't stand much acceleration. He *might* die in the tank."

"I still don't think it would be any loss. But I'll be careful."

"Good."

"I'm ready to enter the tank," Waldo called out. "Will you help me with the straps, Uncle Gus?"

The tank was not a standard deceleration type, but a modification built for this one trip. The tank was roughly the shape of an oversized coffin and was swung in gimbals to keep it always normal to the axis of absolute acceleration. Waldo floated in water—the specific gravity of his fat hulk was low—from which he was separated by the usual flexible, gasketed tarpaulin. Supporting his head and shoulders was a pad shaped to his contour. A mechanical artificial resuscitator was built into the tank, the back pads being under water, the breast pads out of the water but retracted out of the way.

Grimes stood by with neoadrenalin; a saddle had been provided for him on the left side of the tank. Baldur was strapped to a shelf on the right side of the tank; he acted as a counterweight to Grimes.

Grimes assured himself that all was in readiness, then called out to the pilot, "Start when you're ready."

"O.K." He sealed the access port; the entry tube folded itself back against the threshold flat of Freehold, freeing the ship. Gently they got under way.

Waldo closed his eyes; a look of seraphic suffering came over his face.

"Uncle Gus, suppose the deKalbs fail?"

"No matter. Ambulances store six times the normal reserve."

"You're *sure*?"

When Baldur began to feel weight, he started to whimper. Grimes spoke to him; he quieted down. But presently—days later, it seemed to Waldo—as the ship sank farther down into the Earth's gravitational field, the absolute acceleration necessarily increased, although the speed of the ship had not changed materially. The dog felt the weary heaviness creeping over his body. He did not understand it and he liked it even less; it terrified him. He began to howl.

Waldo opened his eyes. "Merciful heavens!" he moaned. "Can't you do something about that? He must be dying."

"I'll see." Grimes undid his safety belt and swung himself across the tank. The shift in weight changed the balance of the load in the gimbals; Waldo was rocked against the side of the tank.

"Oh!" he panted. "Be careful."

"Take it easy." Grimes caressed the dog's head and spoke to him. When he had calmed down, Grimes grabbed a handful of hide between the dog's shoulders, measured his spot, and jabbed in a hypo. He rubbed the area. "There, old fellow! That will make you feel better."

Getting back caused Waldo to be rocked again, but he bore it in martyred silence.

The ambulance made just one jerky maneuver after it entered the atmosphere. Both Waldo and the dog yelped. "Private ship," the pilot yelled back.

"Didn't heed my right-of-way lights." He muttered something about women drivers.

"It wasn't his fault," Grimes told Waldo. "I saw it."

The pilot set them down with exquisite gentleness in a clearing which had been prepared between the highway and Schneider's house. A party of men was waiting for them there; under Grimes's supervision they unslung the tank and carried Waldo out into the open air. The evolution was performed slowly and carefully, but necessarily involved some degree of bumping and uneven movement. Waldo stood it with silent fortitude, but tears leaked out from under his lowered lids.

Once outside he opened his eyes and asked, "Where is Baldur?"

"I unstrapped him," Grimes informed him, "but he did not follow us out."

Waldo called out huskily, "Here, Baldur! Come to me, boy."

Inside the car the dog heard his boss's voice, raised his head, and gave a low bark. He still felt that terrifying sickness, but he inched forward on his belly, attempting to comply. Grimes reached the door in time to see what happened.

The dog reached the edge of his shelf and made a grotesque attempt to launch himself in the direction from which he had heard Waldo's voice. He tried the only method of propulsion he knew; no doubt he expected to sail through the door and arrest his flight against the tank on the ground. Instead he fell several feet to the inner floor plates,

giving one agonized yelp as he did so, and breaking his fall most clumsily with stiffened forelegs.

He lay sprawled where he had landed, making
no noise, but not attempting to move. He was
trembling violently.

Grimes came up to him and examined him
superficially, enough to assure him that the beast
was not really hurt, then returned to the outside.
"Baldur's had a little accident," he told Waldo;
"he's not hurt, but the poor devil doesn't know how
to walk. You had best leave him in the ship."

Waldo shook his head slightly. "I want him with
me. Arrange a litter."

Grimes got a couple of the men to help him,
obtained a stretcher from the pilot of the ambulance, and undertook to move the dog. One of the
men said, "I don't know as I care for this job. That
dog looks vicious. Look't those eyes."

"He's not," Grimes assured him. "He's just scared
out of his wits. Here, I'll take his head."

"What's the matter with him? Same thing as
the fat guy?"

"No, he's perfectly well and strong; he's just
never learned to walk. This is his first trip to
Earth."

"Well, I'll be a cross-eyed owl!"

"I knew a case like it," volunteered the other.
"Dog raised in Lunopolis—first week he was on
Earth he wouldn't move—just squatted down, and
howled, and made messes on the floor."

"So has this one," the first said darkly.

They placed Baldur alongside Waldo's tub. With

great effort Waldo raised himself on one elbow, reached out a hand, and placed it on the creature's head. The dog licked it; his trembling almost ceased. "There! There!" Waldo whispered. "It's pretty bad, isn't it? Easy, old friend, take it easy."

Baldur thumped his tail.

It took four men to carry Waldo and two more to handle Baldur. Gramps Schneider was waiting for them at the door of his house. He said nothing as they approached, but indicated that they were to carry Waldo inside. The men with the dog hesitated. "Him, too," he said.

When the others had withdrawn—even Grimes returned to the neighborhood of the ship—Schneider spoke again. "Welcome, Mr. Waldo Jones."

"I thank you for your welcome, Grandfather Schneider."

The old man nodded graciously without speaking. He went to the side of Baldur's litter. Waldo felt impelled to warn him that the beast was dangerous with strangers, but some odd restraint—perhaps the effect of that enervating gravitational field—kept him from speaking in time. Then he saw that he need not bother.

Baldur had ceased his low whimpering, had raised his head, and was licking Gramps Schneider's chin. His tail thumped cheerfully. Waldo felt a sudden tug of jealousy; the dog had never been known to accept a stranger without Waldo's specific injunction. This was disloyalty—treason! But he suppressed the twinge and coolly assessed the incident as a tactical advantage to him.

Schneider pushed the dog's face out of the way and went over him thoroughly, prodding, thumping, extending his limbs. He grasped Baldur's muzzle, pushed back his lips, and eyed his gums. He peeled back the dog's eyelids. He then dropped the matter and came to Waldo's side. "The dog is not sick," he said; "his mind confuses. What made it?"

Waldo told him about Baldur's unusual background. Schneider nodded acceptance of the matter—Waldo could not tell whether he had understood or not—and turned his attention to Waldo. "It is not good for a sprottly lad to lie abed. The weakness—how long has it had you?"

"All my life, Grandfather."

"That is not good." Schneider went over him as he had gone over Baldur. Waldo, whose feeling for personal privacy was much more intense than that of the ordinarily sensitive man, endured it for pragmatic reasons. It was going to be necessary, he felt, to wheedle and cajole this strange old creature. It would not do to antagonize him.

To divert his own attention from the indignity he chose to submit to, and to gain further knowledge of the old quack, Waldo let his eyes rove the room. The room where they were seemed to be a combination kitchen-living room. It was quite crowded, rather narrow, but fairly long. A fireplace dominated the kitchen end, but it had been bricked up, and a hole for the flue pipe of the baseburner had been let into the chimney. The fireplace was lopsided, as an oven had been included in its left side. The corresponding space at the right was occupied by a short counter which supported a tiny sink. The sink was supplied with water by a small hand pump which grew out of the counter.

Schneider, Waldo decided, was either older than he looked, which seemed incredible, or he had acquired his house from someone now long dead.

The living room end was littered and crowded in the fashion which is simply unavoidable in constricted quarters. Books filled several cases, were piled on the floor, hung precariously on chairs. An ancient wooden desk, crowded with papers and supporting a long-obsolete mechanical typewriter, filled one corner. Over it, suspended from the wall, was an ornate clock, carved somewhat like a house. Above its face were two little doors; while Waldo looked at it, a tiny wooden bird painted bright red popped out of the lefthand door, whistled "*Th-wu th-woo!*" four times, and popped frantically back into its hole. Immediately thereafter a little gray bird came out of the righthand door, said "*Cuckoo*" three times in a leisurely manner, and returned to its hole. Waldo decided that he would like to own such a clock; of course its pendulum-and-weight movement would not function in Freehold, but he could easily devise a one-g certrifuge frame to inclose it, wherein it would have a pseudo Earth-surface environment.

It did not occur to him to fake a pendulum movement by means of a concealed power source; he liked things to work properly.

To the left of the clock was an old-fashioned static calendar of paper. The date was obscured, but the letters above the calendar proper were large and legible: New York World's Fair—Souvenir of the World of Tomorrow. Waldo's eyes widened a little and went back to something he had noticed before, sticking into a pincushion on the edge of the desk. It was a round plastic button mounted on a pin whereby it could be affixed to the clothing. It was not far from Waldo's eyes; he could read the lettering on it:

FREE SILVER
SIXTEEN TO ONE

Schneider must be—*old!*

There was a narrow archway, which led into another room. Waldo could not see into it very well; the arch was draped with a fringe curtain of long strings of large ornamental beads.

The room was rich with odors, many of them old and musty, but not dirty.

Schneider straightened up and looked down at Waldo. "There is nought wrong with your body. Up get yourself and walk."

Waldo shook his head feebly. "I am sorry, Grandfather, I cannot."

"You must reach for the power and make it serve you. Try."

"I am sorry. I do not know how."

"That is the only trouble. All matters are doubtful, unless one knows. You send your force into the Other World. You must reach into the Other World and claim it."

"Where is this 'Other World,' Grandfather?"

Schneider seemed a little in doubt as to how to answer this. "The Other World," he said presently, "is the world you do not see. It is here and it is there and it is everywhere. But it is especially *here*." He touched his forehead. "The mind sits in it and sends its messages through it to the body. Wait." He shuffled away to a little cupboard, from which he removed a small jar. It contained a salve, or unguent, which he rubbed on his hands.

He returned to Waldo and knelt down beside him. Grasping one of Waldo's hands in both of his, he began to knead it very gently. "Let the mind be quiet," he directed. "Feel for the power. The Other World is close and full of power. Feel it."

The massage was very pleasant to Waldo's tired muscles. The salve, or the touch of the old man's hand, produced a warm, relaxing tingle. If he were younger, thought Waldo, I would hire him as a masseur. He has a magnetic touch.

Schneider straightened up again and said, "There—that betters you? Now you rest while I some coffee make."

Waldo settled back contentedly. He was very tired. Not only was the trip itself a nervous strain, but he was still in the grip of this damnable, thick gravitational field, like a fly trapped in honey. Gramps Schneider's ministrations had left him relaxed and sleepy.

He must have dozed, for the last thing he

remembered was seeing Schneider drop an egg-shell into the coffeepot. Then the old man was standing before him, holding the pot in one hand and a steaming cup in the other. He set them down, got three pillows, which he placed at Waldo's back, then offered him the coffee. Waldo laboriously reached out both hands to take it.

Schneider held it back. "No," he reproved, "one hand makes plenty. Do as I showed. Reach into the Other World for the strength." He took Waldo's right hand and placed it on the handle of the cup, steadying Waldo's hand with his own. With his other hand he stroked Waldo's right arm gently, from shoulder to finger tips. Again the warm tingle.

Waldo was surprised to find himself holding the cup alone. It was a pleasant triumph; at the time he left Earth, seventeen years before, it had been his invariable habit never to attempt to grasp anything with only one hand. In Freehold, of course, he frequently handled small objects one-handed, without the use of waldoes. The years of practice must have improved his control. Excellent!

So, feeling rather cocky, he drank the cupful with one hand, using extreme care not to slop it on himself. It was good coffee, too, he was bound to admit—quite as good as the sort he himself made from the most expensive syrup extract—better, perhaps.

When Schneider offered him coffeecake, brown with sugar and cinnamon and freshly rewarmed, he swaggeringly accepted it with his left hand, without asking to be relieved of the cup. He continued to eat and drink, between bites and sips resting and steadying his forearms on the edges of the tank.

The conclusion of the *Kaffeeklatsch* seemed a good time to broach the matter of the deKalbs. Schneider admitted knowing McLeod and recalled, somewhat vaguely it seemed, the incident in which he had restored to service McLeod's broomstick. "Hugh Donald is a good boy," he said. "Machines I do not like, but it pleasures me to fix things for boys."

"Grandfather," asked Waldo, "will you tell me how you fixed Hugh Donald McLeod's ship?"

"Have you such a ship you wish me to fix?"

"I have many such ships which I have agreed to fix, but I must tell you that I have been unable to do so. I have come to you to find out the right way."

Schneider considered this. "That is difficult. I could show you, but it is not so much what you do as how you think about it. That makes only with practice."

Waldo must have looked puzzled, for the old man looked at him and added, "It is said that there are two ways of looking at everything. That is true and less than true, for there are many ways. Some of them are good ways and some are bad. One of the ancients said that everything either *is*, or *is not*. That is less than true, for a thing can both *be* and *not be*. With practice one can see it both ways. Sometimes a thing which *is* for this world is a thing which *is not* for the Other World. Which is important, since we live in the Other World."

"We live in the Other World?"

"How else could we live? The mind—not the brain, but the mind—is in the Other World, and reaches this world through the body. That is one true way of looking at it, though there are others."

"Is there more than one way of looking at deKalb receptors?"

"Certainly."

"If I had a set which is not working right brought in here, would you show me how to look at it?"

"It is not needful," said Schneider, "and I do not like for machines to be in my house. I will draw you a picture."

Waldo felt impelled to insist, but he squelched his feeling. "You have come here in humility," he told himself, "asking for instruction. Do not tell the teacher how to teach."

Schneider produced a pencil and a piece of paper, on which he made a careful and very neat sketch of the antennae sheaf and main axis of a skycar. The sketch was reasonably accurate as well, although it lacked several essential minor details.

"These fingers," Schneider said, "reach deep into the Other World to draw their strength. In turn it passes down this pillar"—he indicated the axis— "to where it is used to move the car."

A fair allegorical explanation, thought Waldo. By considering the "Other World" simply a term for the hypothetical ether, it could be considered correct if not complete. But it told him nothing.

"Hugh Donald," Schneider went on, "was tired and fretting. He found one of the bad truths."

"Do you mean," Waldo said slowly, "that McLeod's ship failed because he was worried about it?"

"How else?"

Waldo was not prepared to answer that one. It had become evident that the old man had some quaint superstitions; nevertheless, he might still be able to show Waldo *what* to do, even though Schneider did not know *why*. "And what did you do to change it?"

"I made no change; I looked for the other truth."

"But how? We found some chalk marks——"

"Those? They were but to aid me in concentrating my attention in the proper direction. I drew them down *so*"—he illustrated with pencil on the sketch—"and thought how the fingers reached out for power. And so they did."

"That is all? Nothing more?"

"That is enough."

Either, Waldo considered, the old man did not know how he had accomplished the repair, or he had had nothing to do with it—sheer and amazing coincidence.

He had been resting the empty cup on the rim of his tank, the weight supported by the metal while his fingers merely steadied it. His preoccupation caused him to pay too little heed to it; it slipped from his tired fingers, clattered and crashed to the floor.

He was much chagrined. "Oh, I'm *sorry*, Grandfather. I'll send you another."

"No matter. I will mend." Schneider carefully gathered up the pieces and placed them on the desk. "You have tired," he added. "That is not good. It makes you lose what you have gained. Go back now to your house, and when you have rested, you can practice reaching for the strength by yourself."

It seemed a good idea to Waldo; he was growing very tired, and it was evident that he was to learn nothing specific from the pleasant old fraud. He promised, emphatically and quite insincerely, to practice "reaching for strength," and asked Schneider to do him the favor of summoning his bearers.

The trip back was uneventful. Waldo did not even have the spirit to bicker with the pilot.

Stalemate. Machines that did not work but should, and machines that did work but in an impossible manner. And no one to turn to but one foggy-headed old man. Waldo worked lackadaisically for several days, repeating, for the most part, investigations he had already made rather than admit to himself that he was stuck, that he did not know what to do, that he was, in fact, whipped and might as well call Gleason and admit it.

The two "bewitched" sets of deKalbs continued to work whenever activated, with the same strange and incredible flexing of each antenna. Other deKalbs which had failed in operation and had been sent to him for investigation still refused to function. Still others, which had not yet failed, performed beautifully without the preposterous fidgeting.

For the umpteenth time he took out the little sketch Schneider had made and examined it. There was, he thought, just one more possibility: to return again to Earth and insist that Schneider actually *do*, in his presence, whatever it was he had done which caused the deKalbs to work. He knew now that he should have insisted on it in the first place, but he had been so utterly played out by having to fight that devilish thick field that he had not had the will to persist.

Perhaps he could have Stevens do it and have the process stereophotoed for a later examination. No, the old man had a superstitious prejudice against artificial images.

He floated gently over to the vicinity of one of the inoperative deKalbs. What Schneider had claimed to have done was preposterously simple. He had drawn chalk marks down each antenna *so*, for the purpose of fixing his attention. Then he had gazed down them and thought about them "reaching out for power," reaching into the Other World, stretching—

Baldur began to bark frantically.

"Shut up, you fool!" Waldo snapped, without taking his eyes off the antennae.

Each separate pencil of metal was wiggling, stretching. There was the low, smooth hum of perfect operation.

Waldo was still thinking about it when the televisor demanded his attention. He had never been in any danger of cracking up mentally as Rambeau had done; nevertheless, he had thought about the matter in a fashion which made his head ache. He was still considerably bemused when he cut in his end of the sound-vision. "Yes?"

It was Stevens. "Hello, Mr. Jones. Uh, we wondered...that is———"

"Speak up, man!"

"Well, how close are you to a solution?" Stevens blurted out. "Matters are getting pretty urgent."

"In what way?"

"There was a partial breakdown in Great New York last night. Fortunately it was not at peak load and the ground crew were able to install spares before the reserves were exhausted, but you can imagine what it would have been like during the rush hour. In my own department the crashes have doubled in the past few weeks, and our underwriters have given notice. We need results pretty quick."

"You'll get your results," Waldo said loftily. "I'm in the final stages of the research." He was actually not that confident, but Stevens irritated him even more than most of the smooth apes.

Doubt and reassurance mingled in Stevens's face. "I don't suppose you could care to give us a hint of the general nature of the solution?"

No, Waldo could not. Still—it would be fun to pull Stevens's leg. "Come close to the pickup, Dr. Stevens. I'll tell you." He leaned forward himself, until they were almost nose to nose—in effect. "Magic is loose in the world!"

He cut the circuit at once.

Down in the underground labyrinth of North America's home plant, Stevens stared at the black screen. "What's the trouble, chief?" McLeod inquired.

"I don't know. I don't rightly know. But I *think* that Fatty has slipped his cams, just the way Rambeau did."

McLeod grinned delightedly. "How sweet! I always did think he was a hoot owl."

Stevens looked very sober. "You had better pray that he *hasn't* gone nuts. We're depending on him. Now let me see those operation reports."

Magic loose in the world. It was as good an explanation as any, Waldo mused. Causation gone haywire; sacrosanct physical laws no longer operative. Magic. As Gramps Schneider had put it, it seemed to depend on the way one looked at it.

Apparently Scheider had known what he was talking about, although he naturally had no real grasp of the physical theory involved in the deKalbs.

Wait a minute now! Wait a minute. He had been going at this problem wrongly perhaps. He had approached it with a certain point of view himself, a point of view which had made him critical of the old man's statements—an assumption that he, Waldo, knew more about the whole matter than Schneider did. To be sure he had gone to see

Schneider, but he had thought of him as a back-country hex doctor, a man who might possess one piece of information useful to Waldo, but who was basically ignorant and superstitious.

Suppose he were to review the situation from a different viewpoint. Let it be assumed that everything Schneider had to say was coldly factual and enlightened, rather than allegorical and superstitious—

He settled himself to do a few hours of hard thinking.

In the first place Schneider had used the phrase "the Other World" time and again. What did it mean, literally? A "world" was a space-time-energy continuum; an "Other World" was, therefore, such a continuum, but a different one from the one in which he found himself. Physical theory found nothing repugnant in such a notion; the possibility of infinite numbers of continua was a familiar, orthodox speculation. It was even convenient in certain operations to make such an assumption.

Had Gramps Schneider meant that? A literal physical "Other World"? On reflection, Waldo was convinced that he must have meant just that, even though he had not used conventional scientific phraseology. "Other World" sounds poetical, but to say an "additional continuum" implies physical meaning. The terms had led him astray.

Schneider had said that the Other World was all around, here, there, and everywhere. Well, was not that a fair description of a space superposed and in one-to-one correspondence? Such a space might be so close to this one that the interval between them was an infinitesimal, yet unnoticed and unreachable, just as two planes may be considered as coextensive and separated by an unimaginably short interval, yet be perfectly discrete, one from the other.

The Other Space was not entirely unreachable; Schneider had spoken of reaching into it. The idea was fantastic, yet he must accept it for the purposes of this investigation. Schneider had implied—no—*stated* that it was a matter of mental outlook.

Was that really so fantastic? If a continuum were an unmeasurably short distance away, yet completely beyond one's physical grasp, would it be strange to find that it was most easily reached through some subtle and probably subconscious operation of the brain? The whole matter was subtle—and Heaven knew that no one had any real idea of *how* the brain works. No idea at all. It was laughably insufficient to try to explain the writing of a symphony in terms of the mechanics of colloids. No, nobody knew how the brain worked; one more inexplicable ability in the brain was not too much to swallow.

Come to think of it, the whole notion of consciousness and thought was fantastically improbable.

All right, so McLeod disabled his skycar himself by thinking bad thoughts; Schneider fixed it by thinking the correct thoughts. Then what?

He reached a preliminary conclusion almost at

once; by extension, the other deKalb failures were probably failures on the part of the operators. The operators were probably run-down, tired out, worried about something, and in some fashion still not clear they infected, or affected, the deKalbs with their own troubles. For convenience let us say that the deKalbs were short-circuited into the Other World. Poor terminology, but it helped him to form a picture.

Grimes's hypothesis! "Run-down, tired out, worried about something!" Not proved yet, but he felt sure of it. The epidemic of crashes though material was simply an aspect of the general *myasthenia* caused by short-wave radiation.

If that were true—

He cut in a sight-sound circuit to Earth and demanded to talk with Stevens.

"Dr. Stevens," he began at once, "there is a preliminary precautionary measure which should be undertaken right away."

"Yes?"

"First, let me ask you this: Have you had many failures of deKalbs in private ships? What is the ratio?"

"I can't give you exact figures at the moment," Stevens answered, somewhat mystified, "but there have been practically none. It's the commercial lines which have suffered."

"Just as I suspected. A private pilot won't fly unless he feels up to it, but a man with a job goes ahead no matter how he feels. Make arrangements for special physical and psycho examinations for all commercial pilots flying deKalb-type ships. Ground any who are not feeling in tiptop shape. Call Dr. Grimes. He'll tell you what to look for."

"That's a pretty tall order, Mr. Jones. After all, most of those pilots, practically all of them, aren't our employees. We don't have much control over them."

"That's your problem," Waldo shrugged. "I'm trying to tell you how to reduce crashes in the interim before I submit my complete solution."

"But—"

Waldo heard no more of the remark; he had cut off when he himself was through. He was already calling over a permanently energized, leased circuit which kept him in touch with his terrestrial business office—with his "trained seals." He gave them some very odd instructions—orders for books, old books, rare books. Books dealing with magic.

Stevens consulted with Gleason before attempting to do anything about Waldo's difficult request. Gleason was dubious. "He offered no reason for the advice?"

"None. He told me to look up Dr. Grimes and get his advice as to what specifically to look for."

"Dr. Grimes?"

"The M.D. who introduced me to Waldo— mutual friend."

"I recall. Mm-m-m...it will be difficult to go about grounding men who don't work for us. Still, I suppose several of our larger customers would co-operate if we asked them to and gave them some sort of a reason. What are you looking so odd about?"

Stevens told him of Waldo's last, inexplicable statement. "Do you suppose it could be affecting him the way it did Dr. Rambeau?"

"Mm-m-m. Could be, I suppose. In which case it would not be well to follow his advice. Have you anything else to suggest?"

"No—frankly."

"Then I see no alternative but to follow his advice. He's our last hope. A forlorn one, perhaps, but our only one."

Stevens brightened a little. "I could talk to Doc Grimes about it. He knows more about Waldo than anyone else."

"You have to consult him anyway, don't you? Very well—do so."

Grimes listened to the story without comment. When Stevens had concluded he said, "Waldo must be referring to the symptoms I have observed with respect to shortwave exposure. That's easy; you can have the proofs of the monograph I've been preparing. It'll tell you all about it."

The information did not reassure Stevens; it helped to confirm his suspicion that Waldo had lost his grip. But he said nothing. Grimes continued, "As for the other, Jim, I can't visualize Waldo losing his mind that way."

"He never did seem very stable to me."

"I know what you mean. But his paranoid streak is no more like what Rambeau succumbed to than chicken pox is like mumps. Matter of fact, one psychosis protects against the other. But I'll go see."

"You will? Good!"

"Can't go today. Got a broken leg and some children's colds that'll bear watching. Been some polio around. Ought to be able to make it the end of the week though."

"Doc, why don't you give up G.P. work! It must be deadly."

"Used to think so when I was younger. But about forty years ago I quit treating diseases and started treating people. Since then I've enjoyed it."

Waldo indulged in an orgy of reading, gulping the treatises on magic and related subjects as fast as he could. He had never been interested in such subjects before; now, in reading about them with the point of view that there might be—and even probably was—something to be learned, he found them intensely interesting.

There were frequent references to another world; sometimes it was called the Other World, sometimes the Little World. Read with the conviction that the term referred to an actual, material, different continuum, he could see that many of the practitioners of the forbidden arts had held the same literal viewpoint. They gave directions for using this other world; sometimes the directions were fanciful, sometimes they were baldly practical.

It was fairly evident that at least 90 per cent of all magic, probably more, was balderdash and sheer mystification. The mystification extended even to the practitioners, he felt; they lacked the scientific method; they employed a single-valued logic as faulty as the two-valued logic of the obsolete Spencer determinism; there was no suggestion of modern extensional, many-valued logic.

Nevertheless, the laws of contiguity, of sympathy, and of homeopathy had a sort of twisted rightness to them when considered in relation to the concept of another, different, but accessible, world. A man who had some access to a different space might well believe in a logic in which a thing could *be*, *not be*, or *be anything* with equal ease.

Despite the nonsense and confusion which characterized the treatments of magic which dated back to the period when the art was in common practice, the record of accomplishment of the art was impressive. There was curare and digitalis, and quinine, hypnotism, and telepathy. There was the hydraulic engineering of the Egyptian priests. Chemistry itself was derived from alchemy; for that matter, most modern science owed its origins to the magicians. Science had stripped off the surplusage, run it through the wringer of two-valued logic, and placed the knowledge in a form in which anyone could use it.

Unfortunately, that part of magic which refused to conform to the neat categories of the nineteenth-century methodologists was lopped off and left out of the body of science. It fell into disrepute, was forgotten save as fable and superstition.

Waldo began to think of the arcane arts as

aborted sciences, abandoned before they had been clarified.

And yet the manifestations of the sort of uncertainty which had characterized some aspects of magic and which he now attributed to hypothetical additional continua had occurred frequently, even in modern times. The evidence was overwhelming to anyone who approached it with an *open mind: Poltergeisten,* stones falling from the sky, apportation, "bewitched" persons—or, as he thought of them, persons who for some undetermined reason were loci of uncertainty—"haunted" houses, strange fires of the sort that would have once been attributed to salamanders. There were hundreds of such cases, carefully recorded and well vouched for, but ignored by orthodox science as being impossible. They *were* impossible, by known law, but considered from the standpoint of a coextensive additional continuum, they became entirely credible.

He cautioned himself not to consider his tentative hypothesis of the Other World as proved; nevertheless, it was an adequate hypothesis even if it should develop that it did not apply to some of the cases of strange events.

The Other Space might have different physical laws—no reason why it should not. Nevertheless, he decided to proceed on the assumption that it was much like the space he knew.

The Other World might even be inhabited. That was an intriguing thought! In which case anything could happen through "magic." Anything!

Time to stop speculating and get down to a little solid research. He had previously regretfully given up trying to apply the formulas of the medieval magicians. It appeared that they never wrote down *all* of a procedure; some essential—so the reports ran and so his experience confirmed—was handed down verbally from master to student. His experience with Schneider confirmed this; there were things, *attitudes*, which must needs be taught directly.

He regretfully set out to learn what he must unassisted.

"Gosh, Uncle Gus, I'm glad to see you!"

"Decided I'd better look in on you. You haven't phoned me in weeks."

"That's true, but I've been working awfully hard, Uncle Gus."

"Too hard, maybe. Mustn't overdo it. Lemme see your tongue."

"I'm O.K." But Waldo stuck out his tongue just the same; Grimes looked at it and felt his pulse.

"You seem to be ticking all right. Learning anything?"

"Quite a lot. I've about got the matter of the deKalbs whipped."

"That's good. The message you sent Stevens seemed to indicate that you had found some hookup that could be used on my pet problem too."

"In a way, yes; but around from the other end. It begins to seem as if it was your problem which created Stevens's problem."

"Huh?"

"I mean it. The symptoms caused by ultra short-wave radiation may have had a lot to do with the erratic behavior of the deKalbs."

"How?"

"I don't know myself. But I've rigged up a working hypothesis and I'm checking it."

"Hm-m-m. Want to talk about it?"

"Certainly—to you." Waldo launched into an account of his interview with Schneider, concerning which he had not previously spoken to Grimes, even though Grimes had made the trip with him. He never, as Grimes knew, discussed anything until he was ready to.

The story of the third set of deKalbs to be infected with the incredible writhings caused Grimes to raise his eyebrows. "Mean to say you caught on to how to do *that*?"

"Yes indeed. Not '*how*,' maybe, but I can do it. I've done it more than once. I'll show you." He drifted away toward one side of the great room where several sets of deKalbs, large and small, were mounted, with their controls, on temporary guys. "This fellow over on the end, it just came in today. Broke down. I'll give it Gramps Schneider's hocus-pocus and fix it. Wait a minute. I forgot to turn on the power."

He returned to the central ring which constituted his usual locus and switched on the beamcaster. Since the ship itself effectively shielded anything in the room from outer radiation, he had installed a small power plant and caster similar in type to NAPA's giant ones; without it he would have had no way to test the reception of the deKalbs.

He rejoined Grimes and passed down the line of deKalbs, switching on the activizing circuits. All save two began to display the uncouth motions he had begun to think of as the Schneider flex. "That one on the far end," he remarked, "is in operation but doesn't flex. It has never broken down, so it's never been treated. It's my control; but this one"—he touched the one in front of him—"needs fixing. Watch me."

"What are you going to do?"

"To tell the truth, I don't quite know. But I'll do it." He did not know. All he knew was that it was necessary to gaze down the antennae, think about them reaching into the Other World, think of them reaching for power, reaching—

The antennae began to squirm.

"That's all there is to it—strictly between ourselves. I learned it from Schneider." They had returned to the center of the sphere, at Grimes's suggestion, on the pretext of wanting to get a cigarette. The squirming deKalbs made him nervous, but he did not want to say so.

"How do you explain it?"

"I regard it as an imperfectly understood phenomenon of the Other Space. I know less about it than Franklin knew about lightning. But I will know—I will! I could give Stevens a solution right now for his worries if I knew some way to get around your problem too."

"I don't see the connection."

"There ought to be some way to do the whole thing through the Other Space. Start out by radiating power into the Other Space and pick up it up from there. Then the radiation could not harm human beings. It would never get at them; it would duck around them. I've been working on my caster, but with no luck so far. I'll crack it in time."

"I hope you do. Speaking of that, isn't the radiation from your own caster loose in this room?"

"Yes."

"Then I'll put on my shield coat. It's not good for you either."

"Never mind. I'll turn it off." As he turned to do so there was the sound of a sweet, chirruping whistle. Baldur barked. Grimes turned to see what caused it.

"What," he demanded, "have you got there?"

"Huh? Oh, that's my cuckoo clock. Fun, isn't it?" Grimes agreed that it was, although he could not see much use for it. Waldo had mounted it on the edge of a light metal hoop which spun with a speed just sufficient to produce a centrifugal force of one g.

"I rigged it up," Waldo continued, "while I was bogged down in this problem of the Other Space. Gave me something to do."

"This 'Other Space' business—I still don't get it."

"Think of another continuum much like our own and superposed on it the way you might lay one sheet of paper on another. The two spaces aren't

identical, but they are separated from each other
by the smallest interval you can imagine—coextensive but not touching—usually. There is an
absolute one-to-one, point-for-point correspondence, as I conceive it, between the two spaces,
but they are not necessarily the same size or
shape."

"Hey? Come again—they would *have* to be."

"Not at all. Which has the larger number of
points in it? A line an inch long, or a line a mile
long?"

"A mile long, of course."

"No. They have exactly the same number of
points. Want me to prove it?"

"I'll take your word for it. But I never studied
that sort of math."

"All right. Take my word for it then. Neither
size nor shape is any impediment to setting up a
full, point-for-point correspondence between two
spaces. Neither of the words is really appropriate.
'Size' has to do with a space's own inner structure,
its dimensions in terms of its own unique constants. 'Shape' is a matter which happens inside
itself—or at least not inside *our* space—and has
to do with how it is curved, open or closed, expand-
ing or contracting."

Grimes shrugged. "It all sounds like gibberish
to me." He returned to watching the cuckoo clock
swing round and round its wheel.

"Sure it does," Waldo assented cheerfully. "We
are limited by our experience. Do you know how
I think of the Other World?" The question was

purely rhetorical. "I think of it as about the size
and shape of an ostrich egg, but nevertheless a
whole universe, existing side by side with our own,
from here to the farthest star. I know that it's a
false picture, but it helps me to think about it that
way."

"I wouldn't know," said Grimes, and turned
himself around in the air. The compound motion
of the clock's pendulum was making him a little
dizzy. "Say! I thought you turned off the caster?"

"I did," Waldo agreed, and looked where Grimes
was looking. The deKalbs were still squirming. "I
thought I did," he said doubtfully, and turned to
the caster's control board. His eyes then opened
wider. "But I *did*. It *is* turned off."

"Then what the devil—"

"Shut up!" He had to think—think hard. Was
the caster actually out of operation? He floated
himself over to it, inspected it. Yes, it was dead,
dead as the dinosaurs. Just to make sure he went
back, assumed his primary waldoes, cut in the
necessary circuits, and partially disassembled it.
But the deKalbs still squirmed.

The one deKalb set which had not been subjected to the Schneider treatment was dead; it gave
out no power hum. But the others were working
frantically, gathering power from—*where*?

He wondered whether or not McLeod had said
anything to Gramps Schneider about the casters
from which the deKalbs were intended to pick up
their power. Certainly he himself had not. It simply had not come into the conversation. But

Schneider had said something. "The Other World is close by and full of power!"

In spite of his own intention of taking the old man literally he had ignored that statement. The Other World is full of power. "I am sorry I snapped at you, Uncle Gus," he said.

"'S all right."

"But what do you make of that?"

"Looks like you've invented perpetual motion, son."

"In a way, perhaps. Or maybe we've repealed the law of conservation of energy. Those deKalbs are drawing energy that was never before in this world!"

"Hm-m-m!"

To check his belief he returned to the control ring, donned his waldoes, cut in a mobile scanner, and proceeded to search the space around the deKalbs with the most sensitive pickup for the radio power band he had available. The needles never jumped; the room was dead in the wave lengths to which the deKalbs were sensitive. The power came from Other Space.

The power came from Other Space. Not from his own beamcaster, not from NAPA's shiny stations, but from Other Space. In that case he was not even close to solving the problem of the defective deKalbs; he might never solve it. Wait, now— just what had he contracted to do? He tried to recall the exact words of the contract.

There just might be a way around it. Maybe. Yes, and this newest cockeyed trick of Gramps

Schneider's little pets could have some very tricky
aspects. He began to see some possibilities, but he
needed to think about it.

"Uncle Gus—"

"Yes, Waldo?"

"You can go back and tell Stevens that I'll be
ready with the answers. We'll get his problem
licked, and yours too. In the meantime I've got to
do some really heavy thinking, so I want to be by
myself, please."

"Greetings, Mr. Gleason. *Quiet, Baldur!* Come
in. Be comfortable. How do you do, Dr. Stevens."

"How do you do, Mr. Jones."

"This," said Gleason, indicating a figure trailing him, "is Mr. Harkness, head of our legal staff."

"Ah, yes indeed. There will be matters of contract to be discussed. Welcome to Freehold, Mr.
Harkness."

"Thank you," Harkness said coldly. "Will your
attorneys be present?"

"They are present." Waldo indicated a stereo
screen. Two figures showed in it; they bowed and
murmured polite forms.

"This is most irregular," Harkness complained.
"Witnesses should be present in person. Things
seen and heard by television are not evidence."

Waldo drew his lips back. "Do you wish to make
an issue of it?"

"Not at all," Gleason said hastily. "Never mind,
Charles." Harkness subsided.

"I won't waste your time, gentlemen," Waldo

began. "We are here in order that I may fulfill my contract with you. The terms are known—we will pass over them." He inserted his arms into his primary waldoes. "Lined up along the far wall you will see a number of radiant power receptors, commonly called deKalbs. Dr. Stevens may, if he wishes, check their serial numbers——"

"No need to."

"Very well. I shall start my local beamcaster, in order that we may check the efficiency of their operation." His waldoes were busy as he spoke. "Then I shall activate the receptors, one at a time." His hands pawed the air; a little pair of secondaries switched on the proper switches on the control board of the last set in line. "This is an ordinary type, supplied to me by Dr. Stevens, which has never failed in operation. You may assure yourself that it is now operating in the normal manner, if you wish, Doctor."

"I can see that it is."

"We will call such a receptor a 'deKalb' and its operation 'normal.'" The small waldoes were busy again. "Here we have a receptor which I choose to term a 'Schneider-deKalb' because of certain treatment it has received"—the antennae began to move—"and its operation 'Schneider-type' operation. Will you check it, Doctor?"

"O.K."

"You fetched with you a receptor set which has failed?"

"As you can see."

"Have you been able to make it function?"

"No, I have not."

"Are you sure? Have you examined it carefully?"

"Quite carefully," Stevens acknowledged sourly. He was beginning to be tired of Waldo's pompous flubdubbery.

"Very well. I will now proceed to make it operative." Waldo left his control ring, shoved himself over to the vicinity of the defective deKalb, and placed himself so that his body covered his exact actions from the sight of the others. He returned to the ring and, using waldoes, switched on the activating circuit of the deKalb.

It immediately exhibited Schneider-type activity.

"That is my case, gentlemen," he announced. "I have found out how to repair deKalbs which become spontaneously inoperative. I will undertake to apply the Schneider treatment to any receptors which you may bring to me. That is included in my fee. I will undertake to train others in how to apply the Schneider treatment. That is included in my fee, but I cannot guarantee that any particular man will profit by my instruction. Without going into technical details I may say that the treatment is very difficult, much harder than it looks. I think that Dr. Stevens will confirm that." He smiled thinly. "I believe that completes my agreement with you."

"Just a moment, Mr. Jones," put in Gleason. "Is a deKalb foolproof, once it has received the Schneider treatment?"

"Quite. I guarantee it."

They went into a huddle while Waldo waited. At last Gleason spoke for them. "These are not quite the results we had expected, Mr. Jones, but we agree that you have fulfilled your commission—with the understanding that you will Schneider-treat any receptors brought to you and instruct others, according to their ability to learn."

"That is correct."

"Your fee will be deposited to your account at once."

"Good. That is fully understood and agreed? I have completely and successfully performed your commission?"

"Correct."

"Very well then. I have one more thing to show you. If you will be patient——" A section of the wall folded back; gigantic waldoes reached into the room beyond and drew forth a large apparatus, which resembled somewhat in general form an ordinary set of deKalbs, but which was considerably more complicated. Most of the complications were sheer decoration, but it would have taken a skilled engineer a long time to prove the fact.

The machine did contain one novel feature: a built-in meter of a novel type, whereby it could be set to operate for a predetermined time and then destroy itself, and a radio control whereby the time limit could be varied. Furthermore, the meter would destroy itself and the receptors if tampered with by any person not familiar with its design.

It was Waldo's tentative answer to the problem of selling free and unlimited power.

But of these matters he said nothing. Small waldoes had been busy attaching guys to the apparatus; when they were through he said, "This gentlemen, is an instrument which I choose to call a Jones-Schneider-deKalb. And it is the reason why you will not be in the business of selling power much longer."

"So?" said Gleason. "May I ask why?"

"Because," he was told, "I can sell it more cheaply and conveniently and under circumstances you cannot hope to match."

"That is a strong statement."

"I will demonstrate. Dr. Stevens, you have noted that the other receptors are operating. I will turn them off." The waldoes did so. "I will now stop the beamcast and I will ask you to assure yourself, by means of your own instruments, that there is *no* radiant power, other than ordinary visible light in this room."

Somewhat sullenly Stevens did so. "The place is dead," he announced some minutes later.

"Good. Keep your instruments in place, that you may be sure it remains dead. I will now activate my receptor." Little mechanical hands closed the switches. "Observe it, Doctor. Go over it thoroughly."

Stevens did so. He did not trust the readings shown by its instrument board; he attached his own meters in parallel. "How about it, James?" Gleason whispered.

121

Stevens looked disgusted. "The damn thing draws power from nowhere?"

They all looked at Waldo. "Take plenty of time, gentlemen," he said grandly. "Talk it over."

They withdrew as far away as the room permitted and whispered. Waldo could see that Harkness and Gleason were arguing, that Stevens was noncommittal. That suited him. He was hoping that Stevens would not decide to take another look at the fancy gadget he had termed a Jones-Schneider-deKalb. Stevens must not learn too much about it—yet. He had been careful to say nothing but the truth about it, but perhaps he had not said all of the truth; he had not mentioned that *all* Schneider-treated deKalbs were sources of free power.

Rather embarrassing if Stevens should discover that!

The meter-and-destruction device Waldo had purposely made mysterious and complex, but it was not useless. Later he would be able to point out, quite correctly, that without such a device NAPA simply could not remain in business.

Waldo was not easy. The whole business was a risky gamble; he would have much preferred to know more about the phenomena he was trying to peddle, but—he shrugged mentally while preserving a smile of smug confidence—the business had dragged on several months already, and the power situation really was critical. This solution would do—if he could get their names on the dotted line quickly enough.

For he had no intention of trying to compete with NAPA.

Gleason pulled himself away from Stevens and Harkness, came to Waldo. "Mr. Jones, can't we arrange this amicably?"

"What have you to suggest?"

It was quite an hour later that Waldo, with a sigh of relief, watched his guests' ship depart from the threshold flat. A fine caper, he thought, and it had worked; he had gotten away with it. He had magnanimously allowed himself to be persuaded to consolidate, provided—he had allowed himself to be quite temperamental about this—the contract was concluded at once, no fussing around and fencing between lawyers. Now or never—put up or shut up. The proposed contract, he had pointed out virtuously, gave him nothing at all unless his allegations about the Jones-Schneider-deKalb were correct.

Gleason considered this point and had decided to sign, had signed.

Even then Harkness had attempted to claim that Waldo had been an employee of NAPA. Waldo had written that first contract himself—a specific commission for a contingent fee. Harkness did not have a leg to stand on; even Gleason had agreed to that.

In exchange for all rights to the Jones-Schneider-deKalb, for which he agreed to supply drawings—wait till Stevens saw, and understood, those sketches!—for that he had received the promise of senior stock in NAPA, non-voting, but fully paid up and nonassessable. The lack of active participation in the company had been his own idea. There were going to be more headaches in the power business, headaches aplenty. He could see them coming—bootleg designs, means of outwitting the metering, lots of things. Free power had come, and efforts to stop it would in the long run, he believed, be fruitless.

Waldo laughed so hard that he frightened Baldur, who set up an excited barking.

He could afford to forget Hathaway now.

His revenge on NAPA contained one potential flaw; he had assured Gleason that the Schneider-treated deKalbs would continue to operate, would not come unstuck. He believed that to be true simply because he had faith in Gramps Schneider. But he was not prepared to prove it. He knew himself that he did not know enough about the phenomena associated with the Other World to be sure that something would, or would not, happen. It was still going to be necessary to do some hard, extensive research.

But the Other World was a devilishly difficult place to investigate!

Suppose, he speculated, that the human race were blind, had never developed eyes. No matter how civilized, enlightened, and scientific the race might have become, it is difficult to see how such a race could ever have developed the concepts of astronomy. They might know of the Sun as a cyclic source of energy having a changing, directional character, for the Sun is so overpowering that it may be "seen" with the skin. They would notice it and invent instruments to trap it and examine it.

But the pale stars, would they ever notice them? It seemed most unlikely. The very notion of the celestial universe, its silent depths and starlit grandeur, would be beyond them. Even if one of their scientists should have the concept forced on him in such a manner that he was obliged to accept the fantastic, incredible thesis as fact, how then would he go about investigating its details?

Waldo tried to imagine an astronomical phototelescope, conceived and designed by a blind man, intended to be operated by a blind man, and capable of collecting data which could be interpreted by a blind man. He gave it up; there were too many hazards. It would take a subtlety of genius far beyond his own to deal with the inescapably tortuous concatenations of inferential reasoning necessary to the solution of such a problem. It would strain him to invent such instruments *for* a blind man; he did not see how a blind man could ever overcome the difficulties unassisted.

In a way that was what Schneider had done for him; alone, he would have bogged down.

But even with Schneider's hints the problem of investigating the Other World was still much like the dilemma of the blind astronomer. He could not *see* the Other World; only through the Schneider treatment had he been able to contact it. Damnation! how could he design instruments to study it?

He suspected that he would eventually have to go back to Schneider for further instruction, but that was an expedient so distasteful that he refused to think much about it. Furthermore, Gramps Schneider might not be able to teach him much; they did not speak the same language.

This much he did know: the Other Space was there and it could be reached sometimes by proper orientation of the mind, deliberately as Schneider had taught him, or subconsciously as had happened to McLeod and others.

He found the idea distasteful. That thought and thought alone should be able to influence physical phenomena was contrary to the whole materialistic philosophy in which he had grown up. He had a prejudice in favor of order and invariable natural laws. His cultural predecessors, the experimental philosphers who had built up the world of science and its concomitant technology, Galileo, Newton, Edison, Einstein, Steinmetz, Jeans, and their myriad colleagues—these men had thought of the physical universe as a mechanism proceeding by inexorable necessity. Any apparent failure to proceed thus was regarded as an error in observation, an insufficient formulation of hypothesis, or an insufficiency of datum.

Even the short reign of the Heisenberg uncertainty principle had not changed the fundamental orientation toward Order and Cosmos; the Heisenberg uncertainty was one they were certain of!

It could be formulated, expressed, and a rigorous statistical mechanics could be built from it. In 1958 Horowitz's reformulation of wave mechanics had eliminated the concept. Order and causation were restored.

But this damned business! One might as well pray for rain, wish on the Moon, go to faith healers, surrender whole hog to Bishop Berkely's sweetly cerebral world-in-your-head. "—the tree's not a tree, when there's no one about the quad!"

Waldo was not emotionally wedded to Absolute Order as Rambeau had been; he was in no danger of becoming mentally unbalanced through a failure of his basic conceptions; nevertheless, consarn it, it was convenient for things to work the way one expected them to. On order and natural law was based predictability; without predictability it was impossible to live. Clocks should run evenly; water should boil when heat is applied to it; food should nourish, not poison; deKalb receptors should *work*, work the way they were designed to; Chaos was insupportable—it could not be lived with.

Suppose Chaos *were* king and the order we thought we detected in the world about us a mere phantasm of the imagination; where would that lead us? In that case, Waldo decided, it was entirely possible that a ten-pound weight *did* fall ten times as fast as a one-pound weight until the day the audacious Galileo decided in his mind that it was not so. Perhaps the whole meticulous science of ballistics derived from the convictions of a few firm-minded individuals who had sold the notion to the world. Perhaps the very stars were held firm in their courses by the unvarying faith of the astronomers. Orderly Cosmos, created out of Chaos—by Mind!

The world was flat before geographers decided to think of it otherwise. The world was flat, and the Sun, tub size, rose in the east and set in the west. The stars were little lights, studding a pellucid dome which barely cleared the tallest mountains. Storms were the wrath of gods and had nothing to do with the calculus of air masses. A Mind-created animism dominated the world then.

More recently it had been different. A prevalent convention of materialistic and invariable causation had ruled the world; on it was based the whole involved technology of a machine-served civilization. The machines *worked*, the way they were designed to work, because everybody believed in them.

Until a few pilots, somewhat debilitated by overmuch exposure to radiation, had lost their confidence and infected their machines with uncertainty—and thereby let magic loose in the world.

He was beginning, he thought, to understand what had happened to magic. Magic was the erratic law of an animistic world; it had been steadily pushed back by the advancing philosophy of invariant causation. It was gone now—until this new outbreak—and its world with it, except for backwaters of "superstition." Naturally an experimental scientist reported failure when investigating haunted houses, apportations, and the like; his convictions prevented the phenomena from happening.

The deep jungles of Africa might be very different places—when there was no white man around to see! The strangely slippery laws of magic might still obtain.

Perhaps these speculations were too extreme; nevertheless, they had one advantage which orthodox concepts had not: they included Gramps Schneider's hexing of the deKalbs. Any working hypothesis which failed to account for Schneider's—and his own—ability to *think* a set of deKalbs into operation was not worth a continental. This one did, and it conformed to Gramps's own statements: "All matters are doubtful" and "A thing can both *be*, *not be*, and *be anything*. There are many true ways of looking at the same thing. Some ways are good, some are bad."

Very well. Accept it. Act on it. The world varied according to the way one looked at it. In that case, thought Waldo, he knew how he wanted to look at it. He cast his vote for order and predictability!

He would *set* the style. He would impress his *own* concept of the Other World on the Cosmos!

It had been a good start to assure Gleason that the Schneider-treated deKalbs were foolproof. Good. So let it be. They were foolproof. They would never get out of order.

He proceeded to formulate and clarify his own concept of the Other World in his mind. He would think of it as orderly and basically similar to this space. The connection between the two spaces lay in the neurological system; the cortex, the thalamus, the spinal cord, and the appended nerve system were closely connected with both spaces. Such a picture was consistent with what Schneider had told him and did not conflict with phenomena as he knew it.

Wait. If the neurological system lay in both spaces, then that might account for the relatively slow propagation of nerve impulses as compared with electromagnetic progression. Yes! If the other space had a c constant relatively smaller than that of this space, such would follow.

He began to feel a calm assurance that it was *so*.

Was he merely speculating—or creating a universe?

Perhaps he would have to abandon his mental picture of the Other Space as being the size and shape of an ostrich egg, since a space with a slower propagation of light is not smaller, but larger, than the space he was used to. No ... no, wait a second, the *size* of a space did not depend on its c constant, but on its radius of curvature in terms of its c constant. Since c was a velocity, size was dependent on the notion of time—in this case time as entropy rate. Therein lay a characteristic which could be compared between the two spaces: they exchanged energy; they affected each other's entropy. The one which degenerated the more rapidly toward a state of level entropy was the "smaller."

He need not abandon his picture of the ostrich egg—good old egg! The Other World was a closed space, with a slow c, a high entropy rate, a short radius, and an entropy state near level—a perfect reservoir of power at every point, ready to spill over into this space wherever he might close the interval. To its inhabitants, if any, it might seem to be hundreds of millions of light years around; to him it was an ostrich egg, turgid to bursting with power.

He was already beginning to think of ways of checking his hypothesis. If, using a Schneider-deKalb, he were to draw energy at the highest rate he could manage, would he affect the local potential? Would it establish an entropy gradient? Could he reverse the process by finding a way to pump power into the Other World? Could he establish different levels at different points and thereby check for degeneration toward level, maximum entropy?

Did the speed of nerve impulse propagation furnish a clue to the c of the Other Space? Could such a clue be combined with the entropy and potential investigations to give a mathematical picture of the Other Space, in terms of its constants and its age?

He set about it. His untrammeled, wild speculations had produced some definite good: he'd tied down at least one line of attack on that Other Space; he'd devised a working principle for his blind man's telescope mechanism. Whatever the truth of the thing was, it was more than *a* truth; it was a complete series of new truths. It was the very complexity of that series of new truths—the truths, the characteristic laws, that were inherent properties of the Other Space, plus the new truth laws resultant from the interaction of the characteristics of the Other Space with Normal Space. No wonder Rambeau had said anything could happen! Almost anything could, in all probability, by a proper application and combination of the three sets of laws: the laws of Our Space, the laws of Other Space, and the co-ordinate laws of Both Spaces.

But before theoreticians could begin work, new data were most desperately needed. Waldo was no theoretician, a fact he admitted left-handedly in thinking of theory as impractical and unnecessary, time waste for him as a consulting engineer. Let the smooth apes work it out.

But the consulting engineer had to find out one thing: would the Schneider-deKalbs continue to function uninterruptedly as guaranteed? If not, what must be done to assure continuous function?

The most difficult and the most interesting aspect of the investigation had to do with the neurological system in relation to Other Space. Neither electromagnetic instruments nor neural surgery was refined enough to do accurate work on the levels he wished to investigate.

But he had waldoes.

The smallest waldoes he had used up to this

time were approximately half an inch across their palms—with micro-scanners to match, of course. They were much too gross for his purpose. He wished to manipulate living nerve tissue, examine its insulation and its performance *in situ*.

He used the tiny waldoes to create tinier ones.

The last stage was tiny metal blossoms hardly an eighth of an inch across. The helices in their stems, or forearms, which served them as pseudo muscles, could hardly be seen by the naked eye—but, then, he used scanners.

His final team of waldoes used for nerve and brain surgery varied in succeeding stages from mechanical hands nearly life-size down to these fairy digits which could manipulate things much too small for the eye to see. They were mounted in bank to work in the same locus. Waldo controlled them all from the same primaries; he could switch from one size to another without removing his gauntlets. The same change in circuits which brought another size of waldoes under control automatically accomplished the change in sweep of scanning to increase or decrease the magnification so that Waldo always saw before him in his stereo receiver a "life-size" image of his other hands.

Each level of waldoes had its own surgical instruments, its own electrical equipment.

Such surgery had never been seen before, but Waldo gave that aspect little thought; no one had told him that such surgery was unheard-of.

He established, to his own satisfaction, the

mechanism whereby short-wave radiation had produced a deterioration in human physical performance. The synapses between dendrites acted as if they were points of leakage. Nerve impulses would sometimes fail to make the jump, would leak off—to where? To Other Space, he was sure. Such leakage seemed to establish a preferred path, a canalization, whereby the condition of the victim became steadily worse. Motor action was not lost entirely, as both paths were still available, but efficiency was lost. It reminded him of a metallic electrical circuit with a partial ground.

An unfortunate cat, which had become dead undergoing the experimentation, had supplied him with much of his data. The kitten had been born and raised free from exposure to power radiation. He subjected it to heavy exposure and saw it acquire a *myasthenia* nearly as complete as his own—while studying in minute detail what actually went on in its nerve tissues.

He felt quite sentimental about it when it died.

Yet, if Gramps Schneider were right, human beings need not be damaged by radiation. If they had the wit to look at it with the proper orientation, the radiation would not affect them; they might even draw power out of the Other World.

That was what Gramps Schneider had told him to do.

That was what Gramps Schneider had told *him* to do!

Gramps Schneider had told him he need not be weak!

That he could be strong—

Strong!

STRONG!

He had never thought of it. Schneider's friendly ministrations to him, his advice about overcoming the weakness, he had ignored, had thrown off as inconsequential. His own weakness, his own peculiarity which made him different from the smooth apes, he had regarded as a basic implicit fact. He had accepted it as established when he was a small child, a final unquestioned factor.

Naturally he had paid no attention to Schneider's words in so far as they referred to him.

To be strong!

To stand alone—to work, to *run*!

Why, he ... he could, he could go down to Earth surface without fear. He wouldn't mind the field. They *said* they didn't mind it; they even *carried* things—great, heavy things. Everybody did. They *threw* things.

He made a sudden convulsive movement in his primary waldoes, quite unlike his normal, beautifully economical rhythm. The secondaries were oversize, as he was making a new setup. The guys tore loose, a brace plate banged against the wall. Baldur was snoozing nearby; he pricked up his ears, looked around, then turned his face to Waldo, questioning him.

Waldo glared at him and the dog whined. "Shut up!"

The dog quieted and apologized with his eyes.

Automatically he looked over the damage—not much, but he would have to fix it. Strength. Why, if he were strong, he could do anything—anything! No. 6 extension waldoes and some new guys——Strong! Absent-mindedly he shifted to the No. 6 waldoes.

Strength!

He could even meet women—be stronger than they were!

He could swim. He could ride. He could fly a ship—run, jump. He could handle things with his bare hands. He could even learn to dance!

Strong!

He would have muscles! He could break things. He could—— He could——

He switched to the great waldoes with hands the size of a man's body. Strong—they were strong! With one giant waldo he hauled from the stock pile a quarter-inch steel plate, held it up, and shook it. A booming rumble. He shook it again. Strong!

He took it on both waldoes, bent it double. The metal buckled unevenly. Convulsively he crumpled it like wastepaper between the two huge palms. The grinding racket raised hackles on Baldur; he himself had not been aware of it.

He relaxed for a moment, gasping. There was sweat on his forehead; blood throbbed in his ears. But he was not spent; he wanted something heavier, *stronger*. Cutting to the adjoining storeroom he selected an L-beam twelve feet long, shoved it through to where the giant hands could reach it, and cut back to them.

The beam was askew in the port; he wrenched it loose, knocking a big dent in the port frame. He did not notice it.

The beam made a fine club in the gross fist. He brandished it. Baldur backed away, placing the control ring between himself and the great hands.

Power! Strength! Smashing, unbeatable strength——

With a spastic jerk he checked his swing just before the beam touched the wall. No—— But he grabbed the other end of the club with the left waldo and tried to bend it. The big waldoes were built for heavy work, but the beam was built to resist. He strained inside the primaries, strove to force the great fists to do his will. A warning light flashed on his control board. Blindly he kicked in the emergency overload and persisted.

The hum of the waldoes and the rasp of his own breath were drowned out by the harsh scrape of metal on metal as the beam began to give way. Exulting, he bore down harder in the primaries. The beam was bending double when the waldoes blew out. The right-hand tractors let go first; the fist flung open. The left fist, relieved of the strain, threw the steel from it.

It tore its way through the thin bulkhead, making a ragged hole, crashed and clanged in the room beyond.

But the giant waldoes were inanimate junk.

He drew his soft pink hands from the waldoes

and looked at them. His shoulders heaved, and racking sobs pushed up out of him. He covered his face with his hands; the tears leaked out between his fingers. Baldur whimpered and edged in closer.

On the control board a bell rang persistently.

The wreckage had been cleared away and an adequate, neat patch covered the place where the L-beam had made its own exit. But the giant waldoes had not yet been replaced; their frame was uninhabited. Waldo was busy rigging a strength tester.

It had been years since he had paid any attention to the exact strength of his body. He had had so little use for strength; he had concentrated on dexterity, particularly on the exact and discriminating control of his namesakes. In the selective, efficient, and accurate use of his muscles he was second to none; he had control—he *had* to have. But he had had no need for strength.

With the mechanical equipment at hand it was not difficult to jerry-rig a device which would register strength of grip as pounds-force on a dial. A spring-loaded scale and a yoke to act on it sufficed. He paused and looked at the contrivance.

He need only take off the primary waldoes, place his bare hand on the grip, bear down—and he would know. Still he hesitated.

It felt strange to handle anything so large with his bare hand. Now. Reach into the Other World for power. He closed his eyes and pressed. He opened them. Fourteen pounds—less than he used to have.

But he had not really tried yet. He tried to imagine Gramps Schneider's hands on his arm, that warm tingle. Power. Reach out and claim it.

Fourteen pounds, fifteen—seventeen, eighteen, twenty, twenty-one! He was winning! He was winning!

Both his strength and his courage failed him, in what order he could not say. The needle spun back to zero; he had to rest.

Had he really shown exceptional strength—or was twenty-one pounds of grip simply normal for him at his present age and weight? A normally strong and active man, he knew, should have a grip on the order of one hundred and fifty pounds.

Nevertheless, twenty-one pounds of grip was six pounds higher than he had ever before managed on test.

Try, again. Ten, eleven—twelve. Thirteen. The needle hesitated. Why, he had just started—this was ridiculous. Fourteen.

There it stopped. No matter how he strained and concentrated his driving will he could not pass that point. Slowly, he dropped back from it.

Sixteen pounds was the highest he managed in the following days. Twenty-one pounds seemed to have been merely a fluke, a good first effort. He ate bitterness.

But he had not reached his present position of wealth and prominence by easy surrender. He persisted, recalling carefully just what Schneider had said to him, and trying to *feel* the touch of Schneider's hands. He told himself now that he really had been stronger under Schneider's touch. But that he had failed to realize it because of the Earth's heavy field. He continued to try.

In the back of his mind he knew that he must eventually seek out Gramps Schneider and ask his help, if he did not find the trick alone. But he was extremely reluctant to do so, not because of the terrible trip it entailed—though that would ordinarily have been more than enough reason— but because if he did so and Schneider was not able to help him, then there would be no hope, no hope at all.

It was better to live with disappointment and frustration than to live without hope. He continued to postpone it.

Waldo paid little attention to Earth time; he ate and slept when he pleased. He might catch a cat nap at any time; however, at fairly regular intervals he slept for longer periods. Not in a bed, of course. A man who floats in air has no need for a bed. But he did make it a habit to guy himself into place before undertaking eight hours of solid sleep, as it prevented him from casual drifting in random air currents which might carry him, unconscious, against controls or switches.

Since the obsession to become strong had possessed him he had frequently found it necessary to resort to soporifics to insure sleep.

Dr. Rambeau had returned and was looking for him. Rambeau—crazy and filled with hate. Rambeau, blaming his troubles on Waldo. He was not safe, even in Freehold, as the crazy physicist had found out how to pass from one space to another. There he was now! Just his head, poked through from the Other World. "I'm going to get you, Waldo!" He was gone—no, there he was behind him! Reaching, reaching out with hands that were writhing antennae. "You, Waldo!" But Waldo's own hands were the giant waldoes; he snatched at Rambeau.

The big waldoes went limp.

Rambeau was at him, was on him; he had him around the throat.

Gramps Schneider said in his ear, in a voice that was calm and strong, "Reach out for the power, my son. Feel it in your fingers." Waldo grabbed at the throttling fingers, strained, tried.

They were coming loose. He was winning. He would stuff Rambeau back into the Other World and keep him there. There! He had one hand free. Baldur was barking frantically; he tried to tell him to shut up, to bite Rambeau, to help—

The dog continued to bark.

He was in his own home, in his own great room. Baldur let out one more yipe. "Quiet!" He looked himself over.

When he had gone to sleep he had been held in place by four light guys, opposed like the axes of a tetrahedron. Two of them were still fastened to his belt; he swung loosely against the control ring. Of the other two, one had snapped off at his belt; its end floated a few feet away. The fourth had been broken in two places, near his belt and again several feet out; the severed piece was looped loosely around his neck.

He looked the situation over. Study as he might, he could conceive no way in which the guys could have been broken save by his own struggles in the nightmare. The dog could not have done it; he had no way to get a purchase. He had done it himself. The lines were light, being intended merely as stays. Still——

It took him a few minutes to rig a testing apparatus which would test pull instead of grip; the yoke had to be reversed. When it was done he cut in a medium waldo pair, fastened the severed pieces of line to the tester, and, using the waldo, pulled.

The line parted at two hundred and twelve pounds.

Hastily, but losing time because of nervous clumsiness, he rerigged the tester for grip. He paused, whispered softly, "Now is the time, Gramps!" and bore down on the grip.

Twenty pounds—twenty-one. Twenty-five!

Up past thirty. He was not even sweating! Thirty-five—forty, -one, -two, -three. Forty-five! And -six! And a half. Forty-seven pounds!

With a great sigh he let his hand relax. He was strong. Strong.

When he had somewhat regained his composure, he considered what to do next. His first impulse was to call Grimes, but he suppressed it. Soon enough when he was sure of himself.

He went back to the tester and tried his left hand. Not as strong as his right, but almost—nearly forty-five pounds. Funny thing, he didn't feel any different. Just normal, healthy. No sensation.

He wanted to try all of his muscles. It would take too long to rig testers for kick, and shove, and back lift, and, oh, a dozen others. He needed a field, that was it, a one-g field. Well, there was the reception room; it could be centrifuged.

But its controls were in the ring and it was long corridors away. There was a nearer one, the centrifuge for the cuckoo clock. He had rigged the wheel with a speed control as an easy way to regulate the clock. He moved back to the control ring and stopped the turning of the big wheel; the clockwork was disturbed by the sudden change; the little red bird popped out, said, "*Th-wu th-woo*" once, hopefully, and subsided.

Carrying in his hand a small control panel radio hooked to the motor which impelled the centrifuge wheel, he propelled himself to the wheel and placed himself inside, planting his feet on the inner surface of the rim and grasping one of the spokes, so that he would be in a standing position with respect to the centrifugal force, once it was impressed. He started the wheel slowly.

Its first motion surprised him and he almost fell off. But he recovered himself and gave it a little more power. All right so far. He speeded it up gradually, triumph spreading through him as he felt the pull of the pseudo gravitational field, felt his legs grow heavy, *but still strong*.

He let it out, one full g. He could take it. He could, indeed! To be sure, the force did not affect the upper part of his body so strongly as the lower, as his head was only a foot or so from the point of rotation. He could fix that; he squatted down slowly, hanging on tight to the spoke. It was all right.

But the wheel swayed and the motor complained. His unbalanced weight, that far out from the center of rotation, was putting too much of a strain on a framework intended to support a cuckoo clock and its counterweight only. He straightened up with equal caution, feeling the fine *shove* of his thigh muscles and calves. He stopped the wheel.

Baldur had been much perturbed by the whole business. He had almost twisted his neck off trying to follow the motions of Waldo.

He still postponed calling Grimes. He wanted to arrange for some selective local controls on the centrifuging of the reception room, in order to have a proper place in which to practice standing up. Then he had to get the hang of this walking business; it looked easy, but he didn't know. Might be quite a trick to learn it.

Thereafter he planned to teach Baldur to walk. He tried to get Baldur into the cuckoo-clock wheel, but the dog objected. He wiggled free and retreated to the farthest part of the room. No matter—when he had the beast in the reception room he would damn well have to learn to walk. Should have seen to it long ago. A big brute like that, and couldn't walk!

He visualized a framework into which the dog could be placed which would force him to stand erect. It was roughly equivalent to a baby's toddler, but Waldo did not know that. He had never seen a baby's toddler.

"Uncle Gus——"

"Oh, hello, Waldo. How you been?"

"Fine. Look, Uncle Gus, could you come up to Freehold—right away?"

Grimes shook his head. "Sorry. My bus is in the shop."

"Your bus is too slow anyhow. Take a taxi, or get somebody to drive you."

"And have you insult 'em when we get there? Huh-uh."

"I'll be sweet as sugar."

"Well, Jimmie Stevens said something yesterday about wanting to see you."

Waldo grinned. "Get him. I'd like to see him."

"I'll try."

"Call me back. Make it soon."

Waldo met them in the reception room, which he had left uncentrifuged. As soon as they came in he started his act. "My, I'm glad you're here. Dr. Stevens—could you fly me down to Earth right away? Something's come up."

"Why—I suppose so."

"Let's go."

"Wait a minute, Waldo. Jimmie's not prepared to handle you the way you have to be handled."

"I'll have to chance it, Uncle Gus. This is urgent."

"But——"

"No 'buts.' Let's leave at once."

They hustled Baldur into the ship and tied him down. Grimes saw to it that Waldo's chair was tilted back in the best approximation of a deceleration rig. Waldo settled himself into it and closed his eyes to discourage questions. He sneaked a look and found Grimes grimly silent.

Stevens made very nearly a record trip, but set them down quite gently on the parking flat over Grimes's home. Grimes touched Waldo's arm. "How do you feel? I'll get someone and we'll get you inside. I want to get you to bed."

"Can't do that, Uncle Gus. Things to do. Give me your arm, will you?"

"Huh?" But Waldo reached for the support requested and drew himself up.

"I'll be all right now, I guess." He let go the physician's arm and started for the door. "Will you untie Baldur?"

"Waldo!"

He turned around, grinning happily. "Yes, Uncle Gus, it's true. I'm not weak any more. *I can walk.*"

Grimes took hold of the back of one of the seats and said shakily, "Waldo, I'm an old man. You ought not to do things like this to me." He wiped at his eyes.

"Yes," agreed Stevens, "it's a damn dirty trick."

Waldo looked blankly from one face to the other.

"I'm sorry," he said humbly. "I just wanted to surprise you."

"It's all right. Let's go downside and have a drink. You can tell us about it then."

"All right. Come on, Baldur." The dog got up and followed after his master. He had a very curious gait; Waldo's trainer gadget had taught him to pace instead of trot.

Waldo stayed with Grimes for days, gaining strength, gaining new reflex patterns, building up his flabby muscles. He had no setbacks; the *myasthenia* was gone. All he required was conditioning.

Grimes had forgiven him at once for his unnecessarily abrupt and spectacular revelation of his cure, but Grimes had insisted that he take it easy and become fully readjusted before he undertook to venture out unescorted. It was a wise precaution. Even simple things were hazards to him. Stairs, for example. He could walk on the level, but going downstairs had to be learned. Going up was not so difficult.

Stevens showed up one day, let himself in, and found Waldo alone in the living room, listening to a stereo show. "Hello, Mr. Jones."

"Oh—hello, Dr. Stevens." Waldo reached down hastily, fumbled for his shoes, zipped them on. "Uncle Gus says I should wear them all the time," he explained. "Everybody does. But you caught me unawares."

"Oh, that's no matter. You don't have to wear them in the house. Where's Doc?"

"Gone for the day. Don't you, really? Seems to me my nurses always wore shoes."

"Oh yes, everybody does—but there's no law to make you."

"Then I'll wear them. But I can't say that I like them. They feel dead, like a pair of disconnected waldoes. But I want to learn how."

"How to wear shoes?"

"How to act like people act. It's really quite difficult," he said seriously.

Stevens felt a sudden insight, a welling of sympathy for this man with no background and no friends. It must be odd and strange to him. He felt an impulse to confess something which had been on his mind with respect to Waldo. "You really are strong now, aren't you?"

Waldo grinned happily. "Getting stronger every day. I gripped two hundred pounds this morning. And see how much fat I've worked off."

"You're looking fit, all right. Here's a funny thing. Every since I first met you I've wished to high heaven that you were as strong as an ordinary man."

"You really did? Why?"

"Well...I think you will admit that you used some pretty poisonous language to me, one time and another. You had me riled up all the time. I wanted you to get strong so that I could just beat the hell out of you."

Waldo had been walking up and down, getting used to his shoes. He stopped and faced Stevens.

He seemed considerably startled. "You mean you wanted to fist-fight me?"

"Exactly. You used language to me that a man ought not to use unless he is prepared to back it up with his fists. If you had not been an invalid I would have pasted you one, oh, any number of times."

Waldo seemed to be struggling with a new concept. "I think I see," he said slowly. "Well—all right." On the last word he delivered a roundhouse swipe with plenty of power behind it. Stevens was not in the least expecting it; it happened to catch him on the button. He went down, out cold.

When he came to he found himself in a chair. Waldo was shaking him. "Wasn't that right?" he said anxiously.

"What did you hit me with?"

"My hand. Wasn't that right? Wasn't that what you wanted?"

"Wasn't that what I——" He still had little bright lights floating in front of his eyes, but the situation began to tickle him. "Look here—is that your idea of the proper way to start a fight?"

"Isn't it?"

Stevens tried to explain to him the etiquette of fisticuffs, contemporary American. Waldo seemed puzzled, but finally he nodded. "I get it. You have to give the other man warning. All right—get up, and we'll do it over."

"Easy, easy! Wait a minute. You never did give me a chance to finish what I was saying. I *was* sore at you, but I'm not any more. That is what I was trying to tell you. Oh, you were utterly poisonous; there is no doubt about that. But you couldn't help being."

"I don't mean to be poisonous," Waldo said seriously.

"I know you don't, and you're not. I rather like you now—now that you're strong."

"Do you really?"

"Yes, I do. But don't practice any more of those punches on me."

"I won't. But I didn't understand. But, do you know, Dr. Stevens, it's——"

"Call me Jim."

"Jim. It's a very hard thing to know just what people do expect. There is so little pattern to it. Take belching; I didn't know it was forbidden to burp when other people are around. It seems obviously necessary to me. But Uncle Gus says not."

Stevens tried to clear up the matter for him— not too well, as he found that Waldo was almost totally lacking in any notion, even theoretical, of social conduct. Not even from fiction had he derived a concept of the intricacies of *mores*, as he had read almost no fiction. He had ceased reading stories in his early boyhood, because he lacked the background of experience necessary to appreciate fiction.

He was rich, powerful, and a mechanical genius, but he still needed to go to kindergarten.

Waldo had a proposition to make. "Jim, you've

been very helpful. You explain these things better than Uncle Gus does. I'll hire you to teach me."

Stevens suppressed a slight feeling of pique. "Sorry. I've got a job that keeps me busy."

"Oh, that's all right. I'll pay you better than they do. You can name your own salary. It's a deal."

Stevens took a deep breath and sighed. "You don't understand. I'm an engineer and I don't hire out for personal service. You can't hire me. Oh, I'll help you all I can, but I won't take money for it."

"What's wrong with taking money?"

The question, Stevens thought, was stated wrongly. As it stood it could not be answered. He launched into a long, involved discussion of professional and business conduct. He was really not fitted for it; Waldo soon bogged down. "I'm afraid I don't get it. But see here—could you teach me how to behave with girls? Uncle Gus says he doesn't dare take me out in company."

"Well, I'll try. I'll certainly try. But, Waldo, I came over to see you about some of the problems we're running into at the plant. About this theory of the two spaces that you were telling me about——"

"It's not theory; it's fact."

"All right. What I want to know is this: When do you expect to go back to Freehold and resume research? We need some help."

"Go back to Freehold? I haven't any idea. I don't intend to resume research."

Robert A. Heinlein

"You don't? But, my heavens, you haven't finished half the investigations you outlined to me."

"You fellows can do 'em. I'll help out with suggestions, of course."

"Well—maybe we could interest Gramps Schneider," Stevens said doubtfully.

"I would not advise it," Waldo answered. "Let me show you a letter he sent me." He left and fetched it back. "Here."

Stevens glanced through it. "—your generous offer of your share in the new power project I appreciate, but, truthfully, I have no interest in such things and would find the responsibility a burden. As for the news of your new strength I am happy, but not surprised. The power of the Other World is his who would claim it—" There was more to it. It was written in a precise Spencerian hand, a trifle shaky; the rhetoric showed none of the colloquialisms with which Schneider spoke.

"Hm-m-m—I think I see what you mean."

"I believe," Waldo said seriously, "that he regards our manipulations with gadgets as rather childish."

"I suppose. Tell me, what do *you* intend to do with yourself?"

"Me? I don't know, exactly. But I can tell you this: I'm going to have fun. I'm going to have lots of fun. I'm just beginning to find out how much fun it is to be a man!"

* * *

His dresser tackled the other slipper. "To tell you just why I took up dancing would be a long story," he continued.

"I want details."

"Hospital calling," someone in the dressing room said.

"Tell 'em I'll be right there, fast. Suppose you come in tomorrow afternoon?" he added to the woman reporter. "Can you?"

"Right."

A man was shouldering his way through the little knot around him. Waldo caught his eye. "Hello, Stanley. Glad to see you."

"Hello, Waldo." Gleason pulled some papers out from under his cape and dropped them in the dancer's lap. "Brought these over myself as I wanted to see your act again."

"Like it?"

"Swell!"

Waldo grinned and picked up the papers. "Where is the dotted line?"

"Better read them first," Gleason cautioned him.

"Oh shucks, no. If it suits you, it suits me. Can I borrow your stylus?"

A worried little man worked his way up to them. "About that recording, Waldo——"

"We've discussed that," Waldo said flatly. "I only perform before audiences."

"We've combined it with the Warm Springs benefit."

"That's different. O.K."

153

"While you're about it, take a look at this lay-out." It was a reduction, for a twenty-four sheet:

THE GREAT WALDO
AND HIS TROUPE

with the opening date and theater left blank, but with a picture of Waldo, as Harlequin, poised high in the air.

"Fine, Sam, fine!" Waldo nodded happily.

"Hospital calling again!"

"I'm ready now," Waldo answered, and stood up. His dresser draped his street cape over his lean shoulders. Waldo whistled sharply. "Here, Baldur! Come along." At the door he stopped an instant, and waved. "Good night, fellows!"

"Good night, Waldo."

They were all such grand guys.

Magic, Inc.

"**W**HOSE SPELLS ARE YOU USING, BUDDY?"

That was the first thing this bird said after coming into my place of business. He had hung around maybe twenty minutes, until I was alone, looking at samples of waterproof pigment, fiddling with plumbing catalogues, and monkeying with the hardware display.

I didn't like his manner. I don't mind a legitimate business inquiry from a customer, but I resent gratuitous snooping.

"Various of the local licensed practitioners of thaumaturgy," I told him in a tone that was chilly but polite. "Why do you ask?"

"You didn't answer my question," he pointed out. "Come on—speak up. I ain't got all day."

I restrained myself. I require my clerks to be polite, and, while I was pretty sure this chap would never be a customer, I didn't want to break my own rules. "If you are thinking of buying anything," I said, "I will be happy to tell you what magic, if any, is used in producing it, and who the magician is."

"Now you're not being co-operative," he complained. "We like for people to be co-operative. You never can tell what bad luck you may run into not co-operating."

"Who d'you mean by 'we,'" I snapped, dropping all pretense of politeness, "and what do you mean by 'bad luck'?"

"Now we're getting somewhere," he said with a nasty grin, and settled himself on the edge of the counter so that he breathed into my face. He was short and swarthy—Sicilian, I judged—and dressed in a suit that was overtailored. His clothes and haberdashery matched perfectly in a color scheme that I didn't like. "I'll tell you what I mean by 'we'; I'm a field representative for an organization that protects people from bad luck—if they're smart, and co-operative. That's why I asked you whose charms you're usin'. Some of the magicians around here aren't co-operative; it spoils their luck, and that bad luck follows their products."

"Go on," I said. I wanted him to commit himself as far as he would.

"I knew you were smart," he answered. "F'r instance—how would you like for a salamander to get loose in your shop, setting fire to your goods and maybe scaring your customers? Or you sell the materials to build a house, and it turns out there's a poltergeist living in it, breaking the dishes and souring the milk and kicking the furniture around. That's what can come of dealing with the wrong magicians. A little of that and your business is ruined. We wouldn't want that to happen, *would we*?" He favored me with another leer.

I said nothing, he went on, "Now, we maintain a staff of the finest demonologists in the business, expert magicians themselves, who can report on how a magician conducts himself in the Half World, and whether or not he's likely to bring his clients bad luck. Then we advise our clients whom to deal with, and keep them from having bad luck. See?"

I saw all right. I wasn't born yesterday. The magicians I dealt with were local men that I had known for years, men with established reputations both here and in the Half World. They didn't do anything to stir up the elementals against them, and they did not have bad luck.

What this slimy item meant was that I should deal only with the magicians they selected at whatever fees they chose to set, and they would take a cut on the fees and also on the profits of my business. If I didn't choose to "co-operate," I'd be persecuted by elementals they had an arrangement with—renegades, probably, with human vices—my stock in trade spoiled and my customers frightened away. If I still held out, I could expect some really dangerous black magic that would injure or kill me. All this under the pretense of selling me protection from men I knew and liked.

A neat racket!

I had heard of something of the sort back East, but had not expected it in a city as small as ours.

He sat there, smirking at me, waiting for my reply, and twisting his neck in his collar, which was too tight. That caused me to notice something. In spite of his foppish clothes a thread showed on his neck just above the collar in back. It seemed likely that it was there to support something next to his skin—an amulet. If so, he was superstitious, even in this day and age.

"There's something you've omitted," I told him. "I'm a seventh son, born under a caul, and I've got second sight. My luck's all right, but I can see bad luck hovering over you like cypress over a grave!" I reached out and snatched at the thread. It snapped and came loose in my hand. There was an amulet on it, right enough, an unsavory little wad of nothing in particular and about as appetizing as the bottom of a bird cage. I dropped it on the floor and ground it into the dirt.

He had jumped off the counter and stood facing me, breathing hard. A knife showed up in his right hand; with his left hand he was warding off the evil eye, the first and little fingers pointed at me, making the horns of Asmodeus. I knew I had him for the time being.

"Here's some magic you may not have heard of," I rapped out, and reached into a drawer behind

158

the counter. I hauled out a pistol and pointed it at his face. "Cold iron! Now go back to your owner and tell him there's cold iron waiting for him, too—both ways!"

He backed away, never taking his eyes off my face. If looks could kill, and so forth. At the door he paused and spat on the doorsill, then got out of sight very quickly.

I put the gun away and went about my work, waiting on two customers who came in just as Mr. Nasty Business left. But I will admit that I was worried. A man's reputation is his most valuable asset. I've built up a name, while still a young man, for dependable products. It was certain that this bird and his pals would do all they could to destroy that name—which might be plenty if they were hooked in with black magicians!

Of course the building-materials game does not involve as much magic as other lines dealing in less durable goods. People like to know, when they are building a home, that the bed won't fall into the basement some night, or the roof disappear and leave them out in the rain.

Besides, building involves quite a lot of iron, and there are very few commercial sorcerers who can cope with cold iron. The few that can are so expensive it isn't economical to use them in building. Of course if one of the café-society crowd, or somebody like that, wants to boast that they have a summerhouse or a swimming pool built entirely by magic, I'll accept the contract, charging accordingly, and sublet it to one of the expensive, first-line magicians. But by and large my business uses magic only in the side issues—perishable items and doodads which people like to buy cheap and change from time to time.

So I was not worried about magic *in* my business, but about what magic could *do* to my business—if someone set out deliberately to do me mischief. I had the subject of magic on my mind anyhow, because of an earlier call from a chap named Ditworth—not a matter of vicious threats, just a business proposition that I was undecided about. But it worried me, just the same....

I closed up a few minutes early and went over to see Jedson—a friend of mine in the cloak-and-suit business. He is considerably older than I am, and quite a student, without holding a degree, in all forms of witchcraft, white and black magic, necrology, demonology, spells, charms, and the more practical forms of divination. Besides that, Jedson is a shrewd, capable man in every way, with a long head on him. I set a lot of store by his advice.

I expected to find him in his office, and more or less free, at that hour, but he wasn't. His office boy directed me up to a room he used for sales conferences. I knocked and then pushed the door.

"Hello, Archie," he called out as soon as he saw who it was. "Come on in. I've got something." And he turned away.

I came in and looked around. Besides Joe Jedson there was a handsome, husky woman about thirty years old in a nurse's uniform, and a fellow named

August Welker, Jedson's foreman. He was a handy all-around man with a magician's license, third class. Then I noticed a fat little guy, Zadkiel Feldstein, who was agent for a good many of the second-rate magicians along the street, and some few of the first-raters. Naturally, his religion prevented him from practicing magic himself, but, as I understand it, there was no theological objection to his turning an honest commission. I had had dealings with him; he was all right.

This ten-percenter was clutching a cigar that had gone out, and watching intently Jedson and another party, who was slumped in a chair.

This other party was a girl, not over twenty-five, maybe not that old. She was blond, and thin to the point that you felt that light would shine through her. She had big, sensitive hands with long fingers, and a big, tragic mouth: Her hair was silver-white, but she was not an albino. She lay back in the chair, awake but apparently done in. The nurse was chafing her wrists.

"What's up?" I asked. "The kid faint?"

"Oh no," Jedson assured me, turning around. "She's a white witch—works in a trance. She's a little tired now, that's all."

"What's her specialty?" I inquired.

"Whole garments."

"Huh?" I had a right to be surprised. It's one thing to create yard goods; another thing entirely to turn out a dress, or a suit, all finished and ready to wear. Jedson produced and merchandised a full line of garments in which magic was used throughout. They were mostly sportswear, novelty goods, ladies' fashions, and the like, in which style, rather than wearing qualities, was the determining factor. Usually they were marked "One Season Only," but they were perfectly satisfactory for that one season, being backed up by the consumers' groups.

But they were not turned out in one process. The yard goods involved were made first, usually by Welker. Dyes and designs were added separately. Jedson had some very good connections among the Little People, and could obtain shades and patterns from the Half World that were exclusive with him. He used both the old methods and magic in assembling garments, and employed some of the most talented artists in the business. Several of his dress designers free-lanced their magic in Hollywood under an arrangement with him. All he asked for was screen credit.

But to get back to the blond girl——

"That's what I said," Jedson answered, "whole garments, with good wearing qualities too. There's no doubt that she is the real McCoy; she was under contract to a textile factory in Jersey City. But I'd give a thousand dollars to see her do that whole-garment stunt of hers just once. We haven't had any luck, though I've tried everything but red-hot pincers."

The kid looked alarmed at this, and the nurse looked indignant. Feldstein started to expostulate, but Jedson cut him short. "That was just a figure of speech; you know I don't hold with black magic.

162

Look, darling," he went on, turning back to the girl, "do you feel like trying again?" She nodded and he added, "All right—sleepy time now!"

And she tried again, going into her act with a minimum of groaning and spitting. The ectoplasm came out freely and sure enough, it formed into a complete dress instead of yard goods. It was a neat little dinner frock, about a size sixteen, sky blue in a watered silk. It had class in a refined way, and I knew that any jobber who saw it would be good for a sizable order.

Jedson grabbed it, cut off a swatch of cloth and applied his usual tests, finishing by taking the swatch out of the microscope and touching a match to it.

He swore. "Damn it," he said, "there's no doubt about it. It's not a new integration at all; she's just reanimated an old rag!"

"Come again," I said. "What of it?"

"Huh? Archie, you really ought to study up a bit. What she just did isn't really creative magic at all. This dress"—he picked it up and shook it— "had a real existence someplace at some time. She's gotten hold of a piece of it, a scrap or maybe just a button, and applied the laws of homeopathy and contiguity to produce a simulacrum of it."

I understood him, for I had used it in my own business. I had once had a section of bleachers, suitable for parades and athletic events, built on my own grounds by old methods, using skilled master mechanics and the best materials—no iron, of course. Then I cut it to pieces. Under the law of contiguity, each piece remained part of the structure it had once been in. Under the law of homeopathy, each piece was potentially the entire structure. I would contract to handle a Fourth of July crowd, or the spectators for a circus parade, and send out a couple of magicians armed with as many fragments of the original stands as we needed sections of bleachers. They would bind a spell to last twenty-four hours around each piece. That way the stands cleared themselves away automatically.

I had had only one mishap with it; an apprentice magician, who had the chore of being on hand as each section vanished and salvaging the animated fragment for further use, happened one day to pick up the wrong piece of wood from where one section had stood. The next time we used it, for the Shrine convention, we found we had thrown up a brand-new four-room bungalow at the corner of Fourteenth and Vine instead of a section of bleachers. It could have been embarrassing, but I stuck a sign on it

MODEL HOME NOW ON DISPLAY

and ran up another section on the end.

An out-of-town concern tried to chisel me out of the business one season, but one of their units fell, either through faulty workmanship on the pattern or because of unskilled magic, and injured several people. Since then I've had the field pretty much to myself.

I could not understand Joe Jedson's objection to reanimation. "What difference does it make?" I persisted. "It's a dress, isn't it?"

"Sure it's a dress, but it's not a new one. That style is registered somewhere and doesn't belong to me. And even if it were one of my numbers she had used, reanimation isn't what I'm after. I can make better merchandise cheaper without it; otherwise I'd be using it now."

The blond girl came to, saw the dress, and said, "Oh, Mr. Jedson, did I do it?"

He explained what had happened. Her face fell, and the dress melted away at once. "Don't you feel bad about it, kid," he added, patting her on the shoulder, "you were tired. We'll try again tomorrow. I know you can do it when you're not nervous and overwrought."

She thanked him and left with the nurse. Feldstein was full of explanations, but Jedson told him to forget it, and to have them all back there at the same time tomorrow. When we were alone I told him what had happened to me.

He listened in silence, his face serious, except when I told him how I had kidded my visitor into thinking I had second sight. That seemed to amuse him.

"You may wish that you really had it—second sight, I mean," he said at last, becoming solemn again. "This is an unpleasant prospect. Have you notified the Better Business Bureau?"

I told him I hadn't.

"Very well then. I'll give them a ring and the

Chamber of Commerce too. They probably can't help much, but they are entitled to notification, so they can be on the lookout for it."

I asked him if he thought I ought to notify the police. He shook his head. "Not just yet. Nothing illegal has been done, and, anyhow, all the chief could think of to cope with the situation would be to haul in all the licensed magicians in town and sweat them. That wouldn't do any good, and would just cause hard feelings to be directed against you by the legitimate members of the profession. There isn't a chance in ten that the sorcerers connected with this outfit are licensed to perform magic; they are almost sure to be clandestine. If the police knew about them, it's because they are protected. If they don't know about them, then they probably can't help you."

"What do you think I ought to do?"

"Nothing just yet. Go home and sleep on it. This Charlie may be playing a lone hand, making small-time shake-downs purely on bluff. I don't really think so; his type sounds like a mobster. But we need more data; we can't do anything until they expose their hand a little more."

We did not have long to wait. When I got down to my place of business the next morning I found a surprise waiting for me—several of them, all unpleasant.

It was as if it had been ransacked by burglars, set fire to, then gutted by a flood. I called up Jedson at once. He came right over. He didn't have anything to say at first, but went poking through the ruins, examining a number of things. He stopped at the point where the hardware storeroom had stood, reached down and gathered up a handful of the wet ashes and muck. "Notice anything?" he asked, working his fingers so that the debris sloughed off and left in the hand some small metal objects—nails, screws, and the like.

"Nothing in particular. This is where the hardware bins were located; that's some of the stuff that didn't burn."

"Yes, I know," he said impatiently, "but don't you see anything else? Didn't you stock a lot of brass fittings?"

"Yes."

"Well, find one!"

I poked around with my toe in a spot where there should have been a lot of brass hinges and drawer pulls mixed in with the ashes. I did not find anything but the nails that had held the bins together. I oriented myself by such landmarks as I could find and tried again. There were plenty of nuts and bolts, casement hooks, and similar junk, but no brass.

Jedson watched me with a sardonic grin on his face.

"Well?" I said, somewhat annoyed at his manner.

"Don't you see?" he answered. "It's magic, all right. In this entire yard there is not one scrap of metal left, *except cold iron!*"

It was plain enough. I should have seen it myself.

He messed around awhile longer. Presently we

came across an odd thing. It was a slimy, wet track that meandered through my property, and disappeared down one of the drains. It looked as if a giant slug, about the size of a Crosley car, had wandered through the place.

"Undine," Jedson announced, and wrinkled his nose at the smell. I once saw a movie, a Megapix superproduction called the *Water King's Daughter*. According to it undines were luscious enough to have interested Earl Carroll, but if they left trails like that I wanted none of them.

He took out his handkerchief and spread it for a clean place to sit down on what had been sacks of cement—a fancy, quick-setting variety, with a trade name of Hydrolith, I had been getting eighty cents a sack for the stuff, now it was just so many big boulders.

He ticked the situation off on his fingers. "Archie, you've been kicked in the teeth by at least three of the four different types of elements— earth, fire, and water. Maybe there was a sylph of the air in on it, too, but I can't prove it. First the gnomes came and cleaned out everything you had that came out of the ground, except cold iron. A salamander followed them and set fire to the place, burning everything that was burnable, and scorching and smoke-damaging the rest. Then the undine turned the place into a damned swamp, ruining anything that wouldn't burn, like cement and lime. You're insured?"

"Naturally." But then I started to think. I carried the usual fire, theft, and flood insurance, but business-risk insurance comes pretty high: I was not covered against the business I would lose in the meantime, nor did I have any way to complete current contracts. It was going to cost me quite a lot to cover those contracts; if I let them slide it would ruin the good will of my business, and lay me open to suits for damage.

The situation was worse than I had thought, and looked worse still the more I thought about it. Naturally I could not accept any new business until the mess was cleaned up, the place rebuilt, and new stock put it. Luckily most of my papers were in a fireproof steel safe; but not all, by any means. There would be accounts receivable that I would never collect because I had nothing to show for them. I work on a slim margin of profit, with all of my capital at work. It began to look as if the firm of Archibald Fraser, Merchant and Contractor, would go into involuntary bankruptcy.

I explained the situation to Jedson.

"Don't get your wind up too fast," he reassured me. "What magic can do, magic can undo. What we need is the best wizard in town."

"Who's going to pay the fee?" I objected. "Those boys don't work for nickels, and I'm cleaned out."

"Take it easy, son," he advised, "the insurance outfit that carries your risks is due to take a bigger loss than you are. If we can show them a way to save money on this, we can do business. Who represents them here?"

I told him—a firm of lawyers downtown in the Professional Building.

I got hold of my office girl and told her to telephone such of our customers as were due for deliveries that day. She was to stall where possible and pass on the business that could not wait to a firm that I had exchanged favors with in the past. I sent the rest of my help home—they had been standing around since eight o'clock, making useless remarks and getting in the way—and told them not to come back until I sent for them. Luckily it was Saturday; we had the best part of forty-eight hours to figure out some answer.

We flagged a magic carpet that was cruising past and headed for the Professional Building. I settled back and determined to enjoy the ride and forget my troubles. I like taxicabs—they give me a feeling of luxury—and I've liked them even better since they took the wheels off them. This happened to be one of the new Cadillacs with the teardrop shape and air cushions. We went scooting down the boulevard, silent as thought, not six inches off the ground.

Perhaps I should explain that we have a local city ordinance against apportation unless it conforms to traffic regulations—ground traffic, I mean, not air. That may surprise you, but it came about as a result of a mishap to a man in my own line of business. He had an order for eleven-odd tons of glass brick to be delivered to a restaurant being remodeled on the other side of town from his yard. He employed a magician with a common carrier's license to deliver for him. I don't know whether he was careless or just plain stupid, but he dropped those eleven tons of brick through the roof the Prospect Boulevard Baptist Church. Anybody knows that magic won't work over consecrated ground; if he had consulted a map he would have seen that the straight-line route took his load over the church. Anyhow, the janitor was killed, and it might just as well have been the whole congregation. It caused such a commotion that apportation was limited to the streets, near the ground.

It's people like that who make it inconvenient for everybody else.

Our man was in—Mr. Wiggin, of the firm Wiggin, Snead, McClatchey & Wiggin. He had already heard about my "fire," but when Jedson explained his conviction that magic was at the bottom of it he balked. It was, he said most irregular. Jedson was remarkably patient.

"Are you an expert in magic, Mr. Wiggin?" he asked.

"I have not specialized in the thaumaturgic jurisprudence, if that is what you mean, sir."

"Well, I don't hold a license myself, but it has been my hobby for a good many years. I'm sure of what I say in this case; you can call in the independent experts you wish—they'll confirm my opinion. Now suppose we stipulate, for the sake of argument, that this damage was caused by magic. If that is true, there is a possibility that we may be able to save much of the loss. You have authority to settle claims, do you not?"

"Well, I think I may say yes to that—bearing in mind the legal restrictions and the terms of the contract." I don't believe he would have conceded that he had five fingers on his right hand without an auditor to back him up.

"Then it is your business to hold your company's losses down to a minimum. If I find a wizard who can undo a part, or all, of the damage, will you guarantee the fee, on behalf of your company, up to a reasonable amount, say 25 percent of the indemnity?"

He hemmed and hawed some more, and said he did not see how he could possibly do it, and that if the fire had been magic, then to restore by magic might be compounding a felony, as we could not be sure what the connections of the magicians involved might be in the Half World. Besides that, my claim had not been allowed as yet; I had failed to notify the company of my visitor of the day before, which possibly might prejudice my claim. In any case, it was a very serious precedent to set; he must consult the home office.

Jedson stood up. "I can see that we are simply wasting each other's time, Mr. Wiggin. Your contention about Mr. Fraser's possible responsibility is ridiculous, and you know it. There is no reason under the contract to notify you, and even if there were, he is within the twenty-four hours allowed for any notification. I think it best that we consult the home office ourselves." He reached for his hat.

Wiggin put up his hand. "Gentlemen, gentlemen, please! Let's not be hasty. Will Mr. Fraser agree to pay half of the fee?"

"No. Why should he? It's your loss, not his. *You* insured *him*."

Wiggin tapped his teeth with his spectacles, then said, "We must make the fee contingent on results."

"Did you ever hear of anyone in his right mind dealing with a wizard on any other basis?"

Twenty minutes later we walked out with a document which enabled us to hire any witch or wizard to salvage my place of business on a contingent fee not to exceed 25 percent of the value reclaimed. "I thought you were going to throw up the whole matter," I told Jedson with a sigh of relief.

He grinned. "Not in the wide world, old son. He was simply trying to horse you into paying the cost of saving them some money. I just let him know that I knew."

It took some time to decide whom to consult. Jedson admitted frankly that he did not know of a man nearer than New York who could, with certainty, be trusted to do the job, and that was out of the question for the fee involved. We stopped in a bar, and he did some telephoning while I had a beer. Presently he came back and said, "I think I've got the man. I've never done business with him before, but he has the reputation and the training, and everybody I talked to seemed to think that he was the one to see."

"Who is it?" I wanted to know.

"Dr. Fortescue Biddle. He's just down the

street—the Railway Exchange Building. Come on, we'll walk it."

I gulped down the rest of my beer and followed him.

Dr. Biddle's place was impressive. He had a corner suite on the fourteenth floor, and he had not spared expense in furnishing and decorating it. The style was modern; it had the austere elegance of a society physician's layout. There was a frieze around the wall of the signs of the zodiac done in intaglio glass, backed up by aluminum. That was the only decoration of any sort, the rest of the furnishing being very plain, but rich, with lots of plate glass and chromium.

We had to wait about thirty minutes in the outer office; I spent the time trying to estimate what I could have done the suite for, subletting what I had to and allowing 10 percent. Then a really beautiful girl with a hushed voice ushered us in. We found ourselves in another smaller room, alone, and had to wait about ten minutes more. It was much like the waiting room, but had some glass bookcases and an old print of Aristotle. I looked at the bookcases with Jedson to kill time. They were filled with a lot of rare old classics on magic. Jedson had just pointed out the *Red Grimoire* when we heard a voice behind us.

"Amusing, aren't they? The ancients knew a surprising amount. Not scientific, of course, but remarkably clever——" The voice trailed off. We turned around; he introduced himself as Dr. Biddle.

He was a nice enough looking chap, really handsome in a spare, dignified fashion. He was about ten years older than I am—fortyish; maybe—with iron-gray hair at the temples and a small, stiff, British major's mustache. His clothes could have been out of the style pages of *Esquire*. There was no reason for me not to like him; his manners were pleasant enough. Maybe it was the supercilious twist to his expression.

He led us into his private office, sat us down, and offered us cigarettes before business was mentioned. He opened up with, "You're Jedson, of course. I suppose Mr. Ditworth sent you?"

I cocked an ear at him; the name was familiar. But Jedson simply answered, "Why, no. Why would you think that he had?"

Biddle hesitated for a moment, then said half to himself, "That's strange. I was certain that I had heard him mention your name. Does either one of you," he added, "know Mr. Ditworth?"

We both nodded at once and surprised each other. Biddle seemed relieved and said, "No doubt that accounts for it. Still—I need some more information. Will you gentlemen excuse me while I call him?"

With that he vanished. I had never seen it done before. Jedson says there are two ways to do it, one is hallucination, the other is an actual exit through the Half World. Whichever way it's done, I think it's bad manners.

"About this chap Ditworth," I started to say to Jedson. "I had intended to ask you——"

175

"Let it wait," he cut me off, "there's not time now."

At this Biddle reappeared. "It's all right," he announced, speaking directly to me. "I can take your case. I suppose you've come about the trouble you had last night with your establishment?"

"Yes," I agreed. "How did you know?"

"Methods," he replied, with a deprecatory little smile. "My profession has its means. Now, about your problem. What is it you desire?"

I looked at Jedson; he explained what he thought had taken place and why he thought so. "Now I don't know whether you specialize in demonology or not," he concluded, "but it seems to me that it should be possible to evoke the powers responsible and force them to repair the damage. If you can do it, we are prepared to pay any reasonable fee."

Biddle smiled at this and glanced rather self-consciously at the assortment of diplomas hanging on the walls of his office. "I feel that there should be reason to reassure you," he purred. "Permit me to look over the ground——" And he was gone again.

I was beginning to be annoyed. It's all very well for a man to be good at his job, but there is no reason to make a side show out of it. But I didn't have time to grouse about it before he was back.

"Examination seems to confirm Mr. Jedson's opinion; there should be no unusual difficulties," he said. "Now as to the...ah...business arrangements——" He coughed politely and gave a little smile, as if he regretted having to deal with such vulgar matters.

Why do some people act as if making money offended their delicate minds? I am out for a legitimate profit, and not ashamed of it; the fact that people will pay money for my goods and services shows that my work is useful.

However, we made a deal without much trouble, then Biddle told us to meet him at my place in about fifteen minutes. Jedson and I left the building and flagged another cab. Once inside I asked him about Ditworth.

"Where'd you run across him?" I said.

"Came to me with a proposition."

"Hm-m-m——" This interested me; Ditworth had made me a proposition, too, and it had worried me. "What kind of a proposition?"

Jedson screwed up his forehead. "Well, that's hard to say—there was so much impressive sales talk along with it. Briefly, he said he was the local executive secretary of a nonprofit association which had as its purpose the improvement of standards of practicing magicians."

I nodded. It was the same story I had heard. "Go ahead."

"He dwelt on the inadequacy of the present licensing laws and pointed out that anyone could pass the examinations and hang out his shingle after a couple of weeks' study of a *grimoire* or black book without any fundamental knowledge of the arcane laws at all. His organization would be a sort of bureau of standards to improve that, like the American Medical Association, or the National Conference of Universities and Colleges, or the Bar Association. If I signed an agreement to patronize only those wizards who complied with their requirements, I could display their certificate of quality and put their seal of approval on my goods."

"Joe, I've heard the same story," I cut in, "and I didn't know quite what to make of it. It sounds all right, but I wouldn't want to stop doing business with men who have given me good value in the past, and I've no way of knowing that the association would approve them."

"What answer did you give him?"

"I stalled him a bit—told him that I couldn't sign anything as binding as that without discussing it with my attorney."

"Good boy! What did he say to that?"

"Well, he was really quite decent about it, and honestly seemed to want to be helpful. Said he thought I was wise and left me some stuff to look over. Do you know anything about him? Is he a wizard himself?"

"No, he's not. But I did find out some things about him. I knew vaguely that he was something in the Chamber of Commerce; what I didn't know is that he is on the board of a dozen or more blue-ribbon corporations. He's a lawyer, but not in practice. Seems to spend all his time on his business interests."

"He sounds like a responsible man."

"I would say so. He seems to have had considerably less publicity than you would expect of a man of his business importance—probably a retiring sort. I ran across something that seemed to confirm that."

"What was it?" I asked.

"I looked up the incorporation papers for his association on file with the Secretary of State. There were just three names, his own and two others. I found that both of the others were employed in his office—his secretary and his receptionist."

"Dummy setup?"

"Undoubtedly. But there is nothing unusual about that. What interested me was this: I recognized one of the names."

"Huh?"

"You know, I'm on the auditing committee for the state committee of my party. I looked up the name of his secretary where I thought I had seen it. It was there all right. His secretary, a chap by the name of Mathias, was down for a whopping big contribution to the governor's personal campaign fund."

We did not have any more time to talk just then, as the cab had pulled up at my place. Dr. Biddle was there before us and had already started his preparations. He had set up a little crystal pavilion, about ten feet square, to work in. The entire lot was blocked off from spectators on the front by an impalpable screen. Jedson warned me not to touch it.

I must say he worked without any of the usual

179

hocus-pocus. He simply greeted us and entered the pavilion, where he sat down on a chair and took a loose-leaf notebook from a pocket and commenced to read. Jedson says he used several pieces of paraphernalia too. If so, I didn't see them. He worked with his clothes on.

Nothing happened for a few minutes. Gradually the walls of the shed became cloudy, so that everything inside was indistinct. It was about then that I became aware that there was something else in the pavilion besides Biddle. I could not see clearly what it was, and, to tell the truth, I didn't want to.

We could not hear anything that was said on the inside, but there was an argument going on—that was evident. Biddle stood up and began sawing the air with his hands. The thing threw back its head and laughed. At that Biddle threw a worried look in our direction and made a quick gesture with his right hand. The walls of the pavilion became opaque at once and we didn't see any more.

About five minutes later Biddle walked out of his workroom, which promptly disappeared behind him. He was a sight—his hair all mussed, sweat dripping from his face, and his collar wrinkled and limp. Worse than that, his aplomb was shaken.

"Well?" said Jedson.

"There is nothing to be done about it, Mr. Jedson—nothing at all."

"Nothing you can do about it, eh?"

He stiffened a bit at this. "Nothing *anyone* can

do about it, gentlemen. Give it up. Forget about it. That is my advice."

Jedson said nothing, just looked at him speculatively. I kept quiet. Biddle was beginning to regain his self-possession. He straightened his hat, adjusted his necktie, and added, "I must return to my office. The survey fee will be five hundred dollars."

I was stonkered speechless at the barefaced gall of the man, but Jedson acted as if he hadn't understood him. "No doubt it would be," he observed. "Too bad you didn't earn it. I'm sorry."

Biddle turned red, but preserved his urbanity. "Apparently you misunderstood me, sir. Under the agreement I have signed with Mr. Ditworth, thaumaturgists approved by the association are not permitted to offer free consultation. It lowers the standards of the profession. The fee I mentioned is the minimum fee for a magician of my classification, irrespective of services rendered."

"I see," Jedson answered calmly; "that's what it costs to step inside your office. But you didn't tell us that, so it doesn't apply. As for Mr. Ditworth, an agreement you sign with him does not bind us in any way. I advise you to return to your office and reread our contract. We owe you nothing."

I thought this time that Biddle would lose his temper, but all he answered was, "I shan't bandy words with you. You will hear from me later." He vanished then without so much as a by-your-leave.

I heard a snicker behind me and whirled around, ready to bite somebody's head off. I had had an

Robert A. Heinlein

upsetting day and didn't like to be laughed at behind my back. There was a young chap there, about my own age. "Who are you, and what are you laughing at?" I snapped. "This is private property."

"Sorry, bud," he apologized with a disarming grin. "I wasn't laughing at you; I was laughing at the stuffed shirt. Your friend ticked him off properly."

"What are you doing here?" asked Jedson.

"Me? I guess I owe you an explanation. You see, I'm in the business myself——"

"Building?"

"No—magic. Here's my card." He handed it to Jedson, who glanced at it and passed it on to me. It read:

JACK BODIE
LICENSED MAGICIAN, 1ST CLASS
TELEPHONE CREST 3840

"You see, I heard a rumor in the Half World that one of the big shots was going to do a hard one here today. I just stopped in to see the fun. But how did you happen to pick a false alarm like Biddle? He's not up to this sort of thing."

Jedson reached over and took the card back. "Where did you take your training, Mr. Bodie?"

"Huh? I took my bachelor's degree at Harvard and finished up postgraduate at Chicago. But that's not important; my old man taught me everything I know, but he insisted on my going to college

182

because he said a magician can't get a decent job these days without a degree. He was right."

"Do you think you could handle this job?" I asked.

"Probably not, but I wouldn't have made the fool of myself that Biddle did. Look here—you want to find somebody who *can* do this job?"

"Naturally," I said. "What do you think we're here for?"

"Well, you've gone about it the wrong way. Biddle's got a reputation simply because he's studied at Heidelberg and Vienna. That doesn't mean a thing. I'll bet it never occurred to you to look up an old-style witch for the job."

Jedson answered this one. "That's not quite true. I inquired around among my friends in the business, but didn't find anyone who was willing to take it on. But I'm willing to learn; whom do you suggest?"

"Do you know Mrs. Amanda Todd Jennings? Lives over in the old part of town, beyond the Congregational cemetery."

"Jennings...Jennings. Hm-m-m—no, can't say that I do. Wait a minute! Is she the old girl they call Granny Jennings? Wears Queen Mary hats and does her own marketing?"

"That's the one."

"But she's not a witch; she's a fortuneteller."

"That's what you think. She's not in regular commercial practice, it's true, being ninety years older than Santy Claus, and feeble to boot. But she's got more magic in her little finger than you'll find in Solomon's Book."

Jedson looked at me. I nodded, and he said:

"Do you think you could get her to attempt this case?"

"Well, I think she might do it, if she liked you."

"What arrangement do you want?" I asked. "Is 10 per cent satisfactory?"

He seemed rather put out at this. "Hell," he said, "I couldn't take a cut; she's been good to me all my life."

"If the tip is good, it's worth paying for," I insisted.

"Oh, forget it. Maybe you boys will have some work in my line someday. That's enough."

Pretty soon we were off again, without Bodie. He was tied up elsewhere, but promised to let Mrs. Jennings know that we were coming.

The place wasn't too hard to find. It was an old street, arched over with elms, and the house was a one-story cottage, set well back. The veranda had a lot of that old scroll-saw gingerbread. The yard was not very well taken care of, but there was a lovely old climbing rose arched over the steps.

Jedson gave a twist to the hand bell set in the door, and we waited for several minutes. I studied the colored-glass triangles set in the door's side panels and wondered if there was anyone left who could do that sort of work.

Then she let us in. She really was something incredible. She was so tiny that I found myself staring down at the crown of her head, and noting that the clean pink scalp showed plainly through the scant, neat threads of hair. She couldn't have weighed seventy pounds dressed for the street, but stood proudly erect in lavender alpaca and white collar, and sized us up with lively black eyes that would have fitted Catherine the Great or Calamity Jane.

"Good morning to you," she said. "Come in."

She led us through a little hall, between beaded portieres, said, "Scat, Seraphin!" to a cat on a chair, and sat us down in her parlor. The cat jumped down, walked away with an unhurried dignity, then sat down, tucked his tail neatly around his carefully placed feet, and stared at us with the same calm appraisal as his mistress.

"My boy Jack told me that you were coming," she began. "You are Mr. Fraser and you are Mr. Jedson," getting us sorted out correctly. It was not a question; it was a statement. "You want your futures read, I suppose. What method do you prefer—your palms, the stars, the sticks?"

I was about to correct her misapprehension when Jedson cut in ahead of me. "I think we'd best leave the method up to you, Mrs. Jennings."

"All right, we'll make it tea leaves then. I'll put the kettle on; 'twon't take a minute." She bustled out. We could hear her in the kitchen, her light footsteps clicking on the linoleum, utensils scraping and clattering in a busy, pleasant disharmony.

When she returned I said, "I hope we aren't putting you out, Mrs. Jennings."

"Not a bit of it," she assured me. "I like a cup of tea in the morning; it does a body comfort. I just had to set a love philter off the fire—that's what took me so long."

"I'm sorry——"

"'Twon't hurt it to wait."

"The Zekerboni formula?" Jedson inquired.

"My goodness gracious, no!" She was plainly upset by the suggestion. "I wouldn't kill all those harmless little creatures. Hares and swallows and doves—the very idea! I don't know what Pierre Mora was thinking about when he set that recipe down. I'd like to box his ears!

"No, I use Emula campana, orange, and ambergris. It's just as effective."

Jedson then asked if she had ever tried the juice of vervain. She looked closely into his face before replying, "You have the sight yourself, son. Am I not right?"

"A little, mother," he answered soberly, "a little, perhaps."

"It will grow. Mind how you use it. As for vervain, it is efficacious, as you know."

"Wouldn't it be simpler?"

"Of course it would. But if that easy a method became generally known, anyone and everyone would be making it and using it promiscuously— a bad thing. And witches would starve for want of clients—perhaps a good thing!" She flicked up one white eyebrow. "But if it is simplicity you want, there is no need to bother even with vervain. Here——" she reached out and touched me on the hand. "'*Bestarberto corrumpit viscera ejus virilis*.'"

That is as near as I can reproduce her words. I may have misquoted it.

But I had no time to think about the formula she had pronounced. I was fully occupied with the startling thing that had come over me. I was in love, ecstatically, deliciously in love—with Granny Jennings! I don't mean that she suddenly looked like a beautiful young girl—she didn't. I still saw her as a little, old, shriveled-up woman with the face of a shrewd monkey, and ancient enough to be my great-grandmother. It didn't matter. She was she—the Helen that all men desire, the object of romantic adoration.

She smiled into my face with a smile that was warm and full of affectionate understanding. Everything was all right, and I was perfectly happy. Then she said, "I would not mock you, boy," in a gentle voice, and touched my hand a second time while whispering something else.

At once it was all gone. She was just any nice old woman, the sort that would bake a cake for a grandson or sit up with a sick neighbor. Nothing was changed, and the cat had not even blinked. The romantic fascination was an emotionless memory. But I was poorer for the difference.

The kettle was boiling. She trotted out to attend to it, and returned shortly with a tray of tea things, a plate of seed cake, and thin slices of homemade bread spread with sweet butter.

When we had drunk a cup apiece with proper ceremony, she took Jedson's cup from him and examined the dregs. "Not much money there," she announced, "but you shan't need much; it's a fine full life." She touched the little pool of tea with the tip of her spoon and sent tiny ripples across it. "Yes, you have the sight, and the need for understanding that should go with it, but I find you in business instead of pursuing the great art, or even the lesser arts. Why is that?"

Jedson shrugged his shoulders and answered half apologetically, "There is work at hand that needs to be done. I do it."

She nodded. "That is well. There is understanding to be gained in any job, and you will gain it. There is no hurry; time is long. When your own work comes you will know it and be ready for it. Let me see your cup," she finished, turning to me.

I handed it to her. She studied it for a moment and said, "Well, you have not the clear sight such as your friend has, but you have the insight you need for your proper work. And more would make you dissatisfied, for I see money here. You will make much money, Archie Fraser."

"Do you see any immediate setback in my business?" I said quickly.

"No. See for yourself." She motioned toward the cup. I leaned forward and stared at it. For a matter of seconds it seemed as if I looked through the surface of the dregs into a living scene beyond. I recognized it readily enough. It was my own place of business, even to the scars on the driveway gateposts where clumsy truck drivers had clipped the corner too closely.

But there was a new annex wing on the east

side of the lot, and there were two beautiful new five-ton dump trucks drawn up in the yard with my name painted on them!

While I watched I saw myself step out of the office door and go walking down the street. I was wearing a new hat, but the suit was the one I was wearing in Mrs. Jennings's parlor, and so was the necktie—a plaid one from the tartan of my clan. I reached up and touched the original.

Mrs. Jennings said, "That will do for now," and I found myself staring at the bottom of the teacup. "You have seen," she went on, "your business need not worry you. As for love and marriage and children, sickness and health and death—let us look." She touched the surface of the dregs with a finger tip; the tea leaves moved gently. She regarded them closely for a moment. Her brow puckered; she started to speak, apparently thought better of it, and looked again. Finally she said, "I do not fully understand this. It is not clear; my own shadow falls across it."

"Perhaps I can see," offered Jedson.

"Keep your peace!" She surprised me by speaking tartly, and placed her hand over the cup. She turned back to me with compassion in her eyes. "It is not clear. You have two possible futures. Let your head rule your heart, and do not fret your soul with that which cannot be. Then you will marry, have children, and be content." With that she dismissed the matter, for she said at once to both of us, "You did not come here for divination;

189

you came here for help of another sort." Again it was a statement, not a question.

"What sort of help, mother?" Jedson inquired.

"For this." She shoved my cup under his nose.

He looked at it and answered, "Yes, that is true. Is there help?" I looked into the cup, too, but saw nothing but tea leaves.

She answered, "I think so. You should not have employed Biddle, but the mistake was natural. Let us be going." Without further parley she fetched her gloves and purse and coat, perched a ridiculous old hat on the top of her head, and bustled us out of the house. There was no discussion of terms; it didn't seem necessary.

When we got back to the lot her workroom was already up. It was not anything fancy like Biddle's, but simply an old, square tent, like a gypsy's pitch, with a peaked top and made in several gaudy colors. She pushed aside the shawl that closed the door and invited us inside.

It was gloomy, but she took a big candle, lighted it and stuck it in the middle of the floor. By its light she inscribed five circles on the ground— first a large one, then a somewhat smaller one in front of it. Then she drew two others, one on each side of the first and biggest circle. These were each big enough for a man to stand in, and she told us to do so. Finally she made one more circle off to one side and not more than a foot across.

I've never paid much attention to the methods of magicians, feeling about them the way Thomas

Edison said he felt about mathematicians—when he wanted one he could hire one. But Mrs. Jennings was different. I wish I could understand the things she did—and why.

I know she drew a lot of cabalistic signs in the dirt within the circles. There were pentacles of various shapes, and some writing in what I judged to be Hebraic script, though Jedson says not. In particular there was, I remember, a sign like a long flat Z, with a loop in it, woven in and out of a Maltese cross. Two more candles were lighted and placed on each side of this.

Then she jammed the dagger—athame, Jedson called it—with which she had scribed the figures into the ground at the top of the big circle so hard that it quivered. It continued to vibrate the whole time.

She placed a little folding stool in the center of the biggest circle, sat down on it, drew out a small book, and commenced to read aloud in a voiceless whisper. I could not catch the words, and presume I was not meant to. This went on for some time. I glanced around and saw that the little circle off to one side was now occupied—by Seraphin, her cat. We had left him shut up in her house. He sat quietly, watching everything that took place with dignified interest.

Presently she shut the book and threw a pinch of powder into the flame of the largest candle. It flared up and threw out a great puff of smoke. I am not quite sure what happened next, as the smoke smarted my eyes and made me blink, besides which, Jedson says I don't understand the purpose of fumigations at all. But I prefer to believe my eyes. Either that cloud of smoke solidified into a body or it covered up an entrance, one or the other.

Standing in the middle of the circle in front of Mrs. Jennings was a short, powerful man about four feet high or less. His shoulders were inches broader than mine, and his upper arms were thick as my thighs, knotted and bowed with muscle. He was dressed in a breechcloth, buskins, and a little hooded cap. His skin was hairless, but rough and earthy in texture. It was dull, lusterless. Everything about him was the same dull monotone, except his eyes, which shone green with repressed fury.

"Well!" said Mrs. Jennings crisply, "you've been long enough getting here! What have you to say for yourself?"

He answered sullenly, like an incorrigible boy caught but not repentant, in a language filled with rasping gutturals and sibilants. She listened awhile, then cut him off.

"I don't care who told you to; you'll account to me! I require this harm repaired—in less time than it takes to tell it!"

He answered back angrily, and she dropped into his language, so that I could no longer follow the meaning. But it was clear that I was concerned in it; he threw me several dirty looks, and finally glared and spat in my direction.

Mrs. Jennings reached out and cracked him

across the mouth with the back of her hand. He looked at her, killing in his eyes, and said something.

"So?" she answered, put out a hand and grabbed him by the nape of the neck and swung him across her lap, face down. She snatched off a shoe and whacked him soundly with it. He let out one yelp, then kept silent, but jerked every time she struck him.

When she was through she stood up, spilling him to the ground. He picked himself up and hurriedly scrambled back into his own circle, where he stood, rubbing himself. Mrs. Jennings's eyes snapped and her voice crackled; there was nothing feeble about her now. "You gnomes are getting above yourselves," she scolded. "I never heard of such a thing! One more slip on your part and I'll fetch your people to see you spanked! Get along with you. Fetch your people for your task, and summon your brother and your brother's brother. By the great Tetragrammaton, get hence to the place appointed for you!"

He was gone.

Our next visitant came almost at once. It appeared first as a tiny spark hanging in the air. It grew into a living flame, a fireball, six inches or more across. It floated above the center of the second circle at the height of Mrs. Jennings's eyes. It danced and whirled and flamed, feeding on nothing. Although I had never seen one, I knew it to be a salamander. It couldn't be anything else.

Mrs. Jennings watched it for a little time before

speaking. I could see that she was enjoying its dance, as I was. It was a perfect and beautiful thing, with no fault in it. There was life in it, a singing joy, with no concern for—with no *relation* to—matters of right and wrong, or anything human. Its harmonies of color and curve were their own reason for being.

I suppose I'm pretty matter-of-fact. At least I've always lived by the principle of doing my job and letting other things take care of themselves. But here was something that was worthwhile in itself, no matter what harm it did by my standards. Even the cat was purring.

Mrs. Jennings spoke to it in a clear, singing soprano that had no words to it. It answered back in pure liquid notes while the colors of its nucleus varied to suit the pitch. She turned to me and said, "It admits readily enough that it burned your place, but it was invited to do so and is not capable of appreciating your point of view. I dislike to compel it against its own nature. Is there any boon you can offer it?"

I thought for a moment. "Tell it that it makes me happy to watch it dance." She sang again to it. It spun and leaped, its flame tendrils whirling and floating in intricate, delightful patterns.

"That was good, but not sufficient. Can you think of anything else?"

I thought hard. "Tell it that if it likes, I will build a fireplace in my house where it will be welcome to live whenever it wishes."

She nodded approvingly and spoke to it again.

I could almost understand its answer, but Mrs. Jennings translated. "It likes you. Will you let it approach you?"

"Can it hurt me?"

"Not here."

"All right then."

She drew a T between our two circles. It followed closely behind the athame, like a cat at an opening door. Then it swirled about me and touched me lightly on my hands and face. Its touch did not burn, but tingled, rather, as if I felt its vibrations directly instead of sensing them as heat. It flowed over my face. I was plunged into a world of light, like the heart of the aurora borealis. I was afraid to breathe at first, finally had to. No harm came to me, though the tingling was increased.

It's an odd thing, but I have not had a single cold since the salamander touched me. I used to sniffle all winter.

"Enough, enough," I heard Mrs. Jennings saying. The cloud of flame withdrew from me and returned to its circle. The musical discussion resumed, and they reached an agreement almost at once, for Mrs. Jennings nodded with satisfaction and said:

"Away with you then, fire child, and return when you are needed. Get hence—" She repeated the formula she had used on the gnome king.

The undine did not show up at once. Mrs. Jennings took out her book again and read from it in a monotonous whisper. I was beginning to be a bit sleepy—the tent was stuffy—when the cat commenced to spit. It was glaring at the center circle, claws out, back arched, and tail made big.

There was a shapeless something in that circle, a thing that dripped and spread its slimy moisture to the limit of the magic ring. It stank of fish and kelp and iodine, and shone with a wet phosphorescence.

"You're late," said Mrs. Jennings. "You got my message; why did you wait until I compelled you?"

It heaved with a sticky, sucking sound, but made no answer.

"Very well," she said firmly, "I shan't argue with you. You know what I want. You will do it!" She stood up and grasped the big center candle. Its flame flared up into a torch a yard high, and hot. She thrust it past her circle at the undine.

There was a hiss, as when water strikes hot iron, and a burbling scream. She jabbed at it again and again. At last she stopped and stared down at it, where it lay, quivering and drawing into itself. "That will do," she said. "Next time you will heed your mistress. Get hence!" It seemed to sink into the ground, leaving the dust dry behind it.

When it was gone she motioned for us to enter her circle, breaking our own with the dagger to permit us. Seraphin jumped lightly from his little circle to the big one and rubbed against her ankles, buzzing loudly. She repeated a meaningless series of syllables and clapped her hands smartly together.

There was a rushing and roaring. The sides of the tent billowed and cracked. I heard the chuckle of water and the crackle of flames, and, through that, the bustle of hurrying footsteps. She looked from side to side, and wherever her gaze fell the wall of the tent became transparent. I got hurried glimpses of unintelligible confusion.

Then it all ceased with a suddenness that was startling. The silence rang in our ears. The tent was gone; we stood in the loading yard outside my main warehouse.

It was there! It was back—back unharmed, without a trace of damage by fire or water. I broke away and ran out the main gate to where my business office had faced on the street. It was there, just as it used to be, the show windows shining in the sun, the Rotary Club emblem in one corner, and up on the roof my big two-way sign:

ARCHIBALD FRASER
BUILDING MATERIALS & GENERAL CONTRACTING

Jedson strolled out presently and touched me on the arm. "What are you bawling about, Archie?"

I stared at him. I wasn't aware that I had been.

We were doing business as usual on Monday morning. I thought everything was back to normal and that my troubles were over. I was too hasty in my optimism.

It was nothing you could put your finger on at first—just the ordinary vicissitudes of business, the little troubles that turn up in any line of work and slow up production. You expect them and

Robert A. Heinlein

charge them off to overhead. No one of them would
be worth mentioning alone, except for one thing:
they were happening too frequently.

You see, in any business run under a consistent
management policy the losses due to unforeseen
events should average out in the course of a year
to about the same percentage of total cost. You
allow for that in your estimates. But I started
having so many small accidents and little difficulties that my margin of profit was eaten up.

One morning two of my trucks would not start.
We could not find the trouble; I had to put them
in the shop and rent a truck for the day to sup-
plement my one remaining truck. We got our
deliveries made, but I was out the truck rent, the
repair bill, and four hours' overtime for drivers at
time and a half. I had a net loss for the day.

The very next day I was just closing a deal with
a man I had been trying to land for a couple of
years. The deal was not important, but it would
lead to a lot more business in the future, for he
owned quite a bit of income property—some courts
and an apartment house or two, several commercial corners, and held title or options on well-
located lots all over town. He always had repair
jobs to place and very frequently new building
jobs. If I satisfied him, he would be a steady customer with prompt payment, the kind you can
afford to deal with on a small margin of profit.

We were standing in the showroom just outside
my office and talking, having about reached an
agreement. There was a display of Sunprufe paint

about three feet from us, the cans stacked in a neat pyramid. I swear that neither one of us touched it, but it came crashing to the floor, making a din that would sour milk.

That was nuisance enough, but not the pay-off. The cover flew off one can, and my prospect was drenched with red paint. He let out a yelp; I thought he was going to faint. I managed to get him back into my office, where I dabbed futilely at his suit with my handkerchief, while trying to calm him down.

He was in a state, both mentally and physically. "Fraser," he raged, "you've got to fire the clerk that knocked over those cans! Look at me! Eighty-five dollars worth of suit ruined!"

"Let's not be hasty," I said soothingly, while holding my own temper in. I won't discharge a man to suit a customer, and don't like to be told to do so. "There wasn't anyone near those cans but ourselves."

"I suppose you think I did it?"

"Not at all. I know you didn't." I straightened up, wiped my hands, and went over to my desk and got out my checkbook.

"Then you must have done it!"

"I don't think so," I answered patiently. "How much did you say your suit was worth?"

"Why?"

"I want to write you a check for the amount." I was quite willing to; I did not feel to blame, but it had happened through no fault of his in my shop.

"You can't get out of it as easily as that!" he

answered unreasonably. "It isn't the cost of the suit I mind—" He jammed his hat on his head and stumped out. I knew his reputation; I'd seen the last of him.

This is the sort of thing I mean. Of course it could have been an accident caused by clumsy stacking of the cans. But it might have been a poltergeist. Accidents don't make themselves.

Ditworth came to see me a day or so later about Biddle's phony bill. I had been subjected night and morning to this continuous stream of petty annoyances, and my temper was wearing thin. Just that day a gang of colored bricklayers had quit one of my jobs because some moron had scrawled some chalk marks on some of the bricks. "Voodoo marks," they said they were, and would not touch a brick. I was in no mood to be held up by Mr. Ditworth; I guess I was pretty short with him.

"Good day to you, Mr. Fraser," he said quite pleasantly, "can you spare me a few minutes?"

"Ten minutes, perhaps," I conceded, glancing at my wrist watch.

He settled his brief case against the legs of his chair and took out some papers. "I'll come to the point at once then. It's about Dr. Biddle's claim against you. You and I are both fair men; I feel sure that we can come to some equitable agreement."

"Biddle has no claim against me."

He nodded. "I know just how you feel. Certainly there is nothing in the written contract obligating you to pay him. But there can be implied contracts just as binding as written contracts."

"I don't follow you. All my business is done in writing."

"Certainly," he agreed; "that's because you are a businessman. In the professions the situation is somewhat different. If you go to a dental surgeon and ask him to pull an aching tooth, and he does, you are obligated to pay his fee, even though a fee has never been mentioned—"

"That's true," I interrupted, "but there is no parallel. Biddle didn't 'pull the tooth.'"

"In a way he did," Ditworth persisted. "The claim against you is for the survey, which was a service rendered you before this contract was written."

"But no mention was made of a service fee."

"That is where the implied obligation comes in, Mr. Fraser; you told Dr. Biddle that you had talked with me. He assumed quite correctly that I had previously explained to you the standard system of fees under the association—"

"But I did not join the association!"

"I know, I know. And I explained that to the other directors, but they insist that some sort of an adjustment must be made. I don't feel myself that you are fully to blame, but you will understand our position, I am sure. We are unable to accept you for membership in the association until this matter is adjusted—in fairness to Dr. Biddle."

"What makes you think I intend to join the association?"

He looked hurt. "I had not expected you to take

that attitude, Mr. Fraser. The association needs men of your caliber. But in your own interest, you will necessarily join, for presently it will be very difficult to get efficient thaumaturgy except from members of the association. We want to help you. Please don't make it difficult for us."

I stood up. "I am afraid you had better sue me and let a court decide the matter, Mr. Ditworth. That seems to be the only satisfactory solution."

"I am sorry," he said, shaking his head. "It will prejudice your position when you come up for membership."

"Then it will just have to do so," I said shortly, and showed him out.

After he had gone I crabbed at my office girl for doing something I had told her to do the day before, and then had to apologize. I walked up and down a bit, stewing, although there was plenty of work I should have been doing. I was nervous; things had begun to get my goat—a dozen things that I haven't mentioned—and this last unreasonable demand from Ditworth seemed to be the last touch needed to upset me completely. Not that he could collect by suing me—that was preposterous—but it was an annoyance just the same. They say the Chinese have a torture that consists in letting one drop of water fall on the victim every few minutes. That's the way I felt.

Finally I called up Jedson and asked him to go to lunch with me.

I felt better after lunch. Jedson soothed me down, as he always does, and I was able to forget and put in the past most of the things that had been annoying me simply by telling him about them. By the time I had had a second cup of coffee and smoked a cigarette I was almost fit for polite society.

We strolled back toward my shop, discussing his problems for a change. It seems the blond girl, the white witch from Jersey City, had finally managed to make her synthesis stunt work on footgear. But there was still a hitch; she had turned out over eight hundred left shoes—and no right ones.

We were just speculating as to the probable causes of such a contretemps when Jedson said, "Look, Archie. The candid-camera fans are beginning to take an interest in you."

I looked. There was a chap standing at the curb directly across from my place of business and focusing a camera on the shop.

Then I looked again. "Joe," I snapped, "that's the bird I told you about, the one that came into my shop and started the trouble!"

"Are you sure?" he asked, lowering his voice.

"Positive." There was no doubt about it; he was only a short distance away on the same side of the street that we were. It was the same racketeer who had tried to blackmail me into buying "protection," the same Mediterranean look to him, the same flashy clothes.

"We've got to grab him," whispered Jedson.

But I had already thought of that. I rushed at him and had grabbed him by his coat collar and the slack of his pants before he knew what was happening, and pushed him across the street ahead of me. We were nearly run down, but I was so mad I didn't care. Jedson came pounding after us.

The yard door of my office was open. I gave the mug a final heave that lifted him over the threshold and sent him sprawling on the floor. Jedson was right behind; I bolted the door as soon as we were both inside.

Jedson strode over to my desk, snatched open the middle drawer, and rummaged hurriedly through the stuff that accumulates in such places. He found what he wanted, a carpenter's blue pencil, and was back alongside our gangster before he had collected himself sufficiently to scramble to his feet. Jedson drew a circle around him on the floor, almost tripping over his own feet in his haste, and closed the circle with an intricate flourish.

Our unwilling guest screeched when he saw what Joe was doing, and tried to throw himself out of the circle before it could be finished. But Jedson had been too fast for him—the circle was closed and sealed; he bounced back from the boundary as if he had struck a glass wall, and stumbled again to his knees. He remained so for the time, and cursed steadily in a language that I judged to be Italian, although I think there were bad words in it from several other languages— certainly some English ones.

He was quite fluent.

Jedson pulled out a cigarette, lighted it, and handed me one. "Let's sit down, Archie," he said, "and rest ourselves until our boy friend composes himself enough to talk business."

I did so, and we smoked for several minutes while the flood of invective continued. Presently Jedson cocked one eyebrow at the chap and said, "Aren't you beginning to repeat yourself?"

That checked him. He just sat and glared. "Well," Jedson continued, "haven't you anything to say for yourself?"

He growled under his breath and said, "I want to call my lawyer."

Jedson looked amused. "You don't understand the situation," he told him. "You're not under arrest, and we don't give a damn about your legal rights. We might just conjure up a hole and drop you in it, then let it relax." The guy paled a little under his swarthy skin. "Oh yes," Jedson went on, "we are quite capable of doing that—or worse. You see, we don't like you."

"Of course," he added meditatively, "we might just turn you over to the police. I get a soft streak now and then." The chap looked sour. "You don't like that either? Your fingerprints, maybe?" Jedson jumped to his feet and in two quick strides was standing over him, just outside the circle. "All right then," he rapped, "answer up and make 'em good! Why were you taking photographs?"

The chap muttered something, his eyes lowered. Jedson brushed it aside. "Don't give me that stuff— we aren't children! Who told you to do it?"

He looked utterly panic-stricken at that and shut up completely.

"Very well," said Jedson and turned to me. "Have you some wax, or modeling clay, or anything of the sort?"

"How would putty do?" I suggested.

"Just the thing." I slid out to the shed where we stow glaziers' supplies and came back with a five-pound can. Jedson pried it open and dug out a good big handful, then sat at my desk and worked the linseed oil into it until it was soft and workable. Our prisoner watched him with silent apprehension.

"There! That's about right," Jedson announced at and slapped the soft lump down on my blotter pad. He commenced to fashion it with his fingers, and it took shape slowly as a little doll about ten inches high. It did not look like much of anything or anybody. Jedson is no artist—but Jedson kept glancing from the figurine to the man in the circle and back again, like a sculptor making a clay sketch directly from a model. You could see the chap's nervous terror increase by the minute.

"Now!" said Jedson, looking once more from the putty figure to his model. "It's just as ugly as you are. Why did you take that picture?"

He did not answer, but slunk farther back in the circle, his face nastier than ever.

"Talk!" snorted Jedson, and twisted a foot of the doll between a thumb and forefinger. The corresponding foot of our prisoner jerked out from under him and twisted violently. He fell heavily to the floor with a yelp of pain.

"You were going to cast a spell on this place, weren't you?"

He made his first coherent answer. "No, no, mister! Not me!"

"Not you? I see. You were just the errand boy. Who was to do the magic?"

"I don't know—Ow! Oh, God!" He grabbed at his left calf and nursed it. Jedson had jabbed a pen point into the leg of the dolly. "I really *don't* know. Please, please!"

"Maybe you don't," Jedson grudged, "but at least you know who gives you your orders, and who some of the other members of your gang are. Start talking."

He rocked back and forth and covered his face with his hands. "I don't dare, mister," he groaned. "Please don't try to make me——" Jedson jabbed the doll with the pen again; he jumped and flinched, but this time he bore it silently with a look of gray determination.

"O.K.," said Jedson, "if you insist——" He took another drag from his cigarette, then brought the lighted end slowly toward the face of the doll. The man in the circle tried to shrink away from it, his hands up to protect his face, but his efforts were futile. I could actually see the skin turn red and angry and the blisters blossom under his hide. It made me sick to watch it, and, while I didn't feel any real sympathy for the rat, I turned to Jedson and was about to ask him to stop when he took the cigarette away from the doll's face.

"Ready to talk?" he asked. The man nodded feebly, tears pouring down his scorched cheeks. He seemed about to collapse. "Here—don't faint," Jedson added, and slapped the face of the doll with a finger tip. I could hear the smack land, and the chap's head rocked to the blow, but he seemed to take a brace from it.

"All right, Archie, you take it down." He turned back. "And you, my friend, talk—and talk lots. Tell us everything you know. If you find your memory failing you, stop to think how you would like my cigarette poked into dolly's eyes!"

And he did talk—babbled, in fact. His spirit seemed to be completely broken, and he even seemed anxious to talk, stopping only occasionally to sniffle, or wipe at his eyes. Jedson questioned him to bring out points that were not clear.

There were five others in the gang that he knew about, and the setup was roughly as we had guessed. It was their object to levy tribute on everyone connected with magic in this end of town, magicians and their customers alike. No, they did not have any real protection to offer except from their own mischief. Who was his boss? He told us. Was his boss the top man in the racket? No, but he did not know who the top man was. He was quite sure that his boss worked for someone else, but he did not know who. Even if we burned him again he could not tell us. But it was a big organization—he was sure of that. He himself had been brought from a city in the East to help organize here.

Was he a magician? So help him, no! Was his

section boss one? No—he was sure; all that sort of thing was handled from higher up. That was all he knew, and could he go now? Jedson pressed him to remember other things; he added a number of details, most of them insignificant, but I took them all down. The last thing he said was that he thought both of us had been marked down for special attention because we had been successful in overcoming our first "lesson."

Finally, Jedson let up on him. "I'm going to let you go now," he told him. "You'd better get out of town. Don't let me see you hanging around again. But don't go too far; I may want you again. See this?" He held up the doll and squeezed it gently around the middle. The poor devil immediately commenced to gasp for breath as if he were being compressed in a strait jacket. "Don't forget that I've got you anytime I want you." He let up on the pressure, and his victim panted his relief. "I'm going to put your alter ego—doll to you!—where it will be safe, behind cold iron. When I want you, you'll feel a pain like that"—he nipped the doll's left shoulder with his fingernails; the man yelped—"then you telephone me, no matter where you are."

Jedson pulled a penknife from his vest pocket and cut the circle three times, then joined the cuts. "Now get out!"

I thought he would bolt as soon as he was released, but he did not. He stepped hesitantly over the pencil mark, stood still for a moment, and shivered. Then he stumbled toward the door. He turned just before he went through it and looked back at us, his eyes wide with fear. There was a look of appeal in them, too, and he seemed about to speak. Evidently he thought better of it, for he turned and went on out.

When he was gone I looked back at Jedson. He had picked up my notes and was glancing through them. "I don't know," he mused, "whether it would be better to turn his stuff at once over to the Better Business Bureau and let them handle it, or whether to have a go at it ourselves. It's a temptation."

I was not interested just then. "Joe," I said, "I wish you hadn't burned him!"

"Eh? How's that?" He seemed surprised and stopped scratching his chin. "I didn't burn him."

"Don't quibble," I said, somewhat provoked. "You burned him through the doll, I mean with magic."

"But I didn't, Archie. Really I didn't. He did that to himself—and it wasn't magic. I didn't do a thing!"

"What the hell do you mean?"

"Sympathetic magic isn't really magic at all, Archie. It's just an application of neuropsychology and colloidal chemistry. He did all that to himself, because he believed in it. I simply correctly judged his mentality."

The discussion was cut short; we heard an agony-loaded scream from somewhere outside the building. It broke off sharply, right at the top. "What was that?" I said, and gulped.

"I don't know," Jedson answered, and stepped to the door. He looked up and down before continuing. "It must be some distance away. I didn't see anything." He came back into the room. "As I was saying, it would be a lot of fun to——"

This time it was a police siren. We heard it from far away, but it came rapidly nearer, turned a corner, and yowled down our street. We looked at each other. "Maybe we'd better go see," we both said, right together, then laughed nervously.

It was our gangster acquaintance. We found him half a block down the street, in the middle of a little group of curious passers-by who were being crowded back by cops from the squad car at the curb.

He was quite dead.

He lay on his back, but there was no repose in the position. He had been raked from forehead to waist, laid open to the bone in three roughly parallel scratches, as if slashed by the talons of a hawk or an eagle. But the bird that made those wounds must have been the size of a five-ton truck.

There was nothing to tell from his expression. His face and throat were covered by, and his mouth choked with, a yellowish substance shot with purple. It was about the consistency of thin cottage cheese, but it had the most sickening smell I have ever run up against.

I turned to Jedson, who was not looking any too happy himself, and said, "Let's get back to the office."

We did.

* * *

We decided at last to do a little investigating on our own before taking up what we had learned with the Better Business Bureau or with the police. It was just as well that we did; none of the gang whose names we had obtained was any longer to be found in the haunts which we had listed. There was plenty of evidence that such persons had existed and that they had lived at the addresses which Jedson had sweated out of their pal. But all of them, without exception, had done a bunk for parts unknown the same afternoon that their accomplice had been killed.

We did not go to the police, for we had no wish to be associated with an especially unsavory sudden death. Instead, Jedson made a cautious verbal report to a friend of his at the Better Business Bureau, who passed it on secondhand to the head of the racket squad and elsewhere, as his judgment indicated.

I did not have any more trouble with my business for some time thereafter, and I was working very hard, trying to show a profit for the quarter in spite of setbacks. I had put the whole matter fairly well out of my mind, except that I dropped over to call on Mrs. Jennings occasionally and that I had used her young friend Jack Bodie once or twice in my business, when I needed commercial magic. He was a good workman—no monkey business and value received.

I was beginning to think I had the world on a leash when I ran into another series of accidents. This time they did not threaten my business; they threatened *me*—and I'm just as fond of my neck as the next man.

In the house where I live the water heater is installed in the kitchen. It is a storage type, with a pilot light and a thermostatically controlled main flame. Right alongside it is a range with a pilot light.

I woke up in the middle of the night and decided that I wanted a drink of water. When I stepped into the kitchen—don't ask me why I did not look for a drink in the bathroom, because I don't know—I was almost gagged by the smell of gas. I ran over and threw the window wide open, then ducked back out the door and ran into the living room, where I opened a big window to create a cross draft.

At that point there was a dull *whoosh* and a *boom*, and I found myself sitting on the living-room rug.

I was not hurt, and there was no damage in the kitchen except for a few broken dishes. Opening the windows had released the explosion, cushioned the effect. Natural gas is not an explosive unless it is confined. What had happened was clear enough when I looked over the scene. The pilot light on the heater had gone out; when the water in the tank cooled, the thermostat turned on the main gas jet, which continued immediately to pour gas into the room. When an explosive mixture was reached, the pilot light of the stove was waiting, ready to set it off.

Apparently I wandered in at the zero hour.

I fussed at my landlord about it, and finally we made a dicker whereby he installed one of the electrical water heaters which I supplied at cost and for which I donated the labor.

No magic about the whole incident, eh? That is what I thought. Now I am not so sure.

The next thing that threw a scare into me occurred the same week with no apparent connection. I keep dry mix—sand, rock, gravel—in the usual big bins set up high on concrete stanchions so that the trucks can drive under the hoppers for loading. One evening after closing time I was walking past the bins when I noticed that someone had left a scoop shovel in the driveway pit under the hoppers.

I have had trouble with my men leaving tools out at night; I decided to put this one in my car and confront someone with it in the morning. I was about to jump down into the pit when I heard my name called.

"Archibald!" it said—and it sounded remarkably like Mrs. Jennings's voice. Naturally I looked around. There was no one there. I turned back to the pit in time to hear a cracking sound and to see that scoop covered with twenty tons of medium gravel.

A man can live through being buried alive, but not when he has to wait overnight for someone to miss him and dig him out. A crystallized steel forging was the prima-facie cause of the mishap. I suppose that will do.

There was never anything to point to but natural causes, yet for about two weeks I stepped on banana peels both figuratively and literally. I saved my skin with a spot of fast footwork at least a dozen times. I finally broke down and told Mrs. Jennings about it.

"Don't worry too much about it, Archie," she reassured me. "It is not too easy to kill a man with magic unless he himself is involved with magic and sensitive to it."

"Might as well kill a man as scare him to death!" I protested.

She smiled that incredible smile of hers and said, "I don't think you have been really frightened, lad. At least you have not shown it."

I caught an implication in that remark and taxed her with it. "You've been watching me and pulling me out of jams, haven't you?"

She smiled more broadly and replied, "That's my business, Archie. It is not well for the young to depend on the old for help. Now get along with you. I want to give this matter more thought."

A couple of days later a note came in the mail addressed to me in a spidery, Spencerian script. The penmanship had the dignified flavor of the last century, and was the least bit shaky, as if the writer were unwell or very elderly. I had never seen the hand before, but guessed who it was before I opened it. It read:

My dear Archibald: This is to introduce my esteemed friend, Dr. Royce Worthington. You will

*find him staying at the Belmont Hotel; he is
expecting to hear from you. Dr. Worthington is
exceptionally well qualified to deal with the matters that have been troubling you these few weeks
past. You may repose every confidence in his
judgment, especially where unusual measures
are required.*

*Please to include your friend, Mr. Jedson, in
this introduction, if you wish.*

> *I am, sir,*
> *Very sincerely yours,*
> *Amanda Todd Jennings*

I rang up Joe Jedson and read the letter to him.
He said that he would be over at once, and for me
to telephone Worthington.

"Is Dr. Worthington there?" I asked as soon as
the room clerk had put me through.

"Speaking," answered a cultured British voice
with a hint of Oxford in it.

"This is Archibald Fraser, Doctor. Mrs. Jennings has written to me, suggesting that I look
you up."

"Oh yes!" he replied, his voice warming considerably. "I shall be delighted. When will be a convenient time?"

"If you are free, I could come right over."

"Let me see——" He paused about long enough
to consult a watch. "I have occasion to go to your
side of the city. Might I stop by your office in thirty
minutes, or a little later?"

"That will be fine, Doctor, if it does not discommode you——"

"Not at all. I will be there."

Jedson arrived a little later and asked me at once about Dr. Worthington. "I haven't seen him yet," I said, "but he sounds like something pretty swank in the way of an English-university don. He'll be here shortly."

My office girl brought in his card a half hour later. I got up to greet him and saw a tall, heavy-set man with a face of great dignity and evident intelligence. He was dressed in rather conservative, expensively tailored clothes and carried gloves, stick, and a large brief case. But he was black as draftsman's ink!

I tried not to show surprise. I hope I did not, for I have an utter horror of showing that kind of rudeness. There was no reason why the man should not be a Negro. I simply had not been expecting it.

Jedson helped me out. I don't believe he would show surprise if a fried egg winked at him. He took over the conversation for the first couple of minutes after I introduced him; we all found chairs, settled down, and spent a few minutes in the polite, meaningless exchanges that people make when they are sizing up strangers.

Worthington opened the matter. "Mrs. Jennings gave me to believe," he observed, "that there was some fashion in which I might possibly be of assistance to one, or both, of you——"

I told him that there certainly was, and sketched

out the background for him from the time the racketeer contact man first showed up at my shop. He asked a few questions, and Jedson helped me out with some details. I got the impression that Mrs. Jennings had already told him most of it, and that he was simply checking.

"Very well," he said at last, his voice a deep, mellow rumble that seemed to echo in his big chest before it reached the air, "I am reasonably sure that we will find a way to cope with your problems, but first I must make a few examinations before we can complete the diagnosis." He leaned over and commenced to unstrap his brief case.

"Uh . . . Doctor," I suggested, "hadn't we better complete our arrangements before you start to work?"

"Arrangements?" He looked momentarily puzzled, then smiled broadly. "Oh, you mean payment. My dear sir, it is a privilege to do a favor for Mrs. Jennings."

"But . . . but . . . see here, Doctor, I'd feel better about it. I assure you I am quite in the habit of paying for magic——"

He held up a hand. "It is not possible, my young friend, for two reasons: In the first place, I am not licensed to practice in your state. In the second place, I am not a magician."

I suppose I looked as inane as I sounded. "Huh? What's that? Oh! Excuse me, Doctor, I guess I just naturally assumed that since Mrs. Jennings had sent you, and your title, and all——"

He continued to smile, but it was a smile of

understanding rather than amusement at my discomfiture. "That is not surprising; even some of your fellow citizens of my blood make that mistake. No, my degree is an honorary doctor of laws of Cambridge University. My proper pursuit is anthropology, which I sometimes teach at the University of South Africa. But anthropology has some odd bypaths; I am here to exercise one of them."

"Well, then, may I ask——"

"Certainly, sir. My avocation, freely translated from its quite unpronounceable proper name, is 'witch smeller.'"

I was still puzzled. "But doesn't that involve magic?"

"Yes and no. In Africa the hierarchy and the categories in these matters are not the same as in this continent. I am not considered a wizard, or witch doctor, but rather an antidote for such."

Something had been worrying Jedson. "Doctor," he inquired, "you were not originally from South Africa?"

Worthington gestured toward his own face. I suppose that Jedson read something there that was beyond my knowledge. "As you have discerned. No, I was born in a bush tribe south of the Lower Congo."

"From there, eh? That's interesting. By any chance, are you nganga?"

"Of the Ndembo, but not by chance." He turned to me and explained courteously. "Your friend asked me if I was a member of an occult fraternity which extends throughout Africa, but which has the bulk of its members in my native territory. Initiates are called nganga."

Jedson persisted in his interest. "It seems likely to me, Doctor, that Worthington is a name of convenience—that you have another name."

"You are again, right—naturally. My tribal name—do you wish to know it?"

"If you will."

"It is"—I cannot reproduce the odd clicking, lip-smacking noise he uttered—"or it is just as proper to state it in English, as the meaning is what counts—Man-Who-Asks-Inconvenient-Questions. Prosecuting attorney is another reasonably idiomatic, though not quite literal, translation, because of the tribal function implied. But it seems to me," he went on, with a smile of unmalicious humor, "that the name fits you even better than it does me. May I give it to you?"

Here occurred something that I did not understand, except that it must have its basis in some African custom completely foreign to our habits of thought. I was prepared to laugh at the doctor's witticism, and I am sure he meant it to be funny, but Jedson answered him quite seriously:

"I am deeply honored to accept."

"It is you who honor me, brother."

From then on, throughout our association with him, Dr. Worthington invariably addressed Jedson by the African name he had formerly claimed as his own, and Jedson called him "brother" or "Royce." Their whole attitude toward each other underwent a change, as if the offer and acceptance of a name had in fact made them brothers, with all the privileges and obligations of the relationship.

"I have not left you without a name," Jedson added. "You had a third name, your real name?"

"Yes, of course," Worthington acknowledged, "a name which we need not mention."

"Naturally," Jedson agreed, "a name which must not be mentioned. Shall we get to work, then?"

"Yes, let us do so." He turned to me. "Have you someplace here where I may make my preparations? It need not be large——"

"Will this do?" I offered, getting up and opening the door of a cloak- and washroom which adjoins my office.

"Nicely, thank you," he said, and took himself and his brief case inside, closing the door after him. He was gone ten minutes at least.

Jedson did not seem disposed to talk, except to suggest that I caution my girl not to disturb us or let anyone enter from the outer office. We sat and waited.

Then he came out of the cloakroom, and I got my second big surprise of the day. The urbane Dr. Worthington was gone. In his place was an African personage who stood over six feet tall in his bare black feet, and whose enormous, arched chest was overlaid with thick, sleek muscles of polished obsidian. He was dressed in a loin skin of leopard, and carried certain accouterments, notably a pouch, which hung at his waist.

But it was not his equipment that held me, nor

yet the John Henrylike proportions of that warrior frame, but the face. The eyebrows were painted white and the hairline had been outlined in the same color, but I hardly noticed these things. It was the expression—humorless, implacable, filled with a dignity and strength which must be felt to be appreciated. The eyes gave a conviction of wisdom beyond my comprehension, and there was no pity in them—only a stern justice that I myself would not care to face.

We white men in this country are inclined to underestimate the black man—I know I do—because we see him out of his cultural matrix. Those we know have had their own culture wrenched from them some generations back and a servile pseudo culture imposed on them by force. We forget that the black man has a culture of his own, older than ours and more solidly grounded, based on character and the power of the mind rather than the cheap, ephemeral tricks of mechanical gadgets. But it is a stern, fierce culture with no sentimental concern for the weak and the unfit, and it never quite dies out.

I stood up in involuntary respect when Dr. Worthington entered the room.

"Let us begin," he said in a perfectly ordinary voice, and squatted down, his great toes spread and grasping the floor. He took several things out of the pouch—a dog's tail, a wrinkled black object the size of a man's fist, and other things hard to identify. He fastened the tail to his waist so that it hung down behind. Then he picked up one of the things that he had taken from the pouch—a small item, wrapped and tied in red silk—and said to me, "Will you open your safe?"

I did so, and stepped back out of his way. He thrust the little bundle inside, clanged the door shut, and spun the knob. I looked inquiringly at Jedson.

"He has his ... well ... soul in that package, and has sealed it away behind cold iron. He does not know what dangers he may encounter," Jedson whispered. "See?" I looked and saw him pass his thumb carefully all around the crack that joined the safe to its door.

He returned to the middle of the floor and picked up the wrinkled black object and rubbed it affectionately. "This is my mother's father," he announced. I looked at it more closely and saw that it was a mummified human head with a few wisps of hair still clinging to the edge of the scalp! "He is very wise," he continued in a matter-of-fact voice, "and I shall need his advice. Grandfather, this is your new son and his friend." Jedson bowed, and I found myself doing so. "They want our help."

He started to converse with the head in his own tongue listening from time to time, and then answering. Once they seemed to get into an argument, but the matter must have been settled satisfactorily, for the palaver soon quieted down. After a few minutes he ceased talking and glanced around the room. His eye lit on a bracket shelf intended for an electric fan, which was quite high off the floor.

"There!" he said. "That will do nicely. Grand-father needs a high place from which to watch." He went over and placed the little head on the bracket so that it faced out into the room.

When he returned to his place in the middle of the room he dropped to all fours and commenced to cast around with his nose like a hunting dog trying to pick up a scent. He ran back and forth, snuffling and whining, exactly like a pack leader worried by mixed trails. The tail fastened to his waist stood up tensely and quivered, as if still part of a live animal. His gait and his mannerisms mimicked those of a hound so convincingly that I blinked my eyes when he sat down suddenly and announced:

"I've never seen a place more loaded with traces of magic. I can pick out Mrs. Jennings' very strongly and your own business magic. But after I eliminate them the air is still crowded. You must have had everything but a rain dance and a sabbat going on around you!"

He dropped back into his character of a dog without giving us a chance to reply, and started making his casts a little wider. Presently he appeared to come to some sort of an impasse, for he settled back, looked at the head, and whined vigorously. Then he waited.

The reply must have satisfied him; he gave a sharp bark and dragged open the bottom drawer of a file cabinet, working clumsily, as if with paws instead of hands. He dug into the back of the drawer eagerly and hauled out something which he popped into his pouch.

After that he trotted very cheerfully around the place for a short time, until he had poked his nose into every odd corner. When he had finished he returned to the middle of the floor, squatted down again, and said, "That takes care of everything here for the present. This place is the center of their attack, so grandfather has agreed to stay and watch here until I can bind a cord around your place to keep witches out."

I was a little perturbed at that. I was sure the head would scare my office girl half out of her wits if she saw it. I said so as diplomatically as possible.

"How about that?" he asked the head, then turned back to me after a moment of listening. "Grandfather says it's all right; he won't let anyone see him he has not been introduced to." It turned out that he was perfectly correct; nobody noticed it, not even the scrubwoman.

"Now then," he went on, "I want to check over my brother's place of business at the earliest opportunity, and I want to smell out both of your homes and insulate them against mischief. In the meantime, here is some advice for each of you to follow carefully: Don't let anything of yourself fall into the hands of strangers—nail parings, spittle, hair cuttings—guard it all. Destroy them by fire, or engulf them in running water. It will make our task much simpler. I am finished." He got up and strode back into the cloakroom.

Ten minutes later the dignified and scholarly

Dr. Worthington was smoking a cigarette with us. I had to look up at his grandfather's head to convince myself that a jungle lord had actually been there.

Business was picking up at that time, and I had no more screwy accidents after Dr. Worthington cleaned out the place. I could see a net profit for the quarter and was beginning to feel cheerful again. I received a letter from Ditworth, dunning me about Biddle's phony claim, but I filed it in the wastebasket without giving it a thought.

One day shortly before noon Feldstein, the magicians' agent, dropped into my place. "Hi, Zack!" I said cheerfully when he walked in. "How's business?"

"Mr. Fraser, of all questions, that you should ask me that one," he said, shaking his head mournfully from side to side. "Business—it is terrible."

"Why do you say that?" I asked. "I see lots of signs of activity around——"

"Appearances are deceiving," he insisted, "especially in my business. Tell me—have you heard of a concern calling themselves 'Magic, Incorporated'?"

"That's funny," I told him. "I just did, for the first time. This just came in the mail"—and I held up an unopened letter. It had a return address on it of "Magic, Incorporated, Suite 700, Commonwealth Building."

Feldstein took it gingerly, as if he thought it

might poison him, and inspected it. "That's the parties I mean," he confirmed. "The gonophs!"

"Why, what's the trouble, Zack?"

"They don't want that a man should make an honest living——Mr. Fraser," he interrupted himself anxiously, "you wouldn't quit doing business with an old friend who had always done right by you?"

"Of course not, Zack, but what's it all about?"

"Read it. Go ahead." He shoved the letter back to me.

I opened it. The paper was a fine quality, watermarked, rag bond, and the letterhead was chaste and dignified. I glanced over the stuffed-shirt committee and was quite agreeably impressed by the caliber of men they had as officers and directors—big men, all of them, except for a couple of names among the executives that I did not recognize.

The letter itself amounted to an advertising prospectus. It was a new idea; I suppose you could call it a holding company for magicians. They offered to provide any and all kinds of magical service. The customer could dispense with shopping around; he could call this one number, state his needs, and the company would supply the service and bill him. It seemed fair enough—no more than an incorporated agency.

I glanced on down. "—fully guaranteed service, backed by the entire assets of a responsible company——" "—surprisingly low standard fees, made possible by elimination of fee splitting with agents and by centralized administration——" "The gratifying response from the members of the great profession enables us to predict that Magic, Incorporated, will be the natural source to turn to for competent thaumaturgy in any line—probably the only source of truly first-rate magic——"

I put it down. "Why worry about it, Zack? It's just another agency. As for their claims—I've heard you say that you have all the best ones in your stable. You didn't expect to be believed, did you?"

"No," he conceded, "not quite, maybe—among us two. But this is really serious, Mr. Fraser. They've hired away most of my really first-class operators with salaries and bonuses I can't match. And now they offer magic to the public at a price that undersells those I've got left. It's ruin, I'm telling you."

It was hard lines. Feldstein was a nice little guy who grabbed the nickels the way he did for a wife and five beady-eyed kids, to whom he was devoted. But I felt he was exaggerating; he has a tendency to dramatize himself. "Don't worry," I said. "I'll stick by you, and so, I imagine, will most of your customers. This outfit can't get all the magicians together; they're too independent. Look at Ditworth. He tried with his association. What did it get him?"

"Ditworth—aagh!" He started to spit, then remembered he was in my office. "This *is* Ditworth—this company!"

"How do you figure that? He's not on the letterhead."

"I found out. You think he wasn't successful
228

because you held out. They held a meeting of the directors of the association—that's Ditworth and his two secretaries—and voted the contracts over to the new corporation. Then Ditworth resigns and his stooge steps in as front for the non-profit association, and Ditworth runs both companies. You will see! If we could open the books of Magic, Incorporated, you will find he has voting control, I know it!"

"It seems unlikely." I said slowly.

"You'll see! Ditworth with all his fancy talk about a no-profit service for the improvement of standards shouldn't be any place around Magic, Incorporated, should he, now? You call up and ask for him——"

I did not answer, but dialed the number on the letterhead. When a girl's voice said, "Good morning—Magic, Incorporated," I said:

"Mr. Ditworth, please."

She hesitated quite a long time, then said, "Who is calling, please?"

That made it my turn to hesitate. I did not want to talk to Ditworth; I wanted to establish a fact. I finally said, "Tell him it's Dr. Biddle's office."

Whereupon she answered readily enough, but with a trace of puzzlement in her voice, "But Mr. Ditworth is not in the suite just now; he was due in Dr. Biddle's office half an hour ago. Didn't he arrive?"

"Oh," I said, "perhaps he's with the chief and I didn't see him come in. Sorry." And I rang off.

"I guess you are right," I admitted, turning back to Feldstein.

He was too worried to be pleased about it. "Look," he said, "I want you should have lunch with me and talk about it some more."

"I was just on my way to the Chamber of Commerce luncheon. Come along and we'll talk on the way. You're a member."

"All right," he agreed dolefully. "Maybe I can't afford it much longer."

We were a little late and had to take separate seats. The treasurer stuck the kitty under my nose and "twisted her tail." He wanted a ten-cent fine from me for being late. The kitty is an ordinary frying pan with a mechanical bicycle bell mounted on the handle. We pay all fines on the spot, which is good for the treasury and a source of innocent amusement. The treasurer shoves the pan at you and rings the bell until you pay up.

I hastily produced a dime and dropped it in. Steve Harris, who has an automobile agency, yelled, "That's right! Make the Scotchman pay up!" and threw a roll at me.

"Ten cents for disorder," announced our chairman, Norman Somers, without looking up. The treasurer put the bee on Steve. I heard the coin clink into the pan, then the bell was rung again.

"What's the trouble?" asked Somers.

"More of Steve's tricks," the treasurer reported in a tired voice. "Fairy gold, this time." Steve had chucked in a synthetic coin that some friendly magician had made up for him. Naturally, when it struck cold iron it melted away.

"Two bits more for counterfeiting," decided Somers, "then handcuff him and ring up the United States attorney." Steve is quite a card, but he does not put much over on Norman.

"Can't I finish my lunch first?" asked Steve, in tones that simply dripped with fake self-pity. Norman ignored him and he paid up.

"Steve, better have fun while you can," commented Al Donahue, who runs a string of drive-in restaurants. "When you sign up with Magic, Incorporated, you will have to cut out playing tricks with magic." I sat up and listened.

"Who said I was going to sign up with them?"

"Huh? Of course you are. It's the logical thing to do. Don't be a dope."

"Why should I?"

"Why should you? Why, it's the direction of progress, man. Take my case: I put out the fanciest line of vanishing desserts of any eating place in town. You can eat three of them if you like, and not feel full and not gain an ounce. Now I've been losing money on them, but kept them for advertising because of the way they bring in the women's trade. Now Magic, Incorporated, comes along and offers me the same thing at a price I can make money with them too. Naturally, I signed up."

"You would. Suppose they raise the prices on you after they have hired, or driven out of business, every competent wizard in town?"

Donahue laughed in a superior, irritating way. "I've got a contract."

"So? How long does it run? And did you read the cancellation clause?"

I knew what he was talking about, even if Donahue didn't; I had been through it. About five years ago a Portland cement firm came into town and began buying up the little dealers and cutting prices against the rest. They ran sixty-cent cement down to thirty-five cents a sack and broke their competitors. Then they jacked it back up by easy stages until cement sold for a dollar twenty-five. The boys took a whipping before they knew what had happened to them.

We all had to shut up about then, for the guest speaker, old B. J. Timken, the big subdivider, started in. He spoke on "Cooperation and Service." Although he is not exactly a scintillating speaker, he had some very inspiring things to say about how businessmen could serve the community and help each other; I enjoyed it.

After the clapping died down, Norman Somers thanked B.J. and said, "That's all for today, gentlemen, unless there is some new business to bring before the house—"

Jedson got up. I was sitting with my back to him, and had not known he was present. "I think there is, Mr. Chairman—a very important matter. I ask the indulgence of the Chair for a few minutes of informal discussion."

Somers answered, "Certainly, Joe, if you've got something important."

"Thanks. I think it is. This is really an extension of the discussion between Al Donahue and Steve Harris earlier in the meeting. I think there has been a major change in business conditions going on in this city right under our noses and we haven't noticed it, except where it directly affected our own business. I refer to the trade in commercial magic. How many of you use magic in your business? Put your hands up." All the hands went up, except for a couple of lawyers'. Personally, I had always figured they were magicians themselves.

"O.K.," Jedson went on, "put them down. We knew that; we all use it. I use it for textiles. Hank Manning here uses nothing else for cleaning and pressing, and probably uses it for some of his dye jobs too. Wally Haight's Maple Shop uses it to assemble and finish fine furniture. Stan Robertson will tell you that Le Bon Marché's slick window displays are thrown together with spells, as well as two thirds of the merchandise in his store, especially in the kids' toy department. Now I want to ask you another question: In how many cases is the percentage of your cost charged to magic greater than your margin of profit? Think about it for a moment before answering." He paused, then said: "All right—put up your hands."

Nearly as many hands went up as before.

"That's the point of the whole matter. We've got to have magic to stay in business. If anyone gets a strangle hold on magic in this community, we are all at his mercy. We would have to pay any prices that are handed us, charge the prices we are told to, and take what profits we are allowed to—or go out of business!"

The chairman interrupted him. "Just a minute, Joe. Granting that what you say is true—it is, of course—do you have any reason to feel that we are confronted with any particular emergency in the matter?"

"Yes, I do have." Joe's voice was low and very serious. "Little reasons, most of them, but they add up to convince me that someone is engaged in a conspiracy in restraint of trade." Jedson ran rapidly over the history of Ditworth's attempt to organize magicians and their clients into an association, presumably to raise the standards of the profession, and how alongside the non-profit association had suddenly appeared a capital corporation which was already in a fair way to becoming a monopoly.

"Wait a second, Joe," put in Ed Parmelee, who has a produce jobbing business. "I think that association is a fine idea. I was threatened by some rat who tried to intimidate me into letting him pick my magicians. I took it up with the association, and they took care of it; I didn't have any more trouble. I think an organization which can clamp down on racketeers is a pretty fine thing."

"You had to sign with the association to get their help, didn't you?"

"Why, yes, but that's entirely reasonable——"

"Isn't it possible that your gangster got what he wanted when you signed up?"

"Why, that seems pretty farfetched."

"I don't say," persisted Joe, "that is the explanation, but it is a distinct possibility. It would not be the first time that monopolists used goon squads with their left hands to get by coercion what their right hands could not touch. I wonder whether any of the rest of you have had similar experiences?"

It developed that several of them had. I could see them beginning to think.

One of the lawyers present formally asked a question through the chairman. "Mr. Chairman, passing for the moment from the association to Magic, Incorporated, is this corporation anything more than a union of magicians? If so, they have a legal right to organize."

Norman turned to Jedson. "Will you answer that, Joe?"

"Certainly. It is not a union at all. It is a parallel to a situation in which all the carpenters in town are employees of one contractor; you deal with that contractor or you don't build."

"Then it's a simple case of monopoly—if it is a monopoly. This state has a Little Sherman Act; you can prosecute."

"I think you will find that it is a monopoly. Have any of you noticed that there are no magicians present at today's meeting?"

We all looked around. It was perfectly true. "I think you can expect," he added, "to find magicians represented hereafter in this chamber by some executive of Magic, Incorporated. With respect to the possibility of prosecution"—he

hauled a folded newspaper out of his hip pocket—
"have any of you paid any attention to the governor's call for a special session of the legislature?"

Al Donahue remarked superciliously that he was too busy making a living to waste any time on the political game. It was a deliberate dig at Joe, for everybody knew that he was a committeeman, and spent quite a lot of time on civic affairs. The dig must have gotten under Joe's skin, for he said pityingly, "Al, it's a damn good thing for you that some of us are willing to spend a little time on government, or you would wake up some morning to find they had stolen the sidewalks in front of your house."

The chairman rapped for order; Joe apologized. Donahue muttered something under his breath about the whole political business being dirty, and that anyone associated with it was bound to turn crooked. I reached out for an ash tray and knocked over a glass of water, which spilled into Donahue's lap. It diverted his mind. Joe went on talking.

"Of course we knew a special session was likely for several reasons, but when they published the agenda of the call last night, I found tucked away toward the bottom an item 'Regulation of Thaumaturgy.' I couldn't believe that there was any reason to deal with such a matter in a special session unless something was up. I got on the phone last night and called a friend of mine at the capitol, a fellow committee member. She did not know anything about it, but she called me back later. Here's what she found out: The item was stuck into the

agenda at the request of some of the governor's
campaign backers; he has no special interest in it
himself. Nobody seems to know what it is all about,
but one bill on the subject has already been dropped
in the hopper—" There was an interruption; somebody wanted to know what the bill said.

"I'm trying to tell you," Joe said patiently. "The
bill was submitted by title alone; we won't be likely
to know its contents until it is taken up in committee. But here is the title: 'A Bill to Establish
Professional Standards for Thaumaturgists, Regulate the Practice of the Thaumaturgic Profession,
Provide for the Appointment of a Commission to
Examine, License, and Administer——' and so on.
As you can see, it isn't even a proper title; it's just
an omnibus onto which they can hang any sort of
legislation regarding magic, including an abridge-
ment of anti-monopoly regulation if they choose."

There was a short silence after this. I think all
of us were trying to make up our minds on a subject that we were not really conversant with—
politics. Presently someone spoke up and said,
"What do you think we ought to do about it?"

"Well," he answered, "we at least ought to have
our own representative at the capitol to protect us
in the clinches. Besides that, we at least ought to
be prepared to submit our own bill, if this one has
any tricks in it, and bargain for the best compro-
mise we can get. We should at least get an imple-
menting amendment out of it that would put some
real teeth into the state antitrust act, at least in

so far as magic is concerned." He grinned. "That's four 'at leasts,' I think."

"Why can't the state Chamber of Commerce handle it for us? They maintain a legislative bureau."

"Sure, they have a lobby, but you know perfectly well that the state chamber doesn't see eye to eye with us little businessmen. We can't depend on them; we may actually be fighting them."

There was quite a powwow after Joe sat down. Everybody had his own ideas about what to do and tried to express them all at once. It became evident that there was no general agreement, whereupon Somers adjourned the meeting with the announcement that those interested in sending a representative to the capitol should stay. A few of the diehards like Donahue left, and the rest of us reconvened with Somers again in the chair. It was suggested that Jedson should be the one to go, and he agreed to do it.

Feldstein got up and made a speech with tears in his eyes. He wandered and did not seem to be getting anyplace, but finally he managed to get out that Jedson would need a good big war chest to do any good at the capitol, and also should be compensated for his expenses and loss of time. At that he astounded us by pulling out a roll of bills, counting out one thousand dollars, and shoving it over in front of Joe.

That display of sincerity caused him to be made finance chairman by general consent, and the subscriptions came in very nicely. I held down my

natural impulses and matched Feldstein's dona-
tion, though I did wish he had not been quite so
impetuous. I think Feldstein had a slight change
of heart a little later, for he cautioned Joe to be
economical and not to waste a lot of money buying
liquor for "those schlemiels at the capitol."

Jedson shook his head at this, and said that
while he intended to pay his own expenses, he
would have to have a free hand in the spending
of the fund, particularly with respect to enter-
tainment. He said the time was too short to depend
on sweet reasonableness and disinterested patri-
otism alone—that some of those lunkheads had
no more opinions than a weather vane and would
vote to favor the last man they had had a drink
with.

Someone made a shocked remark about bribery.
"I don't intend to bribe anyone," Jedson answered
with a brittle note in his voice. "If it comes to
swapping bribes, we're licked to start with. I am
just praying that there are still enough unpledged
votes up there to make a little persuasive talking
and judicious browbeating worth while."

He got his own way, but I could not help agree-
ing privately with Feldstein. And I made a resolution to pay a little more attention to politics
thereafter; I did not even know the name of my
own legislator. How did I know whether or not he
was a high-caliber man or just a cheap opportun-
ist?

And that is how Jedson, Bodie, and myself happened to find ourselves on the train, headed for the capitol.

Bodie went along because Jedson wanted a first-rate magician to play bird dog for him. He said he did not know what might turn up. I went along because I wanted to. I had never been to the capitol before, except to pass through, and was interested to see how this lawmaking business is done.

Jedson went straight to the Secretary of State's office to register as a lobbyist, while Jack and I took our baggage to the Hotel Constitution and booked some rooms. Mrs. Logan, Joe's friend the committeewoman, showed up before he got back.

Jedson had told us a great deal about Sally Logan during the train trip. He seemed to feel that she combined the shrewdness of Machiavelli with the greathearted integrity of Oliver Wendell Holmes. I was surprised at his enthusiasm, for I have often heard him grouse about women in politics.

"But you don't understand, Archie," he elaborated. "Sally isn't a woman politician, she is simply a politician, and asks no special consideration because of her sex. She can stand up and trade punches with the toughest manipulators on the Hill. What I said about women politicians is perfectly true, as a statistical generalization, but it proves nothing about any particular woman.

"It's like this: Most women in the United States have a shortsighted, peasant individualism resulting from the male-created romantic tradition of the last century. They were told that they were superior creatures, a little nearer to the angels than their menfolks. They were not encouraged to think, nor to assume social responsibility. It takes a strong mind to break out of that sort of conditioning, and most minds simply aren't up to it, male or female.

"Consequently, women as electors are usually suckers for romantic nonsense. They can be flattered into misusing their ballot even more easily than men. In politics their self-righteous feeling of virtue, combined with their essentially peasant training, resulted in their introducing a type of cut-rate, petty chiseling that should make Boss Tweed spin in his coffin.

"But Sally's not like that. She's got a tough mind which could reject the hokum."

"You're not in love with her, are you?"

"Who, me? Sally's happily married and has two of the best kids I know."

"What does her husband do?"

"Lawyer. One of the governor's supporters. Sally got started in politics through pinch-hitting for her husband one campaign."

"What is her official position up here?"

"None. Right hand for the governor. That's her strength. Sally has never held a patronage job, nor been paid for her services."

After this build-up I was anxious to meet the paragon. When she called I spoke to her over the house phone and was about to say that I would come down to the lobby when she announced that she was coming up, and hung up. I was a little startled at the informality, not yet realizing that politicians did not regard hotel rooms as bedrooms, but as business offices.

When I let her in she said, "You're Archie Fraser, aren't you? I'm Sally Logan. Where's Joe?"

"He'll be back soon. Won't you sit down and wait?"

"Thanks." She plopped herself into a chair, took off her hat and shook out her hair. I looked her over.

I had unconsciously expected something pretty formidable in the way of a mannish matron. What I saw was a young, plump, cheerful-looking blonde, with an untidy mass of yellow hair and frank blue eyes. She was entirely feminine, not over thirty at the outside, and there was something about her that was tremendously reassuring.

She made me think of county fairs and well water and sugar cookies.

"I'm afraid this is going to be a tough proposition," she began at once. "I didn't think so, but just the same someone has a solid bloc lined up for Assembly Bill 22—that's the bill I wired Joe about. What do you boys plan to do, make a straight fight to kill it or submit a substitute bill?"

"Jedson drew up a fair-practices act with the aid of some of our Half World friends and a couple of lawyers. Would you like to see it?"

"Please. I stopped by the State Printing Office and got a few copies of the bill you are against— AB 22. We'll swap."

I was trying to translate the foreign language

lawyers use when they write statutes when Jedson came in. He patted Sally's cheek without speaking, and she reached up and squeezed his hand and went on with her reading. He commenced reading over my shoulder. I gave up and let him have it. It made a set of building specifications look simple.

Sally asked, "What do you think of it, Joe?"

"Worse than I expected," he replied. "Take Paragraph 7——"

"I haven't read it yet."

"So? Well, in the first place it recognizes the association as a semipublic body like the Bar Association or the Community Chest, and permits it to initiate actions before the commission. That means that every magician had better by a damn sight belong to Ditworth's association and be careful not to offend it."

"But how can that be legal?" I asked. "It sounds unconstitutional to me—a private association like that——"

"Plenty of precedent, son. Corporations to promote world's fairs, for example. They're recognized, and even voted tax money. As for unconstitutionality, you'd have to prove that the law was not equal in application—which it isn't!—but awfully hard to prove."

"But, anyhow, a witch gets a hearing before the commission?"

"Sure, but there is the rub. The commission has very broad powers, almost unlimited powers over everything connected with magic. The bill is filled with phrases like 'reasonable and proper,' which means the sky's the limit, with nothing but the good sense and decency of the commissioners to restrain them. That's my objection to commissions in government—the law can never be equal in application under them. They have delegated legislative powers, and the law is what they say it is. You might as well face a drum-head court-martial.

"There are nine commissioners provided for in this case, six of which must be licensed magicians, first-class. I don't suppose it is necessary to point out that a few ill-advised appointments to the original commission will turn it into a tight little self-perpetuating oligarchy—through its power to license."

Sally and Joe were going over to see a legislator whom they thought might sponsor our bill, so they dropped me off at the capitol. I wanted to listen to some of the debate.

It gave me a warm feeling to climb up the big, wide steps of the statehouse. The old, ugly mass of masonry seemed to represent something tough in the character of the American people, the determination of free men to manage their own affairs. Our own current problem seemed a little smaller, not quite so overpoweringly important—still worth working on, but simply one example in a long history of the general problem of self-government.

I noticed something else as I was approaching the great bronze doors; the contractor for the outer construction of the building must have made his pile; the mix for the mortar was not richer than one to six!

I decided on the Assembly rather than the Senate because Sally said they generally put on a livelier show. When I entered the hall they were discussing a resolution to investigate the tarring and feathering the previous month of three agricultural-worker organizers up near the town of Six Points. Sally had remarked that it was on the calendar for the day, but that it would not take long because the proponents of the resolution did not really want it. However, the Central Labor Council had passed a resolution demanding it, and the labor-supported members were stuck with it.

The reason why they could only go through the motions of asking for an investigation was that the organizers were not really human beings at all, but mandrakes, a fact that the state council had not been aware of when they asked for an investigation. Since the making of mandrakes is the blackest kind of black magic, and highly illegal, they needed some way to drop it quietly. The use of mandrakes has always been opposed by organized labor, because it displaces real men— men with families to support. For the same reasons they oppose synthetic facsimiles and homunculi. But it is well known that the unions are not above using mandrakes, or mandragoras, as well as facsimiles, when it suits their purpose, such as for pickets, pressure groups, and the like. I suppose they feel justified in fighting fire with fire.

Homunculi they can't use on account of their size, since they are too small to be passed off as men.

If Sally had not primed me, I would not have understood what took place. Each of the labor members got up and demanded in forthright terms a resolution to investigate. When they were all through, someone proposed that the matter be tabled until the grand jury of the county concerned held its next meeting. This motion was voted on without debate and without a roll call; although practically no members were present except those who had spoken in favor of the original resolution, the motion passed easily.

There was the usual crop of oil-industry bills on the agenda, such as you read about in the newspapers every time the legislature is in session. One of them was the next item on the day's calendar— a bill which proposed that the governor negotiate a treaty with the gnomes, under which the gnomes would aid the petroleum engineers in prospecting and, in addition, would advise humans in drilling methods so as to maintain the natural gas pressure underground needed to raise the oil to the surface. I think that is the idea, but I am no petroleum engineer.

The proponent spoke first. "Mr. Speaker," he said, "I ask for a 'Yes' vote on this bill, AB 79. It's purpose is quite simple and the advantages obvious. A very large part of the overhead cost of recovering crude oil from the ground lies in the uncertainties of prospecting and drilling. With the aid of the Little People this item can be reduced to an estimated 7 per cent of its present dollar cost, and the price of gasoline and other petroleum products to the people can be greatly lessened.

"The matter of underground gas pressure is a little more technical, but suffice it to say that it takes, in round numbers, a thousand cubic feet of natural gas to raise one barrel of oil to the surface. If we can get intelligent supervision of drilling operations far underground, where no human being can go, we can make the most economical use of this precious gas pressure.

"The only rational objection to this bill lies in whether or not we can deal with the gnomes on favorable terms. I believe that we can, for the Administration has some excellent connections in the Half World. The gnomes are willing to negotiate in order to put a stop to the present condition of chaos in which human engineers drill blindly, sometimes wrecking their homes and not infrequently violating their sacred places. They not unreasonably claim everything under the surface as their kingdom, but are willing to make any reasonable concession to abate what is to them an intolerable nuisance.

"If this treaty works out well, as it will, we can expect to arrange other treaties which will enable us to exploit all of the metal and mineral resources of this state under conditions highly advantageous to us and not hurtful to the gnomes. Imagine, if you please, having a gnome with his X-ray eyes peer into a mountainside and locate a rich vein of gold for you!"

It seemed very reasonable, except that, having once seen the king of the gnomes, I would not trust him very far, unless Mrs. Jennings did the negotiating.

As soon as the proponent sat down, another member jumped up and just as vigorously denounced it. He was older than most of the members, and I judged him to be a country lawyer. His accent placed him in the northern part of the state, well away from the oil country. "Mr. Speaker," he bellowed, "I ask for a vote of 'No'! Who would dream that an American legislature would stoop to such degrading nonsense? Have any of you ever seen a gnome? Have you any reason to believe that gnomes exist? This is just a cheap piece of political chicanery to do the public out of its proper share of the natural resources of our great state—"

He was interrupted by a question. "Does the honorable member from Lincoln County mean to imply that he has no belief in magic? Perhaps he does not believe in the radio or the telephone either."

"Not at all. If the Chair will permit, I will state my position so clearly that even my respected colleague on the other side of the house will understand it. There are certain remarkable developments in human knowledge in general use which are commonly referred to by the laity as magic. These principles are well understood and are taught, I am happy to say, in our great publicly owned institutions for higher learning. I have every respect for the legitimate practitioners thereof.

But, as I understand it, although I am not myself a practitioner of the great science, there is nothing in it that requires a belief in the Little People.

"But let us stipulate, for the sake of argument, that the Little People do exist. Is that any reason to pay them blackmail? Should the citizens of this commonwealth pay cumshaw to the denizens of the underworld—" He waited for his pun to be appreciated. It wasn't. "—for that which is legally and rightfully ours? If this ridiculous principle is pushed to its logical conclusion, the farmers and dairymen I am proud to number among my constituents will be required to pay toll to the elves before they can milk their cows!"

Someone slid into the seat beside me. I glanced around, saw that it was Jedson, and questioned him with my eyes. "Nothing doing now," he whispered. "We've got some time to kill and might as well do it here"—and he turned to the debate.

Somebody had gotten up to reply to the old duck with the Daniel Webster complex. "Mr. Speaker, if the honored member is quite through with his speech—I did not quite catch what office he is running for!—I would like to invite the attention of this body to the precedented standing in jurisprudence of elements of every nature, not only in Mosaic law, Roman law, the English common law, but also in the appellate court of our neighboring state to the south. I am confident that anyone possessing even an elementary knowledge of the law will recognize the case I have in mind without citation, but for the benefit of——"

"Mr. Speaker! I move to amend by striking out the last word."

"A strategem to gain the floor," Joe whispered.

"Is it the purpose of the honorable member who preceded me to imply——"

It went on and on. I turned to Jedson and asked, "I can't figure out this chap who is speaking; awhile ago he was hollering about cows. What's he afraid of, religious prejudices?"

"Partly that; he's from a very conservative district. But he's lined up with the independent oilmen. They don't want the state setting the terms; they think they can do better dealing with the gnomes directly."

"But what interest has he got in oil? There's no oil in his district."

"No. But there is outdoor advertising. The same holding company that controls the so-called independent oilmen holds a voting trust in the Countryside Advertising Corporation. And that can be awfully important to him around election time."

The Speaker looked our way, and an assistant sergeant at arms threaded his way toward us. We shut up. Someone moved the order of the day, and the oil bill was put aside for one of the magic bills that had already come out of committee. This was a bill to outlaw every sort of magic, witchcraft, thaumaturgy.

No one spoke for it but the proponent, who launched into a diatribe that was more scholarly than logical. He quoted extensively from Blackstone's *Commentaries* and the recods of the Massachusetts trials, and finished up with his head thrown back, one finger waving wildly to heaven and shouting, "'Thou shalt not suffer a witch to live!'"

No one bothered to speak against it; it was voted on immediately without roll call, and, to my complete bewilderment, passed without a single nay! I turned to Jedson and found him smiling at the expression on my face.

"It doesn't mean a thing, Archie," he said quietly.

"Huh?"

"He's a party wheel horse who had to introduce that bill to please a certain bloc of his constituents."

"You mean he doesn't believe in the bill himself?"

"Oh no, he believes in it all right, but he also knows it is hopeless. It has evidently been agreed to let him pass it over here in the Assembly this session so that he would have something to take home to his people. Now it will go to the senate committee and die there; nobody will ever hear of it again."

I guess my voice carries too well, for my reply got us a really dirty look from the Speaker. We got up hastily and left.

Once outside I asked Joe what had happened that he was back so soon. "He would not touch it," he told me. "Said that he couldn't afford to antagonize the association."

"Does that finish us?"

"Not at all. Sally and I are going to see another member right after lunch. He's tied up in a committee meeting at the moment."

We stopped in a restaurant where Jedson had arranged to meet Sally Logan. Jedson ordered lunch, and I had a couple of cans of devitalized beer, insisting on their bringing it to the booth in the unopened containers. I don't like to get even a little bit tipsy, although I like to drink. On another occasion I had paid for the wizard-processed liquor and had received intoxicating liquor instead. Hence the unopened containers.

I sat there, staring into my glass and thinking about what I had heard that morning, especially about the bill to outlaw all magic. The more I thought about it the better the notion seemed. The country had gotten along all right in the old days before magic had become popular and commercially widespread. It was unquestionably a headache in many ways, even leaving out our present troubles with racketeers and monopolists. Finally I expressed my opinion to Jedson.

But he disagreed. According to him prohibition never does work in any field. He said that anything which can be supplied and which people want will be supplied—law or no law. To prohibit magic would simply be to turn over the field to the crooks and the black magicians.

"I see the drawbacks of magic as well as you do," he went on, "but it is like firearms. Certainly guns made it possible for almost anyone to commit murder and get away with it. But once they were invented the damage was done. All you can do is to try to cope with it. Things like the Sullivan Act—they didn't keep the crooks from carrying guns and using them; they simply took guns out of the hands of honest people.

"It's the same with magic. If you prohibit it, you take from decent people the enormous boons to be derived from a knowledge of the great arcane laws, while the nasty, harmful secrets hidden away in black grimoires and red grimoires will still be bootlegged to anyone who will pay the price and has no respect for law.

"Personally, I don't believe there was any less black magic practiced between, say, 1750 and 1950 than there is now, or was before then. Take a look at Pennsylvania and the hex country. Take a look at the Deep South. But since that time we have begun to have the advantages of white magic too."

Sally came in, spotted us, and slid into one side of the booth. "My," she said with a sigh of relaxation, "I've just fought my way across the lobby of the Constitution. The 'third house' is certainly out in full force this trip. I've never seen 'em so thick, especially the women."

"Third house?" I said.

"She means lobbyists, Archie," Jedson explained. "Yes, I noticed them. I'd like to make a small bet that two thirds of them are synthetic."

"I *thought* I didn't recognize many of them," Sally commented. "Are you sure, Joe?"

"Not entirely. But Bodie agrees with me. He says that the women are almost all mandrakes, or androids of some sort. Real women are never quite so perfectly beautiful—nor so tractable. I've got him checking on them now."

"In what way?"

"He says he can spot the work of most of the magicians capable of that high-powered stuff. If possible we want to prove that all these androids were made by Magic, Incorporated—though I'm not sure just what use we can make of the fact.

"Bodie has even located some zombies," he added.

"Not really!" exclaimed Sally. She wrinkled her nose and looked disgusted. "Some people have odd tastes."

They started discussing aspects of politics that I know nothing about, while Sally put away a very sizable lunch topped off by a fudge ice-cream cake slice. But I noticed that she ordered from the left-hand side of the menu—all vanishing items, like the alcohol in my beer.

I found out more about the situation as they talked. When a bill is submitted to the legislature, it is first referred to a committee for hearings. Ditworth's bill, AB 22, had been referred to the Committee on Professional Standards. Over in the Senate an identical bill had turned up and had been referred by the lieutenant governor, who presides in the Senate, to the Committee on Industrial Practices.

Our immediate object was to find a sponsor for our bill; if possible, one for each house, and preferably sponsors who were members, in their respective houses, of the committees concerned. All of this needed to be done before Ditworth's bills came up for hearing.

I went with them to see their second-choice sponsor for the Assembly. He was not on the Professional Standards Committee, but he was on the Ways and Means Committee, which meant that he carried a lot of weight in any committee.

He was a pleasant chap named Spence—Luther B. Spence—and I could see that he was quite anxious to please Sally—for past favors, I suppose. But they had no more luck with him than with their first-choice man. He said that he did not have time to fight for our bill, as the chairman of the Ways and Means Committee was sick and he was chairman pro tem.

Sally put it to him flatly. "Look here, Luther, when you have needed a hand in the past, you've gotten it from me. I hate to remind a man of obligations, but you will recall that matter of the vacancy last year on the Fish and Game Commission. Now I want action on this matter, and not excuses!"

Spence was plainly embarrassed. "Now, Sally, please don't feel like that. You're getting your feathers up over nothing. You know I'll always do anything I can for you, but you don't really need this, and it would necessitate my neglecting things that I can't afford to neglect."

"What do you mean, I don't need it?"

"I mean you should not worry about AB 22. It's a cinch bill."

Jedson explained that term to me later. A cinch bill, he said, was a bill introduced for tactical reasons. The sponsors never intended to try to get it enacted into law, but simply used it as a bargaining point. It's like an "asking price" in a business deal.

"Are you sure of that?"

"Why, yes, I think so. The word has been passed around that there is another bill coming up that won't have the bugs in it that this bill has."

After we left Spence's office, Jedson said, "Sally, I hope Spence is right, but I don't trust Ditworth's intentions. He's out to get a strangle hold on the industry. I know it!"

"Luther usually has the correct information, Joe."

"Yes, that is no doubt true, but this is a little out of his line. Anyhow, thanks, kid. You did your best."

"Call on me if there is anything else, Joe. And come out to dinner before you go; you haven't seen Bill or the kids yet."

"I won't forget."

Jedson finally gave up as impractical trying to submit our bill, and concentrated on the committees handling Ditworth's bills. I did not see much of him. He would go out at four in the afternoon to a cocktail party and get back to the hotel at three in the morning, bleary-eyed, with progress to report.

He woke me up the fourth night and announced jubilantly, "It's in the bag, Archie!"

"You killed those bills?"

"Not quite. I couldn't manage that. But they will be reported out of committee so amended that we won't care if they do pass. Furthermore, the amendments are different in each committee."

"Well, what of that?"

"That means that even if they do pass their respective houses they will have to go to conference committee to have their differences ironed out, then back for final passage in each house. The chances of that this late in a short session are negligible. Those bills are dead."

Jedson's predictions were justified. The bills came out of committee with a "do pass" recommendation late Saturday evening. That was the actual time; the statehouse clock had been stopped forty-eight hours before to permit first and second readings of an administration "must" bill. Therefore it was officially Thursday. I know that sounds cockeyed, and it is, but I am told that every legislature in the country does it toward the end of a crowded session.

The important point is that, Thursday or Saturday, the session would adjourn sometime that night. I watched Ditworth's bill come up in the Assembly. It was passed, without debate, in the amended form. I sighed with relief. About midnight Jedson joined me and reported that the same thing had happened in the Senate. Sally was on watch in the conference committee room, just to make sure that the bills stayed dead.

Joe and I remained on watch in our respective

houses. There was probably no need for it, but it made us feel easier. Shortly before two in the morning Bodie came in and said we were to meet Jedson and Sally outside the conference committee room.

"What's that?" I said, immediately all nerves. "Has something slipped?"

"No, it's all right and it's all over. Come on."

Joe answered my question, as I hurried up with Bodie trailing, before I could ask it. "It's O.K., Archie. Sally was present when the committee adjourned *sine die*, without acting on those bills. It's all over; we've won!"

We went over to the bar across the street to have a drink in celebration.

In spite of the late hour the bar was moderately crowded. Lobbyists, local politicians, legislative attachés, all the swarm of camp followers who throng the capitol whenever the legislature is sitting—all such were still up and around, and many of them had picked this bar as a convenient place to wait for news of adjournment.

We were lucky to find a stool at the bar for Sally. We three men made a tight little cluster around her and tried to get the attention of the overworked bartender. We had just managed to place our orders when a young man tapped on the shoulder the customer on the stool to the right of Sally. He immediately got down and left. I nudged Bodie to tell him to take the seat.

Sally turned to Joe. "Well, it won't be long now. There go the sergeants at arms." She nodded toward the young man, who was repeating the process farther down the line.

"What does that mean?" I asked Joe.

"It means they are getting along toward the final vote on the bill they were waiting on. They've gone to 'call of the house' now, and the Speaker has ordered the sergeant at arms to send his deputies out to arrest absent members."

"Arrest them?" I was a little bit shocked.

"Only technically. You see, the Assembly has had to stall until the Senate was through with this bill, and most of the members have wandered out for a bite to eat, or drink. Now they are ready to vote, so they round them up."

A fat man took a stool near us which had just been vacated by a member. Sally said, "Hello, Don."

He took a cigar from his mouth and said, "How are yuh, Sally? What's new? Say, I thought you were interested in that bill on magic?"

We were all four alert at once. "I am," Sally admitted. "What about it?"

"Well, then, you had better get over there. They're voting on it right away. Didn't you notice the 'call of the house'?"

I think we set a new record getting across the street, with Sally leading the field in spite of her plumpness. I was asking Jedson how it could be possible, and he shut me up with, "I don't know, man! We'll have to see."

We managed to find seats on the main floor back of the rail. Sally beckoned to one of the pages she knew and sent him up to the clerk's desk for a copy of the bill that was pending. In front of the rail the Assemblymen gathered in groups. There was a crowd around the desk of the administration floor leader and a smaller cluster around the floor leader of the opposition. The whips had individual members buttonholed here and there, arguing with them in tense whispers.

The page came back with the copy of the bill. It was an appropriation bill for the Middle Counties Improvement Project—the last of the "must" bills for which the session had been called—but pasted to it, as a rider, *was Ditworth's bill in its original, most damnable form!*

It had been added as an amendment in the Senate, probably as a concession to Ditworth's stooges in order to obtain their votes to make up the two-thirds majority necessary to pass the appropriation bill to which it had been grafted.

The vote came almost at once. It was evident, early in the roll call, that the floor leader had his majority in hand and that the bill would pass. When the clerk announced its passage, a motion to adjourn *sine die* was offered by the opposition floor leader and it was carried unanimously. The Speaker called the two floor leaders to his desk and instructed them to wait on the governor and the presiding officer of the Senate with notice of adjournment.

The crack of his gavel released us from stunned immobility. We shambled out.

* * *

We got in to see the governor late the next morning. The appointment, squeezed into an overcrowded calendar, was simply a concession to Sally and another evidence of the high regard in which she was held around the capitol. For it was evident that he did not want to see us and did not have time to see us.

But he greeted Sally affectionately and listened patiently while Jedson explained in a few words why we thought the combined Ditworth-Middle Counties bill should be vetoed.

The circumstances were not favorable to reasoned exposition. The governor was interrupted by two calls that he had to take, one from his director of finance and one from Washington. His personal secretary came in once and shoved a memorandum under his eyes, at which the old man looked worried, then scrawled something on it and handed it back. I could tell that his attention was elsewhere for some minutes after that.

When Jedson stopped talking, the governor sat for a moment, looking down at his blotter pad, an expression of deep-rooted weariness on his face. Then he answered in slow words, "No, Mr. Jedson, I can't see it. I regret as much as you do that this business of the regulation of magic has been tied in with an entirely different matter. But I cannot veto part of a bill and sign the rest—even though the bill includes two widely separated subjects.

"I appreciate the work you did to help elect my administration"—I could see Sally's hand in that remark—"and wish that we could agree in this.

But the Middle Counties Project is something that I have worked toward since my inauguration. I hope and believe that it will be the means whereby the most depressed area in our state can work out its economic problems without further grants of public money. If I thought that the amendment concerning magic would actually do a grave harm to the state——"

He paused for a moment. "But I don't. When Mrs. Logan called me this morning I had my legislative counsel analyze the bill. I agree that the bill is unnecessary, but it seems to do nothing more than add a little more bureaucratic red tape. That's not good, but we manage to do business under a lot of it; a little more can't wreck things."

I butted in—rudely, I suppose—but I was all worked up. "But, Your Excellency, if you would just take time to examine this matter yourself, in detail, you would see how much damage it will do!"

I would not have been surprised if he had flared back at me. Instead, he indicated a file basket that was stacked high and spilling over. "Mr. Fraser, there you see fifty-seven bills passed by this session of the legislature. Every one of them has some defect. Every one of them is of vital importance to some, or all, of the people of this state. Some of them are as long to read as an ordinary novel. In the next nine days I must decide what ones shall become law and what ones must wait for revision at the next regular session. During that nine days at least a thousand people will want me to see them about some one of those bills——"

His aide stuck his head in the door. "Twelve-twenty, chief! You're on the air in forty minutes."

The governor nodded absently and stood up. "You will excuse me? I'm expected at a luncheon." He turned to his aide, who was getting out his hat and gloves from a closet. "You have the speech, Jim?"

"Of course, sir."

"Just a minute!" Sally had cut in. "Have you taken your tonic?"

"Not yet."

"You're not going off to one of those luncheons without it!" She ducked into his private washroom and came out with a medicine bottle. Joe and I bowed out as quickly as possible.

Outside I started fuming to Jedson about the way we had been given the run-around, as I saw it. I made some remark about dunderheaded, compromising politicians when Joe cut me short.

"Shut up, Archie! Try running a state sometime instead of a small business and see how easy you find it!"

I shut up.

Bodie was waiting for us in the lobby of the capitol. I could see that he was excited about something, for he flipped away a cigarette and rushed toward us. "Look!" he commanded. "Down there!"

We followed the direction of his finger and saw two figures just going out the big doors. One was Ditworth, the other was a well-known lobbyist with whom he had worked. "What about it?" Joe demanded.

"I was standing here behind this phone booth, leaning against the wall and catching a cigarette. As you can see, from here that big mirror reflects the bottom of the rotunda stairs. I kept an eye on it for you fellows. I noticed this lobbyist, Sims, coming downstairs by himself, but he was gesturing as if he were talking to somebody. That made me curious, so I looked around the corner of the booth and saw him directly. He was not alone; he was with Ditworth. I looked back at the mirror and he appeared to be alone. *Ditworth cast no reflection in the mirror!*"

Jedson snapped his fingers. "A demon!" he said in an amazed voice. "And I never suspected it!"

I am surprised that more suicides don't occur on trains. When a man is down, I know of nothing more depressing than staring at the monotonous scenery and listening to the maddening *lickety-tock* of the rails. In a way I was glad to have this new development of Ditworth's inhuman status to think about; it kept my mind off poor old Feldstein and his thousand dollars.

Startling as it was to discover that Ditworth was a demon, it made no real change in the situation except to explain the efficiency and speed with which we had been outmaneuvered and to confirm as a certainty our belief that the racketeers and Magic, Incorporated, were two heads of the same beast. But we had no way of proving that

Ditworth was a Half World monster. If we tried to haul him into court for a test, he was quite capable of lying low and sending out a facsimile, or a mandrake, built to look like him and immune to the mirror test.

We dreaded going back and reporting our failure to the committee—at least I did. But at least we were spared that. The Middle Counties Act carried an emergency clause which put it into effect the day it was signed. Ditworth's bill, as an amendment, went into action with the same speed. The newspapers on sale at the station when we got off the train carried the names of the new commissioners for thaumaturgy.

Nor did the commission waste any time in making its power felt. They announced their intention of raising the standards of magical practice in all fields, and stated that new and more thorough examinations would be prepared at once. The association formerly headed by Ditworth opened a coaching school in which practicing magicians could take a refresher course in thaumaturgic principles and arcane law. In accordance with the high principles set forth in their charter, the school was not restricted to members of the association.

That sounds bighearted of the association. It wasn't. They managed to convey a strong impression in their classes that membership in the association would be a big help in passing the new examinations. Nothing you could put your finger on to take into court—just a continuous impression. The association grew.

A couple of weeks later all licenses were canceled and magicians were put on a day-to-day basis in their practice, subject to call for re-examination at a day's notice. A few of the outstanding holdouts against signing up with Magic, Incorporated, were called up, examined, and licenses refused them. The squeeze was on. Mrs. Jennings quietly withdrew from any practice. Bodie came around to see me; I had an uncompleted contract with him involving some apartment houses.

"Here's your contract, Archie," he said bitterly. "I'll need some time to pay the penalties for noncompletion; my bond was revoked when they canceled the licenses."

I took the contract and tore in two. "Forget that talk about penalties," I told him. "You take your examinations and we'll write a new contract."

He laughed unhappily. "Don't be a Pollyanna."

I changed my tack. "What are you going to do? Sign up with Magic, Incorporated?"

He straightened himself up. "I've never temporized with demons; I won't start now."

"Good boy," I said. "Well, if the eating gets uncertain, I reckon we can find a job of some sort here for you."

It was a good thing that Bodie had some money saved, for I was a little too optimistic in my offer. Magic, Incorporated, moved quickly into the second phase of their squeeze, and it began to be a matter of speculation as to whether I myself would eat regularly. There were still quite a number of licensed magicians in town who were not employed by Magic, Incorporated—it would have been an evident, actionable frame-up to freeze out everyone—but those available were all incompetent bunglers, not fit to mix a philter. There was no competent, legal magical assistance to be gotten at any price—except through Magic, Incorporated.

I was forced to fall back on old-fashioned methods in every respect. Since I don't use much magic in any case, it was possible for me to do that, but it was the difference between making money and losing money.

I had put Feldstein on as a salesman after his agency folded up under him. He turned out to be a crackajack and helped to reduce the losses. He could smell a profit even farther than I could—farther than Dr. Worthington could smell a witch.

But most of the other businessmen around me were simply forced to capitulate. Most of them used magic in at least one phase of their business; they had their choice of signing a contract with Magic, Incorporated, or closing their doors. They had wives and kids—they signed.

The fees for thaumaturgy were jacked up until they were all the traffic would bear, to the point where it was just cheaper to do business with magic than without it. The magicians got none of the new profits; it all stayed with the corporation. As a matter of fact, the magicians got less of the proceeds than when they had operated independently, but they took what they could get and were glad of the chance to feed their families.

Jedson was hard hit—disastrously hit. He held out, naturally, preferring honorable bankruptcy to dealing with demons, but he used magic throughout his business. He was through. They started by disqualifying August Welker, his foreman, then cut off the rest of his resources. It was intimated that Magic, Incorporated, did not care to deal with him, even had he wished it.

We were all over at Mrs. Jennings's late one afternoon for tea—myself, Jedson, Bodie, and Dr. Royce Worthington, the witch smeller. We tried to keep the conversation away from our troubles, but we just could not do it. Anything that was said led back somehow to Ditworth and his damnable monopoly.

After Jack Bodie had spent ten minutes explaining carefully and mendaciously that he really did not mind being out of witchcraft, that he did not have any real talent for it, and had only taken it up to please his old man, I tried to change the subject. Mrs. Jennings had been listening to Jack with such pity and compassion in her eyes that I wanted to bawl myself.

I turned to Jedson and said inanely, "How is Miss Megeath?"

She was the white witch from Jersey City, the one who did creative magic in textiles. I had no special interest in her welfare.

He looked up with a start. "Ellen? She's ... she's

all right. They took her license away a month ago," he finished lamely.

That was not the direction I wanted the talk to go. I turned it again. "Did she ever manage to do what whole-garment stunt?"

He brightened a little. "Why, yes, she did—once. Didn't I tell you about it?" Mrs. Jennings showed polite curiosity, for which I silently thanked her. Jedson explained to the others what they had been trying to accomplish. "She really succeeded too well," he continued. "Once she had started, she kept right on, and we could not bring her out of her trance. She turned out over thirty thousand little striped sports dresses, all the same size and pattern. My lofts were loaded with them. Nine tenths of them will melt away before I dispose of them.

"But she won't try it again," he added. "Too hard on her health."

"How?" I inquired.

"Well, she lost ten pounds doing that one stunt. She's not hardy enough for magic. What she really needs is to go out to Arizona and lie around in the sun for a year. I wish to the Lord I had the money. I'd send her."

I cocked an eyebrow at him. "Getting interested, Joe?" Jedson is an inveterate bachelor, but it pleases me to pretend otherwise. He generally plays up, but this time he was downright surly. It showed the abnormal state of nerves he was in.

"Oh, for cripes' sake, Archie! Excuse me, Mrs. Jennings! But can't I take a normal humane interest in a person without you seeing an ulterior motive in it?"

"Sorry."

"That's all right." He grinned. "I shouldn't be so touchy. Anyhow, Ellen and I have cooked up an invention between us that might be a solution for all of us. I'd been intending to show it to all of you just as soon as we had a working model. Look, folks!" He drew what appeared to be a fountain pen out of a vest pocket and handed it to me.

"What is it? A pen?"

"No."

"A fever thermometer?"

"No. Open it up."

I unscrewed the cap and found that it contained a miniature parasol. It opened and closed like a real umbrella, and was about three inches across when opened. It reminded me of one of those clever little Japanese favors one sometimes gets at parties, except that it seemed to be made of oiled silk and metal instead of tissue paper and bamboo.

"Pretty," I said, "and very clever. What's it good for?"

"Dip it in water."

I looked around for some. Mrs. Jennings poured some into an empty cup, and I dipped it in.

It seemed to crawl in my hands.

In less than thirty seconds I was holding a full-sized umbrella in my hands and looking as silly as I felt. Bodie smacked a palm with a fist.

"It's a lulu, Joe! I wonder why someone didn't think of it before."

Jedson accepted congratulations with a fatuous grin, then added, "That's not all—look." He pulled a small envelope out of a pocket and produced a tiny transparent raincoat, suitable for a six-inch doll. "This is the same gag. And this." He hauled out a pair of rubber overshoes less than an inch long. "A man could wear these as a watch fob, or a woman could carry them on a charm bracelet. Then, with either the umbrella or the raincoat, one need never be caught in the rain. The minute the rain hits them, presto!—full size. When they dry out they shrink up."

We passed them around from hand to hand and admired them. Joe went on. "Here's what I have in mind. This business needs a magician—that's you, Jack—and a merchandiser—that's you, Archie. It has two major stockholders: that's Ellen and me. She can go take the rest cure she needs, and I'll retire and resume my studies, same as I always wanted to do."

My mind immediately started turning over the commercial possibilities, then I suddenly saw the hitch. "Wait a minute, Joe. We can't set up business in this state."

"No."

"It will take some capital to move out of the state. How are you fixed? Frankly, I don't believe I could raise a thousand dollars if I liquidated."

He made a wry face. "Compared with me you are rich."

I got up and began wandering nervously around the room. We would just have to raise the money

271

somehow. It was too good a thing to be missed, and would rehabilitate all of us. It was clearly patentable, and I could see commercial possibilities that would never occur to Joe. Tents for camping, canoes, swimming suits, traveling gear of every sort. We had a gold mine.

Mrs Jennings interrupted in her sweet and gentle voice. "I am not sure it will be too easy to find a state in which to operate."

"Excuse me, what did you say?"

"Dr. Royce and I have been making some inquiries. I am afraid you will find the rest of the country about as well sewed up as this state."

"What! Forty-eight states?"

"Demons don't have the same limitations in time that we have."

That brought me up short. Ditworth again.

Gloom settled down on us like fog. We discussed it from every angle and came right back to where we had started. It was no help to have a clever, new business; Ditworth had us shut out of every business. There was an awkward silence.

I finally broke it with an outburst that surprised myself. "Look here!" I exclaimed. "This situation is intolerable. Let's quit kidding ourselves and admit it. As long as Ditworth is in control we're whipped. Why don't we do something?"

Jedson gave me a pained smile. "God knows I'd like to, Archie, if I could think of anything useful to do."

"But we know who our enemy is—Ditworth! Let's tackle him—legal or not, fair means or dirty!"

"But that is just the point. Do we know our enemy? To be sure, we know he is a demon, but what demon, and where? Nobody has seen him in weeks."

"Huh? But I thought just the other day——"

"Just a dummy, a hollow shell. The real Ditworth is somewhere out of sight."

"But, look, if he is a demon, can't he be invoked, and compelled——"

Mrs. Jennings answered this time. "Perhaps—though it's uncertain and dangerous. But we lack one essential—his name. To invoke a demon you must know his real name, otherwise he will not obey you, no matter how powerful the incantation. I have been searching the Half World for weeks, but I have not learned that necessary name."

Dr. Worthington cleared his throat with a rumble as deep as a cement mixer, and volunteered, "My abilities are at your disposal, if I can help abate this nuisance——"

Mrs. Jennings thanked him. "I don't see how we can use you as yet, Doctor. I knew we could depend on you."

Jedson said suddenly, "White prevails over black."

She answered, "Certainly."

"Everywhere?"

"Everywhere, since darkness is the absence of light."

He went on, "It is not good for the white to wait on the black."

"It is not good."

Robert A. Heinlein

"With my brother Royce to help, we might carry light into darkness."

She considered this. "It is possible, yes. But very dangerous."

"You have been there?"

"On occasion. But you are not I, nor are these others."

Everyone seemed to be following the thread of the conversation but me. I interrupted with, "Just a minute, please. Would it be too much to explain what you are talking about?"

"There was no rudeness intended, Archibald," said Mrs. Jennings in a voice that made it all right. "Joseph has suggested that, since we are stalemated here, we make a sortie into the Half World, smell out this demon, and attack him on his home ground."

It took me a moment to grasp the simple audacity of the scheme. Then I said, "Fine! Let's get on with it. When do we start?"

They lapsed back into a professional discussion that I was unable to follow. Mrs. Jennings dragged out several musty volumes and looked up references on points that were sheer Sanskrit to me. Jedson borrowed her almanac, and he and the doctor stepped out into the back yard to observe the moon.

Finally it settled down into an argument—or rather discussion; there could be no argument, as they all deferred to Mrs. Jennings's judgment concerning liaison. There seemed to be no satisfactory way to maintain contact with the real world, and

274

Mrs. Jennings was unwilling to start until it was worked out. The difficulty was this: not being black magicians, not having signed a compact with Old Nick, they were not citizens of the Dark Kingdom and could not travel through it with certain impunity.

Bodie turned to Jedson. "How about Ellen Megeath?" he inquired doubtfully.

"Ellen? Why, yes, of course. She would do it. I'll telephone her. Mrs. Jennings, do any of your neighbors have a phone?"

"Never mind," Bodie told him, "just think about her for a few minutes so that I can get a line—" He stared at Jedson's face for a moment, then disappeared suddenly.

Perhaps three minutes later Ellen Megeath dropped lightly out of nothing. "Mr. Bodie will be along in a few minutes," she said. "He stopped to buy a pack of cigarettes." Jedson took her over and presented her to Mrs. Jennings. She did look sickly, and I could understand Jedson's concern. Every few minutes she would swallow and choke a little, as if bothered by an enlarged thyroid.

As soon as Jack was back they got right down to details. He had explained to Ellen what they planned to do, and she was entirely willing. She insisted that one more session of magic would do her no harm. There was no advantage in waiting; they prepared to depart at once. Mrs. Jennings related the marching orders. "Ellen, you will need to follow me in trance, keeping in close rapport. I think you will find that couch near the fireplace a good place to rest your body. Jack, you will remain here and guard the portal." The chimney of Mrs. Jennings's livingroom fireplace was to be used as most convenient. "You will keep in touch with us through Ellen."

"But, Granny, I'll be needed in the Half——"

"No, Jack." She was gently firm. "You are needed here much more. Someone has to guard the way and help us back, you know. Each to his task."

He muttered a bit, but gave in. She went on, "I think that is all. Ellen and Jack here; Joseph, Royce, and myself to make the trip. You will have nothing to do but wait, Archibald, but we won't be longer than ten minutes, world time, if we are to come back." She bustled away toward the kitchen, saying something about the unguent and calling back to Jack to have the candles ready. I hurried after her.

"What do you mean," I demanded, "about me having nothing to do but wait? I'm going along!"

She turned and looked at me before replying, troubled concern in her magnificent eyes. "I don't see how that can be, Archibald."

Jedson had followed us and now took me by the arm. "See here, Archie, do be sensible. It's utterly out of the question. You're not a magician."

I pulled away from him. "Neither are you."

"Not in a technical sense, perhaps, but I know enough to be useful. Don't be a stubborn fool, man; if you come, you'll simply handicap us."

That kind of argument is hard to answer and manifestly unfair. "How?" I persisted.

WALDO & MAGIC, INC.

"Hell's bells, Archie, you're young and strong and willing, and there is no one I would rather have at my back in a roughhouse, but this is not a job for courage, or even intelligence alone. It calls for special knowledge and experience."

"Well," I answered, "Mrs. Jennings has enough of that for a regiment. But—if you'll pardon me, Mrs. Jennings!—she is old and feeble. I'll be her muscles if her strength fails."

Joe looked faintly amused, and I could have kicked him. "But that is not what is required in——"

Dr. Worthington's double-bass rumble interrupted him from somewhere behind us. "It occurs to me, brother, that there may possibly be a use for our young friend's impetuous ignorance. There are times when wisdom is too cautious."

Mrs. Jennings put a stop to it. "Wait—all of you," she commanded, and trotted over to a kitchen cupboard. This she opened, moved aside a package of rolled oats, and took down a small leather sack. It was filled with slender sticks.

She cast them on the floor, and the three of them huddled around the litter, studying the patterns. "Cast them again," Joe insisted. She did so.

I saw Mrs. Jennings and the doctor nod solemn agreement to each other. Jedson shrugged and turned away. Mrs. Jennings addressed me, concern in her eyes. "You will go," she said softly. "It is not safe, but you will go."

We wasted no more time. The unguent was heated and we took turns rubbing it on each oth-

277

er's backbone. Bodie, as gatekeeper, sat in the midst of his pentacles, mekagrans, and runes, and intoned monotonously from the great book. Worthington elected to go in his proper person, ebony in a breechcloth, parasymbols scribed on him from head to toe, his grandfather's head cradled in an elbow.

There was some discussion before they could decide on a final form for Joe, and the metamorphosis was checked and changed several times. He finished up with paper-thin gray flesh stretched over an obscenely distorted skull, a sloping back, the thin flanks of an animal, and a long, bony tail, which he twitched incessantly. But the whole composition was near enough to human to create a revulsion much greater than would be the case for a more outlandish shape. I gagged at the sight of him, but he was pleased. "There!" he exclaimed in a voice like scratched tin. "You'd done a beautiful job, Mrs. Jennings. Asmodeus would not know me from his own nephew."

"I trust not," she said. "Shall we go?"

"How about Archie?"

"It suits me to leave him as he is."

"Then how about your own transformation?"

"I'll take care of that," she answered, somewhat tartly. "Take your places."

Mrs. Jennings and I rode double on the same broom, with me in front, facing the candle stuck in the straws. I've noticed All Hallow's Eve decorations which show the broom with the handle forward and the brush trailing. That is a mistake.

Custom is important in these matters. Royce and Joe were to follow close behind us. Seraphin leaped quickly to his mistress' shoulder and settled himself, his whiskers quivering with eagerness.

Bodie pronounced the word, our candle flared up high, and we were off. I was frightened nearly to panic, but tried not to show it as I clung to the broom. The fireplace gaped at us, and swelled to a monster arch. The fire within roared up like a burning forest and swept us along with it. As we swirled up I caught a glimpse of a salamander dancing among the flames, and felt sure that it was my own—the one that had honored me with its approval and sometimes graced my new fireplace. It seemed a good omen.

We had left the portal far behind—if the word "behind" can be used in a place where directions are symbolic—the shrieking din of the fire was no longer with us, and I was beginning to regain some part of my nerve. I felt a reassuring hand at my waist, and turned my head to speak to Mrs. Jennings.

I nearly fell off the broom.

When we left the house there had mounted behind me an old, old woman, a shrunken, wizened body kept alive by an indomitable spirit. She whom I now saw was a young woman, strong, perfect, and vibrantly beautiful. There is no way to describe her; she was without defect of any sort, and imagination could suggest no improvement.

Have you ever seen the bronze Diana of the Woods? She was something like that, except that

Robert A. Heinlein

metal cannot catch the live, dynamic beauty that I saw.

But it was the same woman!

Mrs. Jennings—Amanda Todd, that was—at perhaps her twenty-fifth year, when she had reached the full maturity of her gorgeous womanhood, and before time had softened the focus of perfection.

I forgot to be afraid. I forgot everything except that I was in the presence of the most compelling and dynamic female I had ever known. I forgot that she was at least sixty years older than myself, and that her present form was simply a triumph of sorcery. I suppose if anyone had asked me at that time if I were I love with Amanda Jennings, I would have answered, "Yes!" But at the time my thoughts were much too confused to be explicit. She was there, and that was sufficient.

She smiled, and her eyes were warm with understanding. She spoke, and her voice was the voice I knew, even though it was rich contralto in place of the accustomed clear, thin soprano. "Is everything all right, Archie?"

"Yes," I answered in a shaky voice. "Yes, Amanda, everything is all right!"

As for the Half World—— How can I describe a place that has no single matching criterion with what I have known? How can I speak of things for which no words have been invented? One tells of things unknown in terms of things which are known. Here there is no relationship by which to link; all is irrelevant. All I can hope to do is tell how matters affected my human senses, how events influenced my human emotions, knowing that there are two falsehoods involved—the falsehood I saw and felt, and the falsehood that I tell.

I have discussed this matter with Jedson, and he agrees with me that the difficulty is insuperable, yet some things may be said with a partial element of truth—truth of a sort, with respect to how the Half World impinged on me.

There is one striking difference between the real world and the Half World. In the real world there are natural laws which persist through changes of custom and culture; in the Half World only custom has any degree of persistence, and of natural law there is none. Imagine, if you please, a condition in which the head of a state might repeal the law of gravitation and have his decree really effective—a place where King Canute could order back the sea and have the waves obey him. A place where "up" and "down" were matters of opinion, and directions might read as readily in days or colors as in miles.

And yet it was not a meaningless anarchy, for they were constrained to obey their customs as unavoidably as we comply with the rules of natural phenomena.

We made a sharp turn to the left in the formless grayness that surrounded us in order to survey the years for a sabbat meeting. It was Amanda's intention to face the Old One with the matter directly rather than to search aimlessly through ever changing mazes of the Half World for a being hard to identify at best.

Royce picked out the sabbat, though I could see nothing until we let the ground come up to meet us and proceeded on foot. Then there was light and form. Ahead of us, perhaps a quarter of a mile away, was an eminence surmounted by a great throne which glowed red through the murky air. I could not make out clearly the thing seated there, but I knew it was "himself"—our ancient enemy.

We were no longer alone. Life—sentient, evil undeadness—boiled around us and fogged the air and crept out of the ground. The ground itself twitched and pulsated as we walked over it. Faceless things sniffed and nibbled at our heels. We were aware of unseen presences about us in the fog-shot gloom: beings that squeaked, grunted, and sniggered; voices that were slobbering whimpers, that sucked and retched and bleated.

They seemed vaguely disturbed by our presence—Heaven knows that I was terrified by them!—for I could hear them flopping and shuffling out of our path, then closing cautiously in behind, as they bleated warnings to one another.

A shape floundered into our path and stopped, a shape with a great bloated head and moist, limber arms. "Back!" it wheezed. "Go back! Candidates for witchhood apply on the lower level." It did not speak English, but the words were clear.

Royce smashed it in the face and we stamped over it, its chalky bones crunching underfoot. It pulled itself together again, whining its submission, then scurried out in front of us and thereafter gave us escort right up to the great throne.

"That's the only way to treat these beings," Joe whispered in my ear. "Kick 'em in the teeth first, and they'll respect you."

There was a clearing before the throne which was crowded with black witches, black magicians, demons in every foul guise, and lesser unclean things. On the left side the caldron boiled. On the right some of the company were partaking of the witches' feast. I turned my head away from that. Directly before the throne, as custom calls for, the witches' dance was being performed for the amusement of the Goat. Some dozens of men and women, young and old, comely and hideous, cavorted and leaped in impossible acrobatic adagio.

The dance ceased and they gave way uncertainly before us as we pressed up to the throne. "What's this? What's this?" came a husky, phlegmfilled voice. "It's my little sweetheart! Come up and sit beside me, my sweet! Have you come at last to sign my compact?"

Jedson grasped my arm; I checked my tongue.

"I'll stay where I am," answered Amanda in a voice crisp with contempt. "As for your compact, you know better."

"Then why are you here? And why such *odd* companions." He looked down at us from the vantage of his throne, slapped his hairy thigh and laughed immoderately. Royce stirred and muttered; his grandfather's head chattered in wrath. Seraphin spat.

Jedson and Amanda put their heads together for a moment, then she answered, "By the treaty with Adam, I claim the right to examine."

He chuckled, and the little devils around him covered their ears. "You claim privileges here? With no compact?"

"Your customs," she answered sharply.

"Ah yes, the customs! Since you invoke them, so let it be. And whom would you examine?"

"I do not know his name. He is one of your demons who has taken improper liberties outside your sphere."

"One of my demons, and you know not his name? I have seven million demons, my pretty. Will you examine them one by one, or all together?" His sarcasm was almost the match of her contempt.

"All together."

"Never let it be said that I would not oblige a guest. If you will go forward—let me see—exactly five months and three days, you will find my gentlemen drawn up for inspection."

I do not recollect how we got there. There was a great, brown plain, and no sky. Drawn up in military order for review by their evil lord were all the fiends of the Half World, legion on legion, wave after wave. The Old One was attended by his cabinet; Jedson pointed them out to me—Lucifugé, the prime minister; Sataniacha, field marshal; Beelzebub and Leviathan, wing commanders; Ashtoreth, Abaddon, Mammon, Theutus, Asmodeus, and Incubus, the Fallen Thrones. The seventy princes each commanded a division, and each remained with his command, leaving only the dukes and the thrones to attend their lord, Satan Mekratrig.

He himself still appeared as the Goat, but his staff took every detestable shape they fancied. Asmodeus sported three heads, each evil and each different, rising out of the hind quarters of a swollen dragon. Mammon resembled, very roughly, a particularly repulsive tarantula. Ashtoreth I cannot describe at all. Only the Incubus affected a semblance of human form, as the only vessel adequate to display his lecherousness.

The Goat glanced our way. "Be quick about it," he demanded. "We are not here for your amusement."

Amanda ignored him, but led us toward the leading squadron. "Come back!" he bellowed. And indeed we were back; our steps had led us no place. "You ignore the customs. Hostages first!"

Amanda bit her lip. "Admitted," she retorted, and consulted briefly with Royce and Jedson. I caught Royce's answer to some argument.

"Since I am to go," he said, "it is best that I choose my companion, for reasons that are sufficient to me. My grandfather advises me to take the youngest. That one, of course, is Fraser."

"What's that?" I said when my name was mentioned. I had been rather pointedly left out of all the discussions, but this was surely my business.

"Royce wants you to go with him to smell out Ditworth," explained Jedson.

285

"And leave Amanda here with these fiends? I don't like it."

"I can look out for myself, Archie," she said quietly. "If Dr. Worthington wants you, you can help me most by going with him."

"What is this hostage stuff?"

"Having demanded the right of examination," she explained, "you must bring back Ditworth—or the hostages are forfeit."

Jedson spoke up before I could protest. "Don't be a hero, son. This is serious. You can serve us all best by going. If you two don't come back, you can bet that they'll have a fight on their hands before they claim their forfeit!"

I went. Worthington and I had hardly left them before I realized acutely that what little peace of mind I had came from the nearness of Amanda. Once out of her immediate influence the whole mind-twisting horror of the place and its grisly denizens hit me. I felt something rub against my ankles and nearly jumped out of my shoes. But when I looked down I saw that Seraphin, Amanda's cat, had chosen to follow me. After that things were better with me.

Royce assumed his dog pose when we came to the first rank of demons. He first handed me his grandfather's head. Once I would have found that mummified head repulsive to touch; it seemed a friendly, homey thing here. Then he was down on all fours, scalloping in and out of the ranks of infernal warriors. Seraphin scampered after him, paired up and hunted with him. The hound seemed quite content to let the cat do half the work, and I have no doubt he was justified. I walked as rapidly as possible down the aisles between adjacent squadrons while the animals cast out from side to side.

It seems to me that this went on for many hours, certainly so long that fatigue changed to a wooden automatism and horror died down to a dull unease. I learned not to look at the eyes of the demons, and was no longer surprised at any *outré* shape.

Squadron by squadron, division by division, we combed them, until at last, coming up the left wing, we reached the end. The animals had been growing increasingly nervous. When they had completed the front rank of the leading squadron, the hound trotted up to me and whined. I suppose he sought his grandfather, but I reached down and patted his head.

"Don't despair, old friend," I said, "we have still these." I motioned toward the generals, princes all, who were posted before their divisions. Coming up from the rear as we had, we had yet to examine the generals of the leading divisions on the left wing. But despair already claimed me; what were half a dozen possibilities against an eliminated seven million?

The dog trotted away to the post of the nearest general, the cat close beside him, while I followed as rapidly as possible. He commenced to yelp before he was fairly up to the demon, and I broke into a run. The demon stirred and commenced to metamorphose. But even in this strange shape there was something familiar about it. "Ditworth!" I yelled, and dived for him.

I felt myself buffeted by leather wings, raked by claws. Royce came to my aid, a dog no longer, but two hundred pounds of fighting Negro. The cat was a ball of fury, teeth and claws. Nevertheless, we would have been lost, done in completely, had not an amazing thing happened. A demon broke ranks and shot toward us. I sensed him rather than saw him, and thought that he had come to succor his master, though I had been assured that their customs did not permit it. But he helped us—us, his natural enemies—and attacked with such vindictive violence that the gage was turned to our favor.

Suddenly it was all over. I found myself on the ground, clutching at not a demon prince but Ditworth in his pseudo-human form—a little mild businessman, dressed with restrained elegance, complete to brief case, spectacles, and thinning hair.

"Take that thing off me," he said testily. "That thing" was grandfather, who was clinging doggedly with toothless gums to his neck.

Royce spared a hand from the task of holding Ditworth and resumed possession of his grandfather. Seraphin stayed where he was, claws dug into our prisoner's leg.

The demon who had rescued us was still with us. He had Ditworth by the shoulders, talons dug into their bases. I cleared my throat and said, "I believe we owe this to you——" I had not the slightest notion of the proper thing to say. I think the situation was utterly without precedent.

The demon made a grimace that may have been intended to be friendly, but which I found frightening. "Let me introduce myself," he said in English. "I'm Federal Agent William Kane, Bureau of Investigation."

I think that was what made me faint.

I came to, lying on my back. Someone had smeared a salve on my wounds and they were hardly stiff, and not painful in the least, but I was mortally tired. There was talking going on somewhere near me. I turned my head and saw all the members of my party gathered together. Worthington and the friendly demon who claimed to be a G-man held Ditworth between them, facing Satan. Of all the mighty infernal army I saw no trace.

"So it was my nephew Nebiros," mused the Goat, shaking his head and clucking. "Nebiros, you are a bad lad and I'm proud of you. but I'm afraid you will have to try your strength against their champion now that they have caught you." He addressed Amanda. "Who is your champion, my dear?"

The friendly demon spoke up. "That sounds like my job."

"I think not," countered Amanda. She drew him to one side and whispered intently. Finally he shrugged his wings and gave in.

Amanda rejoined the group. I struggled to my feet and came up to them. "A trial to the death, I think," she was saying. "Are you ready, Nebiros?"

I was stretched between heart-stopping fear for Amanda and a calm belief that she could do anything she attempted. Jedson saw my face and shook his head. I was not to interrupt.

But Nebiros had no stomach for it. Still in his Ditworth form and looking ridiculously human, he turned to the Old One. "I dare not, Uncle. The outcome is certain. Intercede for me."

"Certainly, Nephew. I had rather hoped she would destroy you. You'll trouble me someday." Then to Amanda, "Shall we say ... ah ... ten thousand thousand years?"

Amanda gathered our votes with her eyes, including me, to my proud pleasure, and answered, "So be it." It was not a stiff sentence as such things go, I'm told—about equal to six months in jail in the real world—but he had not offended their customs; he had simply been defeated by white magic.

Old Nick brought down one arm in an emphatic gesture. There was a crashing roar and a burst of light and Ditworth-Nebiros was spread-eagled before us on a mighty boulder, his limbs bound with massive iron chains. He was again in demon form. Amanda and Worthington examined the bonds. She pressed a seal ring against each hasp and nodded to the Goat. At once the boulder receded with great speed into the distance until it was gone from sight.

"That seems to be about all, and I suppose you will be going now," announced the Goat. "All except this one——" He smiled at the demon G-man. "I have plans for him."

"No." Amanda's tone was flat.

"What's that, my little one? He has not the protection of your party, and he has offended our customs."

"No!"

"Really, I must insist."

"Satan Mekratrig," she said slowly, "do you wish to try your strength with me?"

"With you, madame?" He looked at her carefully, as if inspecting her for the first time. "Well, it's been a trying day, hasn't it? Suppose we say no more about it. Till another time, then——"

He was gone.

The demon faced her. "Thanks," he said simply. "I wish I had a hat to take off." He added anxiously, "Do you know your way out of here?"

"Don't you?"

"No, that's the trouble. Perhaps I should explain myself. I'm assigned to the antimonopoly division; we got a line on this chap Ditworth, or Nebiros. I followed him in here, thinking he was simply a black wizard and that I could use his portal to get back. By the time I knew better it was too late, and I was trapped. I had about resigned myself to an eternity as a fake demon."

I was very much interested in his story. I knew, of course, that all G-men are either lawyers, magicians, or accountants, but all that I had ever met were accountants. This calm assumption of incredible dangers impressed me and increased my already high opinion of Federal agents.

"You may use our portal to return," Amanda

said. "Stick close to us." Then to the rest of us, "Shall we go now?"

Jack Bodie was still intoning the lines from the book when we landed. "Eight and a half minutes," he announced, looking at his wrist watch. "Nice work. Did you turn the trick?"

"Yes, we did," acknowledged Jedson, his voice muffled by the throes of his remetamorphosis. "Everything that——"

But Bodie interrupted. "Bill Kane—you old scoundrel!" he shouted. "How did you get in on this party?" Our demon had shucked his transformation on the way and landed in his natural form—lean, young, and hard-bitten, in a quiet gray suit and snap-brim hat.

"Hi, Jack," he acknowledged. "I'll look you up tomorrow and tell you all about it. Got to report in now." With which he vanished.

Ellen was out of her trance, and Joe was bending solicitously over her to see how she had stood up under it. I looked around for Amanda.

Then I heard her out in the kitchen and hurried out there. She looked up and smiled at me, her lovely face serene and coolly beautiful. "Amanda," I said, "Amanda——"

I suppose I had the subconscious intention of kissing her, making love to her. But it is very difficult to start anything of that sort unless the woman in the case in some fashion indicates her willingness. She did not. She was warmly friendly, but there was a barrier of reserve I could not cross. Instead, I followed her around the kitchen, talking unconsequentially, while she made hot cocoa and toast for all of us.

When we rejoined the others I sat and let my cocoa get cold, staring at her with vague frustration in my heart while Jedson told Ellen and Jack about our experiences. He took Ellen home shortly thereafter, and Jack followed them out.

When Amanda came back from telling them good night at the door, Dr. Royce was stretched out on his back on the hearthrug, with Seraphin curled up on his broad chest. They were both snoring softly. I realized suddenly that I was wretchedly tired. Amanda saw it, too, and said, "Lie down on the couch for a little and nap if you can."

I needed no urging. She came over and spread a shawl over me and kissed me tenderly. I heard her going upstairs as I fell asleep.

I was awakened by sunlight striking my face. Seraphin was sitting in the window, cleaning himself. Dr. Worthington was gone, but must have just left, for the nap on the hearthrug had not yet straightened up. The house seemed deserted. Then I heard her light footsteps in the kitchen. I was up at once and quickly out there.

She had her back toward me and was reaching up to the old-fashioned pendulum clock that hung on her kitchen wall. She turned as I came in—tiny, incredibly aged, her thin white hair brushed neatly into a bun.

It was suddenly clear to me why a motherly good-night kiss was all that I had received the night before; she had had enough sense for two of us, and had refused to permit me to make a fool of myself.

She looked up at me and said in a calm, matter-of-fact voice, "See, Archie, my old clock stopped yesterday"—she reached up and touched the pendulum—"but it is running again this morning."

There is not anything more to tell. With Ditworth gone, and Kane's report, Magic, Incorporated, folded up almost overnight. The new licensing laws were an unenforced dead letter even before they were repealed.

We all hang around Mrs. Jennings's place just as much as she will let us. I'm really grateful that she did not let me get involved with her younger self, for our present relationship is something solid, something to tie to. Just the same, if I had been born sixty years sooner, Mr. Jennings would have had some rivalry to contend with.

I helped Ellen and Joe organize their new business, then put Bodie in as manager, for I decided that I did not want to give up my old line. I've built the new wing and bought those two trucks, just as Mrs. Jennings predicted. Business is good.

About the Author

Robert Anson Heinlein was born in Butler, Missouri, in 1907. A graduate of the U.S. Naval Academy, he was retired, disabled, in 1934. He studied mathematics and physics at the graduate school of the University of California and owned a silver mine before beginning to write science fiction, in 1939. In 1947 his first book of fiction, ROCKET SHIP GALILEO, was published. His novels include DOUBLE STAR (1956), STARSHIP TROOPERS (1959), STRANGER IN A STRANGE LAND (1961), and THE MOON IS A HARSH MISTRESS (1966), all winners of the Hugo Award. Heinlein was guest commentator for the Apollo 11 first lunar landing. In 1975 he received the Grand Master Nebula Award for lifetime achievement. Mr. Heinlein died in 1988.

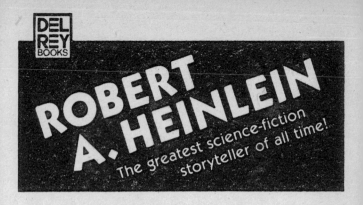